Lest We Fall

GLORIJEAN JOHNSON

Outskirts Press, Inc.
Denver, Colorado

All Bible quotations are taken from the King James Version of the Bible.
Used by permission.

Outskirts Press, Inc.
http://www.outskirtspress.com

ISBN: 978-1-4327-4288-1

Outskirts Press and the "OP" logo are trademarks belonging to Outskirts Press, Inc.

PRINTED IN THE UNITED STATES OF AMERICA

In loving memories of:

The world's greatest mom, my mother, Mattie Louise Palmer,
my dear friend, Dr. Akiba M. Ibura,
my nephew, Timothy Abrams
and my childhood nemesis and dear bubby, the one and only,
Karen Jean Gathren (KJG).
I want to add, "This one is for you Mar-bee"
(my brother, Marvin Palmer).

Acknowledgements

I certainly want to begin by giving all the glory and honor to God the Father, the Son (Jesus Christ) and the Holy Spirit for allowing me to write this book. I thank You, O Great and Mighty God, for trusting me to do it and giving me the courage to dare to be different.

My love and honor goes out to my husband and pastor, John C. Johnson (my sweet Johnny Johnson), for his love, encouragement, patience and for allowing me to dominate the computer. I love you sweet.

To everyone that supported me in writing this book: my sons, Kendall Blunt and Karseeme (Kay) Blunt, heartfelt thanks for your love and support; my son-in-laws, Joseph Gathren and Shaun Crudup, Sr.; to my niece, (child) Latrisha Palmer, thank you for the many hours you sacrificed listen to me go on and on about my stories. To Tanisha Gregory, I hope you are satisfied with this version.

To my grandchildren, my brother, Tony Palmer, my sisters, Jewel Blunt and Andrea Palmer and all my nieces and nephews.

To my dear friends: Detrent Diane Louis and Charlotte Wilson-I can never forget how you stood by me when daring to be different got me (us) in trouble.

Lots of shouts to Dee Chevalier, Janet Moe and Simone (Ce-Girl) Harris: thanks for your friendship and support when my nephew, Tim, passed away. You are the best example of people to work with.

To my pray partners: Josiah Jackson and Artence Johnson

This book is dedicated

To my daughter and agent, Kahesha Gathren: Keek, we did it! The book is a reality just like you said it would be. Thanks for the many, many hours you invested when you came home from work and read my story. Thanks for your love, support, encouragement and listening to your mom go on and on and on about Landis and Pier. You are and always will be more than a reader.

To my daughter, Katrice Crudup: I would never be able to thank you enough, Katrice, for your unselfishness in helping me take care of my mom. You gave up a lot over the years so I could spend the last six years with mama. God bless you my daughter!

To my sister, Lisa Mahmood: Lisa, you have heard my stories since we were children. Thank you for encouraging me all these years.

Wherefore let him that thinketh he standeth take heed lest he fall."
I Corinthians 10:12
King James Version

Prologue

"Ladies and gentlemen, I now present to you Mr. and Mrs. Spencer Trace Mortimer," said Reverend Wright, senior pastor of Solid Foundation Christian Center.

The sleeves of his black and white robe swayed back and forward as he waved his hands toward the happy couple. His eyes shimmered with tears. His grin was from ear to ear. He was very excited to see these fine young people get married. He had known them so long that they were like a son and a daughter to him.

Reverend Wright has been pastor to both their families, the Mortimers and Lovingtons, for ten years. They were fine up standing families. Honest to boot! No job was too big or small for them to do in the church. They tithed and gave without blinking an eye, and *boy*, what money came from these families. Uh-hum, Reverend Wright cleared his throat rubbing his large hand over his shiny baldhead. Not that money was all that or bought his love. *Oh no!* No, it's just good to see people following the biblical example. He counted his blessing, grinning even more.

Landis Renee Lovington, the best man and brother of the bride, moved his tall large muscular frame aside as men, women and children, upon hearing Reverend Wright's official introduction, stood in the sanctuary of the church clapping and cheering the union of Speedy and Micah Rochelle. The organist began to play. Lights flashed from cameras as the wedding party proceeded down the aisle.

He heaved a sigh of relief as he thought to himself; Speedy and Micah Rochelle finally did it. After years of dancing around one another they've finally admitted their love and now they are married. He smiled to himself. Landis was excited for them. Speedy was already like a brother to him.

"They make a good couple, don't they?" said a soft sweet feminine voice behind him.

Recognizing who was speaking, Landis turns with a smile on his face for the lovely maid of honor and sister of the groom, Shannon.

"Yeah they do." He bent his six feet frame down to whisper in her ear. "And you, my sweet, are looking just as beautiful." As he straightened, he once again admired her cornflower blue dress, a couple shades darker than the three bridesmaids. Shannan was a knockout; very beautiful with her hair fashionably cut short and smooth caramel skin color. She wore three-inch stilettos adding height to her five feet four inches frame. As she gazed up at him, she batted her light brown eyes.

"Will you guys stop flirting and get a move on. You're holding up the wedding party," said another feminine voice and sister of

Speedy, disgust vibrating in her tone.

"Sorry, little Pier," said Landis. "Shan, shall we follow the happy couple?" he asked dryly.

The lovely Shannon, smiling, tucked her arm in the crook of his, saying "yes sir, don't wanna make the baby cry." She sticks her tongue out at Pier and receives a returned gesture.

Had Landis and Shannan been looking, they would have seen hurt briefly flashed across Pier's beautiful face. Had either one thought to watch, they would have noticed being young or being called a baby was the last thing the new eighteen-year-old Pier wanted to hear today. After all she had taken special care with her hair and make-up hoping to attract the attention of a certain older male.

Unfortunately as always, being the youngest of the Mortimer clan, Pier Janise was overlooked. Sighing, she turned toward her marching partner, tall dark and good-looking Ace, and plasters a smile on her beautiful young face as he escorts her out the door.

Everyone assembled in front of the church as Speedy and Micah Rochelle stood in front of the white limo smiling happily into the eyes of one another as the photographer snapped away like a wild man.

The bridal party, six bridesmaids and groomsmen, waited patiently until Speedy finally took his eyes off his lovely bride and beckoned for the wedding party to stand with them for pictures.

Next to the happy couple, none were happier than the newly-weds' mothers. They were both in agreement that the two were in love, but more than that they were friends. An enduring and lasting combination to a successful marriage, nodded their mamas.

The reception was held at the extravagant Highlander Inn in Brooklyn Park. The room was huge, holding about two hundred people. Relatives traveled from all over the country to attend the wedding. On the bride's side they traveled as far as from Paris, France.

Speedy had pep in his step as he strutted his tall wiry person over to where Landis stood staring broodingly into the crowd of dancers. With arms stretched out, Speedy hugged his best friend and now, brother-in-law. "Man this is the best day of my life," he said joyfully. "I highly recommend it."

Laughing, Landis pats Speedy on the back. "Well I am happy for you. I couldn't have wished for a better brother-in-law than you bro."

Speedy threw his head back in laughter. "Now you know I was not letting your sister get away from me. I-," he paused in mid sentence and gently pulled his goat-tee as he narrows his light brown eyes. Landis turned around and his eyes followed Speedy's gaze. They fastened on Ace slow dancing with Little Pier. Ace was holding Pier just a little closer than necessary, Landis thought but didn't say anything.

Shaking his head, Speedy said, "I am not going to let Ace ruin my day by dancing with my little sister. Man, if it wasn't for the fact that this is my wedding day I would be all over Ace like a rash and that is for real."

Anyone who knew Speedy knew when it came to his two sisters, his tolerance was low. Very low!

"I didn't get a chance to mention this to you, Landis, with

Pier's graduation and our wedding being in the same month and everyone so busy, but your boy Ace came to me a couple days after Pier's graduation party and had the nerves to say to me he was going to holler at my fine sister now that she's turned eighteen and out of high school. Can you believe this man? Gonna tell me he wants to *date* my sister." Speedy voice dripped with sarcasm.

Landis' gaze still fastened on Ace and Pier, went very still. His expression became bland. "Is that right?" he asked Speedy in a very frozen voice.

"Man I told him he better get a life and leave my little sister alone. I mean how sick is that? He has known Pier since she was four." Speedy sliced the air with his hand. "As if I would let any of my friends talk to my baby sister, especially Ace. Little innocent Pier. Please. Ace would eat her for breakfast. Uh, just the thought of it is making me sick. She is too young and naïve for someone like him. But he's got a lot of guts to say that to me. I almost hit him.

Closing and opening his chocolate eyes, Landis glanced at Speedy and then back at Pier. He exhaled. "I do see your point. Ace does have a lot of nerve, but bro, you must admit, in that dress she doesn't look like a baby sister." Her light blue dress seemed to be glued to her body.

Speedy sighed. "Yeah, I know. What were they thinking letting that kid wear a revealing dress like that? I thought bridesmaid dresses were supposed to be ugly."

"They are. Just not on your sisters," replied Landis, not taking his eyes off Ace and Pier.

The left spaghetti strap of Pier's dress slipped off her shoulder and both men became rigid as they observed Ace carefully placing it back.

"Aw, he didn't mean any harm," Speedy said after a couple of seconds. "Ace ain't crazy.

Landis didn't say anything, all too aware of Speedy's protective streak with those he loved, especially Pier. Clearing his throat he said, "Speedy, she is eighteen and legally there isn't much you can do if Ace or any of our friends wanted to holler at Pier. Man, you gotta accept she isn't a baby anymore."

Speedy's face became as granite. "If any friend of mine ever try to talk to my baby sister, not only will he no longer be my friend, but I will hurt him," he said with finality in his voice.

Landis nodded his head in understanding.

Speedy, changing the subject, said to Landis, "Anyway man I'm glad at least you're cool about me marrying your sister. If you were against it," he sighed noisily, "let's just say it would have been hard choosing." He gave a wicked grin. "I would have hated losing my best friend and brother." He gave Landis a thoughtful look. "You know I'm going to take good care of her, don't you? I'll do everything in my power to make her happy. And," he added with a silly happy grin, "I pray to God for His blessings and that we will always stay as one."

Staring thoughtfully at his best friend of fourteen years, Landis stretched out his arms and pulled Speedy into another hug. "I know man. I know. All I can say is "'bout time."

"Thanks, bro." Speedy's grin quickly turned to a frown as he glanced again at Ace and Pier still dancing to yet another slow song. "Now let me get over here and dance with my sister before I forget how happy I am and kill Ace."

After the final toast and final speech, which happened to come from the father of the groom-who didn't mind giving speeches-long speeches, Landis escaped and sat behind a large green foliage plant trying to come up with a plan to leave because he couldn't take seeing the object of his every wakened thought any longer. This has been pure torture for him. He loved her and there was nothing he could do to stop those feelings. He should know he has been fighting them since his return home. She was so beautiful and probably too young.

Yeah, he sighed. Too young! And watching her glide on the dance floor with every man, young and old, in the room was more pain than he wanted to bear. They all wanted to dance with her including Landis. But he didn't because this was the one thing of the whole day he had control over. Holding her in his arms and knowing nothing could ever come of it was too much even for *St. Landis.*

He was just getting ready to loosen his bow tie when she called him. "Hey Landis, Micah Rochelle wants to take the final group picture; then she's going to change and throw the bouquet," she said in an excited voice.

Landis closed his eyes briefly. When will this torturous day end?

"Okay, ladies! Are you ready?" Asks Micah Rochelle dressed in a lavender two-piece silk suit, standing with bouquet in hand preparing to throw it. Her almond shape chocolate colored eyes filled with amusement as she watched about fifty single women crowd around the band area waiting, smiling as she remembered it was just last year she did the same thing at one of her friend's wedding.

Two things were going on in the back of the crowd that would hinder Micah Rochelle's matchmaking goal of getting Shannan to catch the bouquet and Landis the garter. One, Landis had quietly slipped out of the room. Two, Pier stood next to Shannan and she was taller.

Shaking her head as she turned her back to the women, Micah Rochelle threw the bouquet in Shannan's direction anyway.

Shannan, aware of her new sister-in-law's plan, laughing, side-stepped out of the way-while Pier stretched out her hand and caught it.

"I've got it," she screamed excitedly.

Everyone laughed, although some of the single women had a disgusted look on their face. "What a waste," their expressions seem to emulate.

Speedy was next to throw the garter. Someone had produced a folding chair for Micah Rochelle to sit on while he bent on one knee. The drummer did a drum roll. Micah carefully lifted her skirt a little and Speedy slid the garter down her leg. Good nature laughter filled the room. Some wolfish whistling went out. Speedy raised himself up with garter in hand, turned around and threw it.

Since Landis' day was pretty rough anyway, he wasn't a bit surprise on reentering the room to see two grown men tussling to get a silly garter sailing in the air only to miss, and the garter as if it had an undercover mission landed right at Landis' feet. Landis closed his eyes.

Finally Landis looked down staring at it as if it was a bomb ready to explode. Pier laughingly scoops it up, holding it out to him and showed him her bouquet. Their eyes met. This time her laughter settled down to a soft sweet alluring smile. He felt like his heart and every other organ in his body had stopped. He closes his eyes again hoping when he opens them this time; this hellish nightmare would be over. Landis opened them and she was still standing there.

His best friend's kid sister!
A death wish!

Chapter One

About five years later

This isn't called the Windy City for nothing, Landis Lovington thought to himself as the March wind howled, causing one of the windows in his living room to rattle. He was leaning against the big picture window, watching sheets of rain cascading down like a waterfall and splashing against the windowpanes. Typical March madness. Typical Chicago.

It was a Saturday evening and he didn't have any plans except to stay home. Actually these days the twenty-nine year old would rather stay home. He didn't want to go clubbing, not that he went out all that much. It was like pulling teeth for his co-worker and friend, Keith, to convince him to go out. Once convinced, he usually had a good time. But lately he felt the club scene was getting kind of old. Lately he has been feeling kind of restless.

Just last weekend Jackie, his current girlfriend, had commented on how agitated and edgy he'd been. She hinted that was why they had been arguing a lot lately, which shouldn't be because she was out of town more than in.

Rubbing his brow, something he does when in deep thought, Landis pushed his body away from the window and lowered himself on his navy blue leather couch. Shaking his head as if that would organize his brain, he heaves a sigh; he wasn't sure what to do about Jackie.

Jackie! Just thinking about her made his heart ache. He truly cared for her, wishing with all his heart what he felt for her was love instead of like, that he could just ask her to marry him and they live happily ever after. After all, she was a beautiful woman inside and out, a successful model and genuinely treated him with love and respect. Bottom line she was everything any man would want.

That is if that man's heart didn't belong to someone else, as his did. Pier held his heart. Just thinking about her made him sad. Sad because they could never be, sad because she didn't know he was in love with her. No one knew. For the most part the women he'd dated eventually figured out he was in love with someone else but who is Landis' secret he has carried around for nearly five years.

Shaking himself out of his reminiscing, Landis picks up the television remote control and channel surfed until finally settling for the sports channel. Folding his large hands behind his head, he leaned back on the couch. Saturday night and here he was watching TV. He usually enjoyed watching the sports, but tonight his mind was preoccupied.

"Man, I must be getting old," he muttered to himself. "Landis, man, you need a life."

Actually he had a good life. In spite of the unpredictable weather, Chicago was without a doubt a great place to live. He has a good job. Three years ago, he was promoted as senior vice president of the loan department at Monroe-Phillips' Bank. His financial portfolio couldn't be better. At twenty-nine he was a very wealthy man, thanks to the trust fund he received when he turned twenty-one and wise investments.

Yes, Landis lived a good live. But if he were honest with himself, he would admit lately he's founded himself homesick. He missed his family. He missed his friends. He missed living in Minnesota. He missed her.

Pier!

The name and image flashed quickly once again in his mind. He hadn't seen her in four years, eight months and three days but who was counting?

When Speedy called Landis' office today laughing, talking and jesting about his old married life, Landis felt just a little bit envious and even more homesick. In spite of Speedy's self ridicule, Landis knew how happy he and Micah Rochelle really were. And his son, Landis' nephew-every time Landis talked to that little two years old tyke, he was amazed at how big he sounded. And when he asked his uncle when he was coming to visit, what was left for him to say except soon.

Sighing once again, he realized it was going to be kind of hard visiting with little Pier living back in Minnesota. After all, it was because of her that he quickly packed up and left town again....

Landis and Speedy were eighteen when they went off to college. Everyone had been surprised when they decided to go to different ones. Speedy chose University of Minnesota and Landis chose the University of Colorado. This would be the first time in eight years you would see one and not see the other.

The plan was that Landis and his father were to travel by car to Colorado and once he was settled in, his father would fly back home.

On the day they were leaving, twelve-year-old Pier was at his house bright and early with a present for him. It was a framed picture of her so he wouldn't forget her. Landis stared at the photograph and smiled. Her ebony hair was in two ponytails and her smile in her full little face was sweet and serene. She explained she has also given Speedy one. For some reason, to Pier it seemed like they were deserting her.

He dramatically pressed the picture to his heart and assured Little Pier he would remember her and would see her during breaks and the summer. She wrapped her chubby arms around him and told him she loved him. He watched her skip down the block for home, which were only a few blocks away.

Although that was his intention, it didn't happen quite that way, for Landis ended up visiting home only during Christmas vacations. And as Pier got older, he'd somehow always just missed seeing her.

Keeping in touch with family and friends by letters, cards and e-mails worked out better for a busy Landis. It was during his last year of college when Little Pier, in High School, decided to e-mail him every Friday. Landis found himself picking up the picture she had given him, looking forward to hearing about her week. She was funny and witty. She talked about her friends and *boys.*

"They're such jerks, Landis," she wrote. "I don't know what all the fuss is about having a boyfriend. Dad did start letting me date without Speedy big head double dating. Dad also said no serious dating until after I graduate-*from college!!* Can you believe my father sometimes?"

She would describe in detail her love for their church. She'd also shared with him all the fun things about church and the not so fun things, mainly how her dad, Elder Mortimer, would use her in his messages. The list went on and on. Speedy would tease him about still letting Pier bug him. Landis loved it. He probably knew her better than anyone did. They were pals.

After graduation, Landis decided to stay in Denver another year to work at a bank. He did come home for a couple of weeks, but Little Pier was away on a church tour with the choir. She'd e-mailed him expressing deep regret in not seeing him. She'd hope to see him for Christmas. She sounded like such a mature sixteen years old.

She also shared with him that she had a boyfriend. It was nothing serious.

Landis remembered he laughed and called Speedy asking him if he missed his double dating with Pier. Speedy was not amused. He was, however, getting serious about Micah Rochelle. Landis gave him his approval.

Speedy also informed him he was thinking of going into the ministry. Quick temper-act now-and-think later Speedy a minister? This he had to see! All joking aside, Landis knew his friend would make a good and true preacher. He'd always preached about something.

Finally after five years, Landis was ready to leave Denver and return home. He couldn't have picked a better time because it was a few months before Speedy and Micah Rochelle's wedding and little Pier's high school graduation, as well as her eighteenth birthday party. With plans in motion, he e-mailed his friend, Little Pier. She was excited, stating she hoped he would arrive in time for her big one-eight-birthday party. Landis recalled staring at the picture she'd given him, wondering how much she'd changed. Granted he'd seen pictures of her but she just looked like his Little Pier who trailed behind him and Speedy any and everywhere they would let her.

Landis sold most of his worldly goods and shipped the rest to his parents' home. He made plane reservations two weeks shy of Pier's birthday. She was excited he would be there for the party.

The day Landis Renee Lovington stepped off the plane was the day that changed the course of his life. When the plane stopped, he excitedly grabbed his garment bag and rushed through the gates. He knew his mom had said Speedy insisted on picking him up. He couldn't wait to see his boy. From a distance he recognized Speedy and Shannan standing, waving. Speedy ran to meet him and hugged him.

"That's it, man. No more staying in another state," he said. He was a little shorter than Landis' six feet and a lot slimmer, wiry as ever. He sported a neatly trimmed mustache and goat tee.

Shannan was still waving excitedly. She was taller. Her hair was longer and her... that's not Shannan-it was his Little Pier he realized as he neared. Little Pier had grown up. Staring at her in amazement, he wondered what happened. Where were the pigtails and the chubby face? Who was this talk gorgeous young lady?

"Landis!" She rushed into his arms like a whirlwind. Had he been smaller, she would have knocked him down.

Grinning he looked at Speedy. "Is this our little baby that was our shadow?"

Thumping him on the back, Speedy nodded his head laughing.

"Would you believe I thought she was Shan?"

"A lot of our old male friends do." Speedy made a face. Same old Speedy, as protective of Pier as ever.

Pier looped her arm through Landis' as they made their way to the baggage claim. She talked a mile a minute.

"Oh, Landis, I'm soo glad you're here in time for my birthday party. It's going to be at the house. Ole Shannan had her party at a banquet hall." She made a face. "Why can't I have my party there?" She wanted to know.

"Shannan turned twenty-two, baby. You're still a little girl," Speedy patiently explained.

"I am not a baby, Handsome." She pouted. "Do I look like a baby, Landis?"

He wanted to say *no way* but he merely laughed and said nothing. She was clad in jeans someone had to have poured her in. And her t-shirt should be called *t* because that's how it fitted. No longer pigtails but hair that swung around her shoulders. Unlike the girls he had known at that age, her only make up was lip-gloss.

"I am not a baby. Thank you very much. Just wait 'til you see my dress, Landis. I won't look like a baby in it. It's red. You remember red is my favorite color."

They had reached the baggage claims area and were waiting for his luggage.

Landis held his hands up. "Okay. Okay. Speedy, she is not a baby," he stated with mock sincerity.

All the way home from the Minneapolis/St. Paul airport, Pier talked about her best girlfriends, her new boyfriend, and college. She was going in August to the University of Minnesota like the rest of her bigheaded siblings. She stuck her tongue out at Speedy, who didn't see it because he was driving.

"We're going to drop the baby off first. Our parents are at a church meeting so you'll have to see them later," said a grinning Speedy. "Unless, man, you wanna go to church." He and Landis laughed. Pier made a face.

When the car pulled into the driveway, Pier jumped out yelling, "I got to call my girls. If they think Speedy's a handsome hunk, wait 'til they see you, Landis." He was a super hunk because he wasn't her brother.

Landis looked at Speedy, who made a face and looked heavenward.

Pier turned around and sprinted back down the drive. She tapped the window on Landis side. Speedy automatically rolls it down.

"What, brat?" he asked impatiently.

Shrugging her shoulders Pier replies, "nothing really. I just wanted to let Landis know I'm sooo glad he's back home." She leaned inside and planted a kiss on his full sensuous lips. Waving she jogs back up the driveway and into the house.

Grinning, Speedy commented she didn't even give her brother a kiss. "I see I get no love."

Landis tries to smile but he was still in shocked surprise of that kiss and even more shocking, he nearly responded to it. Shaking his head he blew it off, blaming the plane flight.

He had three weeks before he started his new job at 1st Bank of Minneapolis. He used that time to spend with Speedy and some old high school acquaintances of theirs. They all hung out like old times. He and Speedy doubled dated with Micah Rochelle and Shannnan. Only this time Speedy and Micah were a real couple. And the lovely Shannan usually dropped him like a hot potato when some 'good-looking' male caught her attention. Sometimes when it was just he and Speedy, they would let Pier 'the baby' tags along.

A few times during the weekends when Speedy and Micah Rochelle would go out and Shannan had a date, Landis found himself in the company of Pier. *No big deal.*

He didn't think much about it or her until the night of her birthday party. That night she wore a red dress that hugged her slim curvy figure. And to top it off, it was short. She wore her hair up and for the first time wore lipstick-red. She was drop-dead gorgeous and seemed to be having the time of her life.

Elder and Mrs. Mortimer left after he gave one of his famous long-winded birthday speeches. And man, what a long speech. He and Speedy, along with Micah Rochelle, were to chaperone the party. Landis and Speedy, being the big brothers, cautioned Pier's boyfriend and the others what would happen if they got caught in a corner kissing-especially Pier.

Everything was going smoothly until rebellious Shannan and three of her friends dropped by, one of them by the nickname of Bulldog who took immense pleasure in flirting with Pier. Her boyfriend, Kayvion, was getting upset. Landis didn't like it either and he told Bulldog to quit. Bulldog laughingly threw his hands up and walked away.

Shannan and her friends played loud music as if it were her party. Pier looked as if she was ready for the party to end. She looked relieved when her guests exited around eleven. A few minutes later, Pier thanked the chaperones for helping out and said goodnight.

Without being known to anyone, Bulldog followed her up the stairs.

Landis will never know why he decided to use the upstairs bathroom instead of the guest bathroom downstairs. Upon reaching the upstairs landing, he was grateful he did because he heard Pier saying in a frightened voice "leave me alone". Hearing the fear in her voice made him open the door without knocking. His chocolate colored eyes widened in fury when he saw one of Bulldog's arms around Pier's waist and the other hand caressing her face. The look of relief in her beautiful brown eyes will forever be in his memory when she and Bulldog turned around.

With all his strength, he pulls Bulldog away from Pier by the neck, and Landis was not a small man. He was big and muscular.

"Hey, dude, Whuz up witcha?" Bulldog voice was raspy because Landis was nearly choking the life out of him.

"Man, if you have any sense at all, you'll leave this room, this house, this city, and this state," Landis replied in a quiet deadly voice. "Because if I ever set eyes on you again, I probably will kill you." He paused. "Better yet, I think I might just give her brother a holler."

"Hey, man, it's all straight. I'm straight. I didn't mean anything by it. She's so fine I wanted to give her a goodnight kiss." He hunched his shoulders as Landis reluctantly released him. "It's not like I was trying to rape her or something. What you think, I want to go to jail?" Shaking his head Bulldog said, "I'm outta here. Peace." He exited Pier's bedroom.

The whole time Pier stood statue still, but when she heard the door close, she brokenly whispered "Oh, Landis. I was so scared. I didn't try to lead him on. I'm sorry."

He pulled her into his arms, hugging her closely to his muscular body. "You're sorry? You didn't do anything to be sorry about. He's the one at fault. Not you, Baby." He pulled away to look into her teary eyes. "Do you want me to get Speedy? Shannan? Call the police? You want to press charges?"

She shook her head no to all his questions. "I just want to forget this ever happened. If we say something to Speedy, he'll only rant and rave and fight with Shannan."

Landis stared at her intently for a moment, and then he said, "We'll never speak on it again. You're sure you're alright?" Closing her eyes, Pier nodded her head.

"Thank you Landis. I'm so glad you came when you did. I don't know what would have happened." She shuddered.

Landis hugged her again, intending to press a light feathery kiss on her forehead, but she raised her face up the same time he bent down, causing his lips to land on hers, lingering a little longer than appropriate.

Then and there, Landis knew that what he felt for his best friend's little sister was no brotherly love. Shock and appalled, he quickly released her, wishing her a happy birthday and stumbled down the stairs.

The Mortimers had returned by the time he reached the family room and Shannan and her friends had left. Speedy said he would take Micah Rochelle home. *And Landis.* Landis received the shock of his life. He'd just kissed his best friend's kid sister and knew he was in love.

The ringing of the telephone brought Landis' mind back to the present. Unfolding his hands, he reached for the phone.

"Lovington," he said with a deep firm voice not betraying any of his thoughts.

"Whuz up, man?"

The voice on the other end was just what he needed to shake

him out of this mood.

"Speedy, my man, calling twice in one day. I'm honored. What's up with ya?"

"Nothing's up. I didn't think I'd catch you at home. What? Didn't feel like partying?"

Landis yawns. Thinking about the past had made him sleepy.

"N'all, getting too old. Jackie's out of town and old Keith wanted to go some place. Man, I told him 'see ya!'"

Speedy laughed. "I was calling because the lovely Shannan's birthday's coming up and she wants you here this year. No excuses. I thought I had better call you and let you know she's going to call you." He laughed again. "Tell me I didn't just sound like I did when we were teenagers."

"Okay, I won't tell you." Landis laughed too.

"Yeah, well, expect a call from Shan."

"Is she having a party? And will your dad be there with his speech?"

"Yes. Yes. Her party is at the Park Grand Hotel," said Speedy and Landis whistled. "Yeah, she's going all out this year. Probably because she's getting old." Speedy laughed.

Giving a short laugh, Landis said, "Watch it, bro, we're two years older. I'm already feeling old. Don't need to hear I'm not the only one."

"Y'all speak for yourselves. I, my friend, have never felt younger."

"Okay, okay" Landis laughed again. Pausing, he asked, "How's little Pier settling back home after living in Atlanta?" he tried to make his voice as casual as possible.

"Good. She's such a quiet little thing. Kind of introverted, you know."

Rubbing a brow, Landis closed his eyes, "Is she dating a lot?"

"Nope. Hardly ever dates. This one dude, Devin, got his eyes set on her, but she *wants to just be friends*." Speedy imitating Pier's voice.

Landis couldn't help but laugh at Speedy's imitation of Pier.

"Hey man, I gotta go. Be looking out for Shan's call. You are coming to her birthday party?"

"I'll see."

"Okay. But be warned, Shannan's not taking no for an answer. Alright, Landis."

"Alright, Speed. Talk to you later." He hung up the phone.

Landis went back to the window. Under the street lamp the rain now seemed more like a gentle drizzle. He watched a man and woman rush to their car. Once again his mind drifted down memory lane.

He remembered it was after Speedy and Micah Rochelle's wedding when he knew in his heart he had to leave. He had to get out of Dodge. He couldn't stay, caring about Pier the way he did. Maybe if she was older. Nah, Speedy still would have his head. The previous week he had turned down a job to relocate in Chicago because he wanted to be home. He declined even when one of the bank's owners had assured him it was an opportunity of a lifetime. However, when his feeling for Pier became so profound, he knew he had to leave or be found out. And besides he'd thought to himself, since he'd just moved back, it wasn't like he was uprooting all that much. Shoot, he was still living with his parents.

Landis had always been the planner. He rarely talked to anyone about his problems. As close as he and Speedy were, he did not share everything with him, and under the circumstances Speedy would be the last person he would talk to anyway about Pier. After all, he did want to live.

It was on a Saturday two months after the wedding that he decided to go and talk to Mrs. Mortimer. Throughout the years they had a special bond, and she next to his father had become his confidante. He had called about seven that morning and asked if he could come over and visit. He had something important to discuss with her. They agreed to meet around noon. He remember standing hesitantly and nervous at their back door, moving restlessly as he pressed the bell and waited for the door to be answered.

Mrs. Mortimer might understand his feeling for Pier. She may not hold it against him falling for the youngest instead of Shannan who, after Speedy and Micah marriage, was the parents' ideal choice for him. Yes, maybe she would understand. After all, she has on many occasions got him to open up.

When Ella Mortimer answered the door, his thoughts were once again hidden. She greeted him like always with a wide smile and an invitation into the kitchen. Landis was grinning genuinely- it felt like old times.

It was definably like old times when he walked in and saw Elder Spencer Mortiner sitting at the wooden table reading the newspaper. Looking up, he gestured for Landis to sit down at the table.

After he was seated, Elder, laying the paper down, raised an inquiring brow to Landis. "You said you needed to speak with Mrs. Mortimer on an important matter."

"Yes sir."

"Well, son, what is so urgent that it couldn't wait?"

The Elder had always made Landis feel like he was under a

microscope. It was as if he could see right through him. Landis eyes immediately went to Mrs. Mortimer.

"Spencer, it's time for you to go to church." She shooed him away. "It's Saturday. Remember? One o'clock prayer." Mrs. Mortimer returned to the stove where she was cooking. She had on a big white apron over a blue jean dress with the words *Ella's in Charge* imprinted on it. She turned toward Landis. "Son, want something to eat? I've made Gumbo."

Landis knew it was a time waster to tell her he wasn't hungry. After all he'd been eating in this house for many years. "Yes ma'am," Landis replied.

Elder Mortimer raised his tall sinewy frame and kissed his wife. He had on gray sweat pants, gym shoes and a white t-shirt. He looked more like he was getting ready for a game of ball than going to church. "Landis, I'll see you later. Now don't go making a play for my wife." He winked. Landis laughed. Elder still managed to surprise him. One-minute stern, the next joking. Little Pier was a lot like her father.

After sitting a big bowl of soup in front of Landis, Mrs. Mortimer sat down with a cup of coffee in the seat her husband abandoned. She looked questionably at him.

"So, son, what you want to talk about?" She raised the cup to her lips taking a swallow of the coffee. "You've been a little distracted lately. I noticed it even at the wedding reception. What gives, boy?" Her soft southern drawl was laced with concern.

Landis lost what little appetite he had mustered up. He picked up his spoon as merely something to do with his hand. Setting the spoon back down, he nervously played with the bowl.

"Mrs. Mortimer, I-now that I'm here, I don't know where to begin."

"Always at the beginning. How many times do I have to tell you children?" She gave him a gentle smile. She was in her mid-fifties but looked more like early forties. She wore her slightly gray hair long, framing her oval face. The only wrinkles were the crow's feet in the corner of her light brown eyes. Eyes so like Piers.

Landis cleared his throat and began the story in his mind. He should begin with, *"there's no easy way to say it except just to say it."* He rubbed his hand over his head. *"I think, no- make that I know I'm in love with your daughter."*

She would probably say, *"Don't you think you should be discussing this with Shannan?"*

No doubt this would cause him to stand up and pace the floor. *"That's just it, Mrs. Mortimer. It's not Shannan. It's Pier."*

Knowing her, she wouldn't miss a beat. She probably would calmly sit the cup back down and fold her hands together and say, *"Son, we do seem to have a problem.* She'd unfold her hands. *"Now why don't you tell me how and when this happened? As far as I know you have never treated Pier anyway except like a little sister."*

Without realizing what he was doing, Landis had stood up and was pacing the floor.

"Please, Landis, sit down. You're making me dizzy." He immediately sat down.

"Now tell me, what it is you wanted to talk about."

Losing all his courage of what he would say, Landis slowly exhaled and could only plaster a smile on his face, hoping this perceptive woman didn't see through him.

"I wanted to tell you the good news and get your opinion on it."

Sitting her cup down, Mrs. Mortimer nodded her head for

him to continue.

"I got a job offer at a bank in Chicago. I've accepted it."

She gave him a big grin and a thumb up. "That's wonderful. I'm happy for you son. This is the beginning. But why so secretive? If you've accepted the job, everyone will know." She paused in thought, "there's something else you want to talk about?"

Landis averted his gaze from hers. "No nothing else," he lied. He moved restlessly around in his seat, a dead give away something else was on his mind. "I need to know if you think it's a good idea or should I apply for something else."

"Well, I don't know much about banking but it sounds like a good idea. I hate to see you move from home again. You've just gotten back, but it's what you want that matters."

She got up and poured herself another cup of coffee and a pop for Landis.

"Thank you," he said after receiving the drink. "I'm hesitant about leaving, but I've got to get started if I want to one day co-own a bank."

They laughed. Both knowing co-owning a bank was one of his goals in working toward helping under privileged people. Thank God his father and Mr. Mortimer sold their business and invested the money wisely, causing their children to receive a nice piece of change when they turn twenty-one. Landis had invested his and made a nice profit.

"I, young man, have no doubt you'll be successful in whatever endeavor you plan."

"You have always said that."

"And I mean it." She looked intently at him. "I can't help thinking you have more to say."

He continued the conversation in his mind, *"it's crazy. I'm crazy!*

Mrs. Mortimer, I'm tripping that something like this has happen. I would never have dreamed or planned anything like this. You're right, I've never thought of her as anything except a little sister that is until the night of her birthday. I- She looked so beautiful and innocent. When she smiles, her eyes light up. When she laughs, you laugh. Something happened that night when she looked at me and smiled. Ma'am, I don't know the words to describe her smile except it's like a ray of sunlight in a hundred midnights. I no longer saw this little kid that bugs me with questions when I used to visit. I saw a young lady on the brink of becoming a woman. Something happened that's never happened in all my twenty-four years. I felt like my search was over and this is what I've been looking for. I didn't plan it, nor was I looking for it. It just happened. Now please, ma'am, tell me what to do. Tell me I'm not crazy.

"Landis, is there anything else you want to tell me?" she asked again.

Landis shook himself out of his daydreaming. He looked at Mrs. Mortimer and shook his head no.

He picked up his bowl as he stood up and carried it to the sink. "I appreciate you listening, Mrs. Mortimer. I guess I better go. I still have a lot to do."

"I hate to see you go. It was hard enough when you went away to college."

"Oh, I don't mind leaving," he murmured to himself. "It's coming back that concerns me." He'd bent down and kissed Mrs. Mortimer and quickly exited the back door. He remembered seeing Pier as he left; he told her he was moving to Chicago in a couple of weeks. She'd had momentarily looked in disbelief. Then she hugged him and said she would miss him.

Once again, the ringing telephone brought him back to the present. Landis knew this had to be Shannan.

"Hello."

"What's up player?"

Landis laughed. "Hello Shan. I've been expecting your call."

"Speedy bighead called you, didn't he?"

"Yeah, he did. Just like old times. I got a 'hey man, Shannan's gonna call you.'"

Shannan giggled. "Well, I won't keep you. Just give me a yes or no and I'm off the phone. It better be yes, buddy or you are in some real trouble."

"Hey motor mouth, can I at least say something?"

"As long as it's something, go ahead."

Rubbing his brow, Landis sat back down on the leather couch. "Okay, lovely Shan, you've talked me into it. I'm too scared to say no."

Chapter Two

The April clouds, which hovered all morning, suddenly burst, releasing snowy rain showers all over Pier Mortimer as she made a mad dash from her red Honda to her brother's small front porch. "Just great," she muttered to herself. Now her hair was wet. She decided she should have stayed in bed.

And she would have if this wasn't her Saturday to work at LaKay's Adult Academic Program. She volunteered there twice a month teaching working adults basic math to pass the GED program.

The song, "This is the day that the Lord has made", is what Pier has been singing and reciting every since she woke up late this morning. She sang it when she burned the eggs while boiling them. She did pause to ask the question, how do you burn boiled eggs? Her resounding answer was "let Pier in the kitchen".

She recited it when a student she had worked with for months decided not to take the GED test in fear of failing. She was exhausted after finally convincing her student to take the test.

She bellowed, "This is the day that the Lord has made" as she waited for road service to come and give her a jump because her car wouldn't start. And all of this drama had caused her to arrive late to her brother's house.

She shuddered as a gust of wind blew around her neck and face, causing her to pull up the collar of her red leather jacket. Yesterday was beautiful and she had gladly welcomed the sunny smile of spring; her favorite time of the year, but today winter clearly got the last laugh. Pier shivered as she waited in front of the door. Hurry back, spring, she mumbled to herself as she pressed the doorbell.

A few seconds later, her sister-in-law, Micah Rochelle, opened the door. "Hey girl. Get in here. Can you believe the weatherman? He said sunshine, blue skies. A nice April day he said." She grabbed Pier's arm and pulled her inside the small foyer. She was dressed in blue jeans and a sweatshirt. "Do you think they deliberately lie or they just don't know any better?" Her dark brown almond shaped eyes alight with humor, eyes like her brother, Landis.

Landis!

Where did that come from? She couldn't think of Landis. It was too painful.

Shaking her head, forcing a laugh, Pier hung her coat in the closet. She watched Micah Rochelle through long damp hair, taking in her high cheekbones and ready smile that revealed white even teeth. That smile had been available for many years for Pier. She had always loved Micah Rochelle even before she was her sister-in-law.

"We're in the kitchen," said Micah leading the way. Their house was modern and spacious with three bedrooms, two baths, an enormous living room and dining room. The décor was black and white with splashes of color on the walls and tables. The black and white decorated kitchen was through two big white doors. It was large enough to hold a sitting area containing a couch, chair, coffee table and television.

On entering the kitchen, they found Speedy moving from counter top to stove battering chicken and putting it in the skillet. Chicken was his favorite. His tall wiry body clad in faded jeans and a black t-shirt didn't look at all out of place in the kitchen. He had on one of his famous aprons reading: *I'm Hen-Pecked. I do whatever I'm told.* He looked up and grinned when he saw her.

"There she is. Hey you." He pointed a battered chicken leg at her. "'Bout time for you to get here. I was beginning to think you weren't coming." Light brown eyes smoldered with laughter.

"And miss seeing you in that apron, Handsome?" Sitting at the table, Pier shook her head. "I don't think so. Is it new?"

Ever since returning home from Atlanta, Georgia where she went to college, Pier spent one Saturday out of the month with Spencer and his family. It was usually just them but a couple of times some of their friends were invited.

"Girl, you know it is," said Micah Rochelle coming in the kitchen. "He better wear a sign telling who the boss is." She handed Pier a towel to dry her rain-drenched face and hair.

Speedy finished putting the chicken in the skillet; he raised flour battered hands at Micah Rochelle and leered at her. He went over to the sink and washed his hands with antibacterial soap.

"Whuz up with ya, little Pier?"

Micah Rochelle stepped lightly on his foot as she carried broccoli florets over to the sink for him to wash. "I keep telling you, Speedy, she is not little anymore. She'll soon be twenty-three." Turning to Pier with a wide grin she said, "Gotta forgive your brother, girl, you will always be the 'baby' to him." She took the clean veggies and prepared to cook them. "He drove himself crazy the whole time you were in Atlanta. Then when you did like Landis and stayed an extra year, I thought I was going to be a widow."

"Don't remind me. I can't stand this talk," mocked Speedy, as he flopped down in the kitchen chair across the table from Pier. "Our baby has grown up." He placed his hand over his heart. "I can't take it."

Pier took her hand and dramatically laid it on her brow. In an imitated southern drawl she said, "Well, I declare, Handsome, I better not tell you what I really was doing in Atlanta." At Speedy's look of alarm, she and Micah Rochelle burst out laughing.

"Quit playing, little girl," said Speedy, sounding like their father. "Is this your Saturday to work at the school?"

"Yep. My day has been terrible." She briefly explained her day's events. "And now, I'm having car trouble. I hope it lasts 'til I buy a new one."

"Want me to get it checked out?" Speedy asked.

"Nope. I'm waiting for my birthday. Then I'm buying myself a brand new red convertible." She started to sway and rock to imaginary music.

Anyone who's seen Pier drive would tremble as Speedy and Micah were doing. Not that she was a bad driver. In fact she was rather good. Never had a parking or speeding ticket. She merely pushed to the speed limit and darted in and out of the lanes that could aggravate even a racecar driver.

"Say it ain't so, little Pier," Speedy said with raised eyebrows.

"I sure am."

"Just tell me when you're driving and I'll make sure to be off the road."

"Stop it. I'm a good driver."

"Yeah, if you were on a lone Texas road."

The child monitor on the counter revealed their son, Spency, awakened. "I'll go get him," volunteered Pier. She exited quickly.

She loved her nephew. She found two-year-old Spency sitting up in his bed, with his big chocolate eyes, so like his uncle Landis, filled with tears.

"Hello, lil man. You're glad to see your auntie Pier." She lifts him out of the bed. "Oh boy, somebody's wet." She laid him on the changing table. "You want your auntie to change your diaper? Oops! Excuse me, lil man, you have on pull-ups. I forgot what a big boy you are." She tickles his stomach, provoking a giggle out of him.

"Come on, let's go downstairs and see Mama and Daddy," she said after changing him.

As Pier reentered the kitchen with Spency, the phone rings; Speedy answers with a "yello". "Landis! Whuz up man?" With phone tucked between ear and shoulder, he took Spency out of Pier arms and put him in his high chair.

Pier's heart raced a little. *Landis*. Speedy was talking to Landis. She stilled her trembling hands by placing them on the back of Spency's highchair. Pier hadn't seen Landis for almost five years. But she could visualize like yesterday the day she fell in love with Landis. Simply a schoolgirl crush, she had convinced herself. Whatever it was, it still had her heart pounding like a drum in a jungle. She could feel her palms sweating just knowing he was on the other end of the line talking to Speedy.

When did her feelings change from loving him as a brother to loving him as a man? So long ago it was hard to remember.

Liar. It began when she was sixteen and was e-mailing him. Then, when he returned home, she tried to spend every waking moment with him without revealing her feelings to anyone.

He had always been patient with her. Even as a child, when her own brother didn't have time for her, Landis did, answering all of her questions. One time, to her brother's disgust, he even had imaginary tea with her.

She had to be about five when he would come in and pull her braids and call her Little Pier. The name had stuck with her to this day.

Yes, he was a patient caring man. And that patience spilled over when she e-mailed him about everything. Every Friday after school, she would rush to her room and send him humorous things about her week.

And Landis, being Landis, e-mailed her right back, treating her like a young lady instead of a child. He talked to her, not at her. They were pals.

As well as being Speedy's brother-in-law, they'd been best friends for almost twenty years. Pier was a couple years older than Spency when they first met.

"Oh, nothing much. We're getting ready to eat", Speedy was saying. "The brat's here, dateless as usual. I was hoping she'd take her friend, Devin, out of his misery and invite him." He listened. "Yep it's our once a month Saturday." He was listening to Landis again. He laughed. Getting out of the chair, he propped the cordless phone between shoulder and ear again, as he took the rest of the chicken out and turned the burner off.

"Hey Little Pier, Landis said to tell you hello."

Widening her eyes and clearing her throat, Pier said, "Tell him hi." She was sure he heard her voice tremble.

It had been a couple months after the wedding when he dropped by to tell her mom goodbye that she'd last seen him. He told her he accepted a banker's job in Chicago.

Ironically, because of her feelings for Landis, Pier had snuck and applied for college in Atlanta. This had caused a big family emergency meeting with Speedy ranting about her being too young. If she had known Landis was moving, she would have stayed with the University of Minnesota.

She was in love with him and had known for certain since she saw him at the airport. And he didn't know she existed.

She went with Speedy to pick him up from the airport. She vaguely knew what he looked like after five years living in Colorado. So when she saw him walking toward them, she was not expecting him to be as tall, as big or as handsome as he was.

As she looked into his eyes, she wondered why she never noticed them before. They were the most beautiful eyes she had ever seen. They were melty milk chocolate and smiling at her. After greeting Speedy, Pier ran to him throwing her arms around him, holding him very tight. His laughter was a deep boisterous sound that would make merry the coldest of hearts.

After exclaiming how much she had grown, he told Speedy he thought she was Shannon. She smiled, used to hearing their friends' remark on the likeness. She remembered thinking it's too bad she was just a kid and he a man.

"I hope", Speedy was saying interrupting her thoughts, "when you get here, the ladies, especially Kayla, let you spend some time with your family and not all of it with her." He laughed. "You are tripping out, man. You know that girl likes you." He laughed again. "Come on now, Landis, when you were here for Christmas, that girl took to you like bees to honey." Speedy sat back in the chair laughing. "Nope. I promise I will not try to match make you with Shannan or anyone else." He threw his head back and laughed harder.

The ladies? Who's Kayla? Pier asked herself. She realized she didn't know very much about Landis anymore. Kayla was probably one of his girls in Minnesota. She heard he had lots of girlfriends. If he looked as good as he did five years ago, the rumor probably is true.

As she listened to their conversation, she decided nothing could ever sever Speedy and Landis' friendship. They were as close as brothers. Pier didn't know how close until she started spending her Saturdays with Speedy and his family. Speedy, the great storyteller, had a habit of stretching the truth. Thanks to Micah Rochelle correcting his exaggeration, Pier was pretty sure she had the truth.

Just last month when she was visiting, they filled her in on exactly how Speedy and Landis met. They were around ten when Landis and his family moved into the neighborhood. Speedy was noisy and always laughing. Landis, although he had a sense of humor, was quiet and always seemed to be thinking or planning. He was nicknamed around the hood as "Landis 'I've got a plan' Lovington."

Micah Rochelle explained that Landis was drawn to Speedy; it just took him longer because he didn't make friends easily.

According to Speedy, they didn't hit it off right away. It was only after a bully was messing with Micah and Speedy defended her, that he and Landis became friends. Micah volunteered that's when she "fell in love" with Speedy. And five boyfriends later, they live happily ever after.

"Okay. Okay. Hey man, you're the one who moved out of

town," Pier heard Speedy say, as he moved back to the stove pushing Micah Rochelle out the way with his hip; he stirred the vegetable she deserted. He listened. "Okay, here's Micah." He handed the phone to his wife.

Micah was laughing at him before she could say hello. "What's up brother?" Pier heard Micah say before carrying the cordless phone into the other room. She and Landis were just as close as Speedy and Shannan. Pier was the odd person out because she was a few years younger.

Pier could hear more laughter. She wondered what he was saying that makes everyone laugh. No sooner had the question went through her mind did Micah come back and hand her the phone.

"Landis wants to speak to you."

Pier raised perfectly arched brows. *Really!* "H-hello," she stammered. Great, she was sounding like she was still eighteen.

He repeated, "Hello," and she thought, oh yeah, feelings definitely still there.

"H-Hi Landis, How are you?" She asked just a tad too brightly.

"I'm good. I'm good. How about you, Little Pier?" Still the same smooth timbre voice. Not too deep. Velvet. Sexy. Just right.

"Doing just great." Her chest was really pounding hard. *What do I say to him? Help!* "So you're coming to Shannan's birthday celebration?" Great, what a conversationalist she is.

"Yes. I've missed enough of Shannan's birthdays."

"Oh, that's right. I remember you and Shannan used to date."

"No, little Pier," he said firmly. "We were all just friends. That is until your brother decided to marry my sister." He laughed. She, like Speedy and Micah Rochelle, laughs also. So that's it, she concluded. His laughter makes you want to laugh.

"So tell me, little Pier, how many hearts have you broken since I've seen you?"

"None." *Falling for you has hindered me from having serious relationships.*

"I know you're kidding me. You were breaking hearts when you were just a teenager."

Pier's mind instantly flashed back to the night of her eighteenth birthday, the night she knew beyond a shadow of doubt he was more than just Speedy's friend or Shannon's *boyfriend*. She knew him as a man.

"Well, I look forward to seeing you next week. It has been awhile", Pier said softly.

"Do you really?" The tone of his voice changed.

"Really what?" *Really, let's get off this phone before I make a complete fool of myself,* she was thinking.

"Look forward to seeing me," he answered quietly.

Pier cleared her throat. "Yes, I do."

Landis sighed. "I'm glad," he murmured. "I can't wait to see you either."

"I-I uh-," she stuttered, "h-here's Micah Rochelle." She handed Micah the phone as if it was hot coals.

After eating a leisurely dinner, they watched a movie, some romantic comedy that had Pier thinking about Landis. Speedy and Micah Rochelle were acting like newlyweds. Maybe that's how people in love acted. Pier played with Spency until it was time for him to go to bed. She then decided to go home.

She thanked them for letting her spend Saturday with them as

Speedy helped with her coat.

"Is red still your favorite color?" He's been asking her this question for years.

"Always," was the standard answer.

"I'll walk you to your car," he said. Micah was standing in the doorway waving.

"So little Pier, who are you bringing to Shannan's birthday celebration?"

"No one."

"Why not?" Speedy asked. Not that he was complaining; nobody was good enough for his little sister. But he was concerned about her lack of dates since she had been home.

He opened the car door for her. The rain had stopped. The wind, however, was blowing hard on their faces. Pier leaps into her red sporty car.

She rolled the window down, "You know me. I may not even stay long. I might leave after a couple of hours. Y'all too old for me", she teased. 'Bye Handsome." Pier bagged out the driveway leaving her brother's tall wiry frame waving.

Later that night as Pier prepared for bed, she remembered her conversation with Landis. Why did he ask to speak to her? He had some nerve. She hadn't seen or spoken to Landis for almost five years. He usually sent words of hello through Shannan, Speedy or Micah Rochelle. She always felt like he was avoiding her. He was never in town when she was. The only Christmas he came to town was last year, the one she couldn't make. It didn't take a rocket scientist to figure it out. Maybe he didn't want to be in the same vicinity as she was.

She had been hurt when he couldn't make her college graduation. She remembered calling her brother and excitingly telling him to let Landis know she had an extra ticket just for him. She really wanted him to see her as an adult. He'd regretfully sent best wishes and a beautiful gold bracelet, which she rarely took off, but couldn't make it.

Now he wanted to talk to her. And he was flirting. Or maybe she wished he were. She sometimes wondered if he remembered what happened on her birthday. She did. She'd never forget. Not the Bulldog part but the part where Landis kissed her.

Sighing as she always did when she thought of Landis, she knew she'd never forget the feel of his arms around her, comforting her. And the gentle way he pressed his lips on hers. Apologizing...

Sighing, Pier got into bed and pulled the covers over her shoulders. She shut her mind down on those thoughts. She wondered what Landis was doing on a Saturday night. Probably partying or with his girlfriend. Anything but thinking of his best friend's baby sister. How will she act when she sees him again? Most likely like an adolescent. Whatever, she couldn't wait to see him.

<hr />

Landis lay in his bed thinking about Pier. Almost five years since he'd heard her voice or seen her face. Staying away had been hard. He thought it would be better if he didn't even talk to her. Pier stirred up things best forgotten. Like what happened on her birthday. To this day he remembered it as if it happened a few hours ago. Every time he thought about it he couldn't believe he had actually kissed her. Rubbing his brow, he groaned. Walking away had been hard but not impossible. Just discipline. *Discipline!* Shoot, he should have joined the army or at least got a disciplinary award.

He would casually inquire about her from Speedy or Shannon. He'd drilled poor Micah Rochelle about everything; when did she last visit, about her grades, who was she dating and whether or not it seemed serious, and how did she look? He was surprised no one had a clue of his true feelings for Pier.

The telephone rang. He turned on the bed light and answered to the sound of Jackie's soft voice on the other end.

"Hi sweetie," she said. "What are you doing?"

"I'm in bed. What are doing?" Please, he thought to himself, don't ask to come over, not tonight. He wants to be alone with his thoughts of Pier. Why he asked to speak to her he'd never know. When Speedy said she was there, he should have ended the conversation and called back later. No. He had to talk to her before seeing her.

He needed to get on with his life and get over whatever he was feeling for Pier. Yeah, right. If he hasn't by now, he may never get over her.

"Landis? Did you hear what I said?"

"No. What?"

"I said I wish I was there. Are you sleeping?" Jackie sounded a little irritated.

"No, of course not. I'm daydreaming at night." Landis sighed. He shook himself and closed the door to all thoughts of Pier.

"I can't come over tonight. I'm staying at my sister's giving her and her husband a break with the baby. I just called to let you know I'm thinking about you."

"That's good to know, Jackie." He rubbed his brow. Jackie's a good woman.

"Alright, sweetie. I have to go. Hopefully I'll see you tomorrow before I leave town."

"Okay. Bye." Groaning, Landis hung up the phone. She was good for him. He had been seeing Jackie Reynolds for about a year. Maybe he should reconsider a future with her, since she is the longest relationship he'd had in five years. The rest, after a couple months of dating, he'd end it with a thank you gift. Not that he was careless or an uncaring man. Basically he'd be looking for something he'd already found, someone to spend the rest of his life with. Oh God! Why did it have to be Pier?

Why did he let them talk him into coming? When he sees Pier and nothing has changed, he'll…what? Nothing! She's still Speedy's baby sister and still out of his reach. He remembered, as if it was yesterday, instead of years ago how upset Speedy was when their friend Ace said he wanted to date Pier. Maybe he could call Speedy and talk with him about his feeling. He closed his eyes and visualized Speedy's reaction and shook his head with dismay. He knows Speedy. He wouldn't understand, not his baby sister.

It was useless to try to sleep. Landis frowned and got out of bed. He headed downstairs to the kitchen. The night would be a long familiar one. He grabbed a can of cola out the fridge and picked up the phone and dialed Shannan's number.

"Hello," a sleepy Shannan whispered.

"What's up, Shannan?" Landis sat in the kitchen chair. He took a swig of his drink.

"Who is this and why are you calling me this late?"

"Come now, sweetheart, don't get old on me. It's Saturday night and you're in bed at eleven?"

"Landis? You jerk. Who said I was alone. What's up with you?"

"I'm checking to see if I can bring someone with me to your party."

"And this couldn't wait until morning. Who you wanna bring? A girlfriend? Jackie is her name, right? Finally we get to meet a Chicago woman of yours." Shannan wide awake now. "Sure, you can bring her."

"Yep. Her name is Jackie. We have been dating for about a year. I like her, but there is someone else I have strong feelings for." Great! Where did that come from? He's never blurted anything out in his life.

"What?"

Landis smirked. At least he has her attention. Knowing Shannan, she was sitting straight up in bed, all thoughts of sleep gone. If she was nothing else, she was noisy. They had had a lot of fun growing up and hanging out together, but they could never go past that brother and sister stage. As much as Speedy and Micah tried after they'd became serious, Landis and Shannan had never seen one another as anything except siblings.

"Are you alone?" he wanted to know.

"Yes. What difference does it make? That's not like you. Whose this other girl you want? Why aren't you with her?"

Same old Shannan.

"May I answer one question at a time?" At her grunt of yes, he continued. "First of all, Jackie is a nice beautiful woman I met when her sister came in the bank for a loan. We hit it off right away. One thing led to another."

"And Speedy knows about her?"

"Yeah. She was out of town when they visited. So they've never met her."

"And this other woman. How did you meet her and who is she?"

Landis took another swallow of cola. "It doesn't matter who she is. I can't be with her. I can never be with her. Sometimes I think I just want what I can't have," Landis said sadly.

"Landis! Is she married? Is that what it is?" Shannan asked, voice laced with concern.

"No, she not married. As far as I know, she's not with anyone." Landis immediately shut down. "Listen, Shan, I can't talk about it. I guess I was feeling sorry for myself. I'll let you go."

"No, you will not let me go. If this woman is not married, why can't you be with her? The Landis I know is not a quitter. You're Mr. Fix It. Fight for what you want."

"That's what I said a few years ago. But I can't. There is too much at stake and besides, she doesn't think of me in that way."

"I'm more confused now than before. What is up, brother? Talk to me." Shannan sounded as frustrated as Landis felt.

"I won't say much more. I shouldn't have said anything."

"Boy, this is deep."

"I'm thinking maybe if Jackie will have me, we should get married. I'm twenty-nine. I'm ready to settle down. I want kids. I envy Speedy every time we visit."

"I agree you are feeling sorry for yourself. Marrying someone you don't love," she muttered to herself. "Loving someone who doesn't love you. Settling for something less than love. I guess a big time vice president doesn't have time to plan. I am tripping. You're tripping. I've never heard you talk like this before," she paused as if getting a second wind.

"Okay, enough, Shannan. You, dear sis, don't know the whole story. And I'm not at liberty to tell it all. Now tell me why you're asleep on a Saturday night."

Shannan grudgingly accepted the changed subject. "I guess this coming birthday has made me want to get somewhere and sit down. Now don't go ruining my rep by telling somebody."

"My lips are sealed. Please don't tell on me either."

"You know me better. I'm a quiet noisy person."

Landis threw his can in the recycle bin. "May I get off the phone now, mother?"

"I guess. But Landis, when you come, don't bring Jackie. When girls go out of town to meet the family, they get the idea things are getting serious. Don't do that to her. Okay?"

"Yes, ma'am. I do care for her. Too bad you and I never fell in love, hmm."

"Yeah, right. I don't know what this woman you want is like, but you need someone who is supportive, caring, very loving and able to stand up to you. Someone like, actually like Little Pier. Okay, enough preaching. I love you Bighead. Bye."

Landis hoped she didn't hear him catch his breath. "I love you, too. Maybe Speed's not the only preacher. Bye, sweet heart." He hung the cordless up. So Shannan thinks someone like little Pier is his type. All of a sudden things were looking up. Whistling, he headed back to bed.

Chapter Three

The next morning was Sunday, a church day. Everyone who lived in the Mortimer's' house, which Pier did, went to church. Pier, being a Christian, didn't mind. She dressed in her Sunday best and headed to Sunday school.

Although, Shannan didn't go to church, afterwards she always dropped by faithfully every Sunday to visit. This particular Sunday, Pier was upstairs in her room listening to some gospel music, when Shannan stuck her head in to say hello.

"Hey, Pier. See, I didn't say little." She grinned and sat on the bed. "So what's up Bighead?" Her short-layered hair was immaculately styled as usual. So was her make-up.

Pier, sitting crossed legged on her bed, leaned forward and turned down the music. "Nothing much. What's up with you, Bighead?"

"Nothing much," Shannan mimicked. She pauses, listening to the music. "Girl, you just ain't natural." She stretched out on the bed. "You should be out enjoying your life. Having some fun, but no, you're sitting here listening to church music. Didn't you go to church today? Didn't you have enough?"

Having heard 'you just ain't natural' in every conversation with Shannan since she'd returned home three months ago, Pier learned to tune her out. She turned the music off.

Shannan, at Piers age, gave everyone a hard time. She'd wanted to "party." She was what her mom called, "rebelliously" finding her way. Thank God, her sister was no longer like that. Her argument was, however, that Pier should experience life before living a "good Christian" boring life.

Changing the subject, she asked about the party she was having for her birthday. "You've been kinda hush-hush about this year's party."

"To tell you the truth, I don't really want to go all out celebrating my day this year. I wanted it to be just family and a few friends. But you know how daddy is. He's the one who goes all out on birthdays." Shannan sat up and smoothed her pretty blue cotton sweater over creased jeans.

"I know, I thought I was the only one who felt that way." Pier stood up and stretched. "I guess when your birthdays not recognized as a child, it makes you get a little zealous for your children."

"A little." She looked at Pier as if she was nuts, "girl, you know daddy gets crazy around our birthday times."

They laughed.

"Remember your eighteenth, Daddy had invited all those kids from the church and I, of course, pop in with my "thug" friends. I thought Speedy and Landis were going to kill me. Your boyfriend, what's-his-name, was so jealous of Bulldog. Speedy and Landis spent the whole night being bodyguards. Come to think of it, that was the last house party."

Shannan fell back on the bed giggling. "You were so miserable." Sitting up again, she asked, "Did I ever say sorry?" Pier shook her head no. "I really am sorry, sis. God! I was so crazy a few years ago." She stood up and looked around the bedroom. She gave her usual 'ugh' at the red décor in Pier's room.

"You're so uptight. I just want you to have some fun." Shannan smiled prettily at her young sister.

Pier smiled right back. Shannan had always gotten her way. She did as Landis said and put that night behind her, although, the pain of that night still periodically crept up in her mind. If it had been Speedy instead of Landis who found Bulldog trying to kiss her, she wondered what would have happened. As it was, Landis went berserk.

"So tell me, what are you wearing?" Shannan asked offhandedly as she flopped down in the over stuffed strawberry colored chair.

"I don't know. I really don't have anything. What kind of party is it? How do I need to dress?

"Oh I thought I told you, the dress code is formal. Very formal. We're going to sit at the table and eat and listen to dad's speech. Mingle a little, then when the 'saints' march on, we party." She raised a brow. "What do you think?"

"Sounds like a plan. I guess I'll leave with the saints."

Shannan sighed. "You know, Pier, I hope in the years to come you don't regret not enjoying life while you're young. We are not perfect and we all make mistakes. Sometimes I think you're trying so hard to please everybody that you don't know what Pier wants. And when you do realize what you want, it may be what you least expect and cause you to rethink life."

Groaning, Pier changed the subject by asking, "You're glad

Landis' coming?"

"Sure, why not? It's always good to see Landis. We had fun growing up, the four of us hanging out at the mall, going to the movies, trying to get in clubs. Then when he went away to college, things changed. Speed and Mic decided they were in love."

Shannan made a face and said 'Yuk.' "Landis moved to Colorado, then Chicago. I like visiting him and all but things changed. That's why you should live a little," her answer to every question in life.

Pier pondered on what her sister was saying. Shannan rarely chatted and when she did, Pier enjoyed listening. "You're sounding a little nostalgic about Landis."

"Yeah, I am. You know how the old folks say 'those were the days,' when you're young, which I still am, but you think you'll be young the rest of your life. Something about this birthday that's making me, I guess, grow up. I'll be twenty-seven and I don't know what settling down is. It's time I learn.

"Landis plays an important part in my life because he and Speedy kept us girls together growing up. Landis' always been so level headed.

"You know when he visits, Speedy and Micah drive us crazy trying to mate us."

Pier laughed, "You sound like y'all animals."

"That's how they treat us."

"They just want y'all to be happy like they are. Now listen, I always thought you and Landis were going together when y'all use to kick it."

Shannan pushed herself out the chair. "Get real. Girl that would be like kissing Speedy. Incest," glancing at her watch, "I gotta go." She walked to the door and turned around and pointed a finger at Pier. "I have the perfect dress for you. It's a little big on me so it should fit you just fine. And the day of the party, you, Micah, and I are going to the spa and get the full treatment. Let's call this another coming out party. Speedy gonna trip fighting the men off you." Shaking her head, "Landis too." She winked and was gone.

Pier falling back on the pillows, sighing, she knew the kind of dresses Shannan wears. Landis will get to see her as a woman in a dress to kill. She giggled and bounced up and down on the bed. "For once in my life, I'm going to dress to kill", she sang.

⊰⊱

April 23ʳᵈ, Shannan's birthday, finally arrived. On the day of the party, Shannan, Micah Rochelle and Pier spent the entire day getting ready. As Shannan had promised they went to the spa and got the full treatment. They also went to the hair salon. Shannan wore her hair short and tapered in the back. She had it colored light brown. It went good with her caramel complexion. She was about five feet three inches tall and had a slender figure.

Micah was the shortest of the three, at least five feet two inches. She got her hair swooped into a French roll.

Pier was five feet six inches tall, more curvy and busty than the other two women. She opted to wear her black shoulder length hair straight slightly framing her face.

Looking good but exhausted, they stopped at the Burger Place and ordered diet drinks and one large fry to snack on before heading home to get dressed. The party was schedule to start in a few hours.

"I hadn't heard whether or not Landis was here yet?" Shannan said to Micah Rochelle. "He better not renege on me."

Micah Rochelle laughed. "He should be here by now. Probably hanging out with Speedy. I talked to him last night and he's definitely coming. He's staying at the parent's house. I don't know why he won't stay with us."

"Good, as long as he comes," said Shannan licking the ketchup off her fingers.

At the talk of Landis, Pier once again felt her heart race. She quickly grabbed her diet coke and gulped it. Of course, she choked. "I'm okay", she said at their inquiring look.

"So tell me, Mic, did he bring a date or is he supposed to be mines?" Shannan mocked her sister-in-law.

"No, he didn't. And girl, Speedy and I are done with the match making business. Y'all on your own."

"Why didn't he bring a date?" Pier asked hesitantly. "Doesn't he have a girlfriend?"

"He's seeing some girl name Jackie", replies Micah Rochelle. "She's a model. We didn't meet her when we visited last year. Land doesn't talk much about her. But he doesn't talk much about any of his women." She and Shannan giggled.

They polished their fries off and headed to Shannan's condo, where Pier and Micah had left their cars.

"Hang on, Pier, I'll run upstairs and get your dress." She pointed her index finger at Pier. "You better wear it." They waved Micah off. Shannan ran in the building of her condo. Pier leaned on the door of her car.

"I mean you better wear it," Shannan warned again when she returned with the dress in a garment bag. "Promise me. And don't look at it until it's time to put it on. I know you. One look and you won't wear it. You'll wear something low budget, looking a mess. Promise."

"Alright. Man. I'll wear the dress", trying to hide her excitement. Little did Shannan know, Pier wanted to wear something nice so Landis could see her as a... Shaking her head she hung the garment bag on the hook on the back door of the car and got in waving as she drove off.

Pier arrived home to the sound of laughter. Her dad was getting dressed. From the sound of it, her mom was making fun of him. As far as Pier knew, their marriage was perfect. Her mom, Ella, was about Shannan's height and they were identical in everything but personality. Shannan had her own character.

"Hi Handsome", Pier said to her dad. He was standing in front of the long mirror in the upstairs hallway. Her mom returned to their bedroom to finish getting dress. Her dad was tall gray headed with skin the color of coffee. With the exception of skin color, Speedy looked a lot like him. They both were good looking men.

"Hi, Baby Girl, go get ready," he commanded as he fixed his tie. "We want to be on time."

"Dad, it's only a party", she teased him. "Besides we have a couple more hours."

"Only a party," he frowned. "It's not a party. It's a celebration. We are celebrating the fact that the good Lord let my daughter see another year. Same thing next month when you turn twenty."

"Twenty-three," Pier exclaimed.

He chuckled. "Just checking to see if you are listening." He turned from the mirror to look at Pier. "Voila. How does the old man look?"

"You look tight, dad." At his puzzled look, "handsome."

"Whatever happened to cool?" Shaking his head, "Go get

dress, Pier. You're riding with us. I don't trust your car enough for you to be driving around late at night. Speedy can give you a ride back if you don't want to leave with us."

Nodding her head in agreement, Pier rushed to her room with the dress in hand. She wrapped her hair and took a quick shower and pampered her skin as instructed at the spa. Oh no, she exclaimed. What if she didn't have the right shoes for the dress? All man. Why didn't she think about this before?

Almost afraid now to look at the dress, Pier unzipped the garment bag. Shannan has good taste so there was really no need to worry if it was stylish. If she says she has the perfect dress, you can count on it. Pier pulled out the most beautiful dress she'd ever seen. It was a simple classic long red dress with spaghetti straps and a sheer waist jacket. The neckline was low but tasteful. The sheer jacket clasped together with a silver broach. Pier slipped it over her head hoping she could do the dress justice. Perfect fit. She suspected Shannan bought the dress especially for her. And she did have the perfect shoes-silver stilettos from graduation. Shannan probably checked before getting the dress.

She repaired her make up. Standing in front of the same mirror as her father had, she decided she looked nice. The only thing she didn't like about the dress was the long split on the left side. Every time she walked her leg and thigh would show.

Picking up her sister's gift, she walked downstairs to the den, where she knew her parents would be waiting. "Well how do I look?" Her dad eyes widened and he opened his mouth as if to say something, only to close it after looking at his wife. Her mother clapped her hands, declaring Pier looked gorgeous and she had the perfect wrap for her to wear. Watching her mother leave the room, Pier couldn't help admiring how pretty she looked in a royal blue dress. She hoped she would age as well as her mother.

"You don't think it's a bit too much?" she asked on her mother's return with the wrap. "One of Shannan dresses." She made a face.

"No hon, it's perfect. Shannan has impeccable taste as always."

All the while she was getting dressed, Pier tried not to think of seeing Landis. Now sitting in the back seat of her dad's car, Landis was all she could think about. How will she act? I hope I don't make a fool of myself, she thought. I hope I don't stutter. I hope I don't faint. I hope these feelings are gone. I hope I can get on with my life and get serious about someone--like Devin, for instant.

"We're here," said her dad.

Pier took a deep breath. "Let the games begin", she whispered to herself as she exhaled.

Shannan party was being held at the Park Grand Hotel in Brooklyn Park. Once they reached the designated area, they saw people everywhere. It was almost like at Speedy's wedding. The decorations were done in Shannan's favorite colors, different shades of purple. The tables' centerpiece was lavender and white.

As she glanced around the room, a frown marred Mrs. Mortimer's face. "How long, Spencer, do you think we should stay?" She asked her husband. "A couple of hours?"

"Well this is Shannan's party. We'll play it by ear. Maybe leave after dinner and the presentations." He waved at some of the few people he knew. "Let's go over and say hello to Bobby. Then we'll find the birthday girl."

"You guys go ahead. I'm going to find Speedy and Micah Rochelle." She felt nervous. She always did in big crowds. Shannan must have invited everyone she knew and then some.

————)(●)(————

Landis arrived in time to see the back of a woman in a red dress. He watched her briefly before his eyes scanned the room looking for Speedy. They spotted one another at the same time.

"Whuz up, man?" Speedy rushed toward him. "Just getting here?" They shook hands and hugged.

"Nothing much. Been in town for a couple of hours. What's up with you?"

"Nothing. Just wondering how this party's gonna turn out." Landis gave the expected laugh.

"So you decided to drive instead of flying."

"Yeah. The weather's been good. A long drive usually clears my head."

They were standing near the door entrance, both unaware of the female looks they were getting in their black formal attire. Both wore tailor made Karseeme LaMarr tuxes.

"Where's the birthday girl?"

"She's somewhere. She must have invited every person in the Twin Cities." They laughed.

"So you didn't bring what's her name?" he gave Landis a speculated look.

"Forget what you thinking. Shannan and I will never be anything except brother and sister. And *what's her name* is Jackie," he said slowly. "Has little Pier arrived yet?" he asked striving to be indifferent.

"Hey, that's right", Speedy said with a thoughtful look. "It's been awhile since you seen her." He glanced around the room. "Naa, I don't see her-- man, look what that girl got on."

"Who?" Landis eyes followed Speedy's gaze.

"Pier. There she is talking to Shannan and Micah. I'm surprised Dad let her out the house with that dress on."

Landis looked and did a double take. *The woman in the red dress!* "That's little Pier. She's definitely not little anymore." He was staring as if mesmerized.

Speedy nodded looking at Landis. "Yep. She is something else. Thank God she's not like Shannan at this age. I don't think I could handle that again. Let's go over there."

They walked up as Shannan and Micah Rochelle were giggling about something. Pier didn't look too happy about what was being said. Landis stood behind Shannan and kissed her neck. "What's funny, birthday girl?"

She turned and threw her arms around him. "Landis! Glad you made it. Pier's not too happy about the attention she's drawing in that dress," she answered him. She linked her arm through his.

"Wouldn't have missed it for the world." He looked at his sister. Then his gaze fastened on Little Pier. He stared at her intently for a moment, his heart pounding. She was more beautiful than he had ever imagined she would be. The few pictures he'd seen of her hadn't done her any justice. He forced his gaze back to his sister.

"Hi Sis, what's going on with you?" He leaned over hugging and kissing her and praying she wouldn't feel him trembling.

Micah Rochelle put her arms around her brother as Shannan relinquished her hold. "You. Why aren't you staying with us instead of staying at the parents?" She playfully hit him in the arm.

C'mon, Mic, you know how mom is." Landis rubbed his arm. "I didn't feel like it this time. Remember Christmas." Everyone but Pier laughed. He looked at Pier again. Her eyes were so like the rest of the Mortimer siblings, yet different. The brown is different. That's what it is. Speedy and Shannan eyes were golden brown, whereas Pier's more like warm honey.

"Hello, Little Pier. I hardly recognized you. You're all grown up."

Pier was convinced everyone standing nearby heard her heart pounding and could see the sweat forming on her upper lip. She licked her lips nervously and tried to smile. She hoped she wasn't looking at him like he was the proverbial gift on a silver platter.

She took a deep breath and extended a hand that felt like lead to this handsome man, with laughing brown eyes and a breathtaking smile. He looked first at her hand and then at her face. Taking her trembling hand in his, he pulled her into an embrace.

Home! That's what she felt. Like coming home. *Oh God! Help!* She silently screamed.

"It's good to see you after all these years, Little Pier."

"You too, Landis," she said breathless. She inhaled his clean masculine scent.

"You're looking lovely, baby," he said before releasing her.

Pier gave a small strained smile as she tried to tame her imagination. *I'm just a kid to him* she recited over and over in her mind.

"This is the first time I've seen you dressed like this," said Speedy. "Did you come with Dad?"

Pier sighed heavenward, looking uncomfortable. "Yes. Mom said I looked gorgeous."

"And Dad?"

"Shut up, Speedy. The days of tripping about what we wear are over," Shannan exclaimed. "Now leave us alone. It's my birthday."

Pier was watching Landis. He was watching her. She burst out with nervous laugher. Several people heads turned their way at the musical sound. "Meet my parents," she gestured toward her siblings.

Landis smiled.

An older man and plump lady came over to wish Shannan happy birthday. She thanked them.

"We've attended enough of y'all celebrations to know gifts later," the woman said. "So I put ours over with the others." They talked a few minutes and moved on to the next group of people.

Shannan excused herself and went to greet other people coming in. You could hear her laughter over the soft music and chatter of the people as she stopped at each group. All eyes followed her as she made her way to the entrance. She looked absolutely breathtaking in her purple dress. Yep! Shannan had a real eye for clothes.

Pier moved from one foot to the other. She was scared, scared of her own feelings. Was she going to spend the rest of her life loving someone she couldn't be with? She needed to get away from Landis and sort out her feelings. The last time she felt this excited was at Speedy and Micah's wedding. And yes, Landis was there also.

"I'm going to the bathroom", she whispered to Micah Rochelle and headed toward the exit.

"Wait up. I'll go with you", said Micah Rochelle.

Landis watched them leave. He couldn't take his eyes off Pier. If she smiled at him one more time, he was sure he would pass out from the pure pleasure of it. She'd been such a pretty little girl, a gorgeous young lady, now she was a beautiful woman. He observed the young men smiling and talking to her as she and Micah made their way out the door. Something stirred in him. Jealousy? Nope, he wasn't the jealous type. But then he never had to deal with something like this.

"Oh-oh man, here she comes," said Speedy, shaking him out of his musing. "Look at her, Landis. Headed right your way, Yeah man, she likes you." Shaking his head as he pulled his goat-tee. "Talk about ghetto." Kayla Givens was wearing a black dress that hugged everything, short enough to show everything.

Landis scrutinized Kayla as she approached them. Remembering how she stuck to him like glue his Christmas visit, he whispered, lips not moving, "Spencer, you better not leave me with her. Kayla! How you doing?"

"Landis Lovington. How long have you been in town? You couldda called." She threw her arms around his neck, placing a big kiss on his lips as if it was her right to do so.

Landis looked down at Kayla's five feet. "I'll call next time I visit." *Liar*, he said to himself. He's going to kill Shannan. When Shannan introduced him to her, he'd spent most of the visit avoiding her.

"When you leaving?"

"In a few days. But most of this visit will be with family," Landis added quickly.

Speedy masked his laughter with a cough. Landis leaned over thumping him harder than necessary on his back. "You alright, bro?"

"Yeah."

Kayla asked Speedy where his wife was. "Can't leave you

unattached for long or somebody might snatch you up."

Kayla was the kind of woman that made an art out of flirting. She was a mild nuisance. No one took her serious, least of all Landis. At that moment, Landis saw Pier and Micah Rochelle returning to them. Kayla was pulling on his sleeve to get his attention; his attention was on Pier.

Pier, seeing a woman's hand on Landis paused, looking around as if seeking a haven. Finding none, she continues toward them. Micah Rochelle, seeing the woman, muttered under her breath.

"Micah Rochelle, hey girl, I was just telling Speedy he shouldn't be traveling unattached", Kayla gave what she considered a sexy laugh.

Micah Rochelle looked at her and spoke with scorn. "Didn't you see the leash, Kayla? I always know where my husband is." She rolled her eyes heavenward at Pier.

"Bow-wow, baby," said a giggling Kayla as she winked at Speedy.

"Come on, Micah, let's go over to our table; maybe they will take the hint and start this dinner." Speedy, knowing his wife quickly ushered her over to their table.

"So you're Speedy and Shannan's little sister. I haven't seen you before. I heard a lot about you from your sister." Kayla was eyeing her up and down.

Landis closed his eyes momentarily sensing where this conversation was heading. "That's because Pier's been away to college," he hastily volunteered.

"Oh really? What was it that you majored in?"

"English." Pier swept a glance at her with wide-eyed innocence.

"Whatcha wanna be when you grow up?" Kayla asked with a

dig at her age.

Meow, Landis thought. He was never any good with catty women.

"Oh, I'm sure I'll be successful in something when I reach your age. What do you do?"

"Mostly hair. I'm a cosmetologist"

Pier looked thoughtfully at her hair. "Ohhh-you're still in school?" she asked dryly.

Landis mustache twitched while he tried to keep from laughing. "Okay, Kayla, we'll see you later." He clasped Pier hand in his and led her to the table where they were supposed to sit.

"Little Pier, you must behave yourself," he murmured in her ear as he held out her chair.

"What? What are you talking about?" Pier feigned innocence. Sighing. "She deserved it."

"We'll leave it for now. Maybe I can switch seats with", he looked at the name card, "Devin. That will give us a chance to chat. I'll be back."

He strolled over to Shannan's seat observing his name next to Kayla at her table. "Your sense of humor stinks," he whispered. "I refuse to sit next to Kayla during this dinner."

Shannan raised an eyebrow. "Now Landis, calm down," she whispered back. "I was only trying to help you with your situation. Kayla's a lot of fun. You need fun."

"I took your advice and didn't bring Jackie." *Thank God for that.* "The least you can do is let me enjoy sitting with little Pier. So switch now." He walked back and sat next to Pier.

Pier had no idea how she would be able to consume a bite sitting next to Landis. She was nervous, her hands felt clammy, and her cheeks hurt from all the polite smiling. She was torn between getting right up and going home to refocus or sit there and take whatever crumbs tossed her way. One thing for sure, this was no childish emotion. They were mature adult feelings, feelings she had no business feeling for her brother's best friend.

A couple more hours and I'm outta here. That Kayla woman and Landis can do whatever.

Shannan came over to Pier. "Landis wants to sit with you. He's spoil and usually gets what he wants. Do you mind?"

"As long as he behaves himself, it shouldn't be a problem," Pier answered back striving to act blasé.

Landis raised a brow. "Ladies, please don't talk about me as if I weren't here."

"Why not?" Shannan inquired. "Men do it all the time." She waved to a man at another table. "Excuse me, people. Talk to y'all later." She headed toward the man.

Landis turned in his seat to look at Pier. "I understand from Speedy you loved Atlanta. I'm surprise to see you back. I thought we'd have to come and get you."

She looked down at her hands. "Yes, I do. I almost came close to staying another year, but I got homesick. What about you? Are you going to spend the rest of your life in Chicago?"

He gave her one of those nerve-racking stares and a slow smile. "You never know, Little Pier. You never know."

Elder Mortimer went up to the podium. "Ladies and gentlemen," he spoke into the microphone. "Thank you so much for coming and celebrating with us the birthday of our daughter, Shannan. For those of you here who know me knows how much birthdays mean to us. As you know, when I was a child we didn't celebrate birthdays. It was too many of us and we were too poor…"

Pier eyes were on Landis as he sat listening to every word in her father's routine birthday speech as if he'd never heard it before. Giving his undivided attention was as much a part of him as his chocolate eyes or his broad shoulders or sexy smile. He was breathtaking in his designer tux. Turning his head, he caught her staring. He winked and looks back at her father. Pier felt like she couldn't breathe. Gasping for breath, she quickly looked away.

".... So on behalf of my family and me, we thank you and hope you enjoy yourselves." Elder Mortimer took his seat. Everyone clapped and sang 'Happy Birthday' to Shannan.

Dinner was served. The menu consisted of cream of chicken soup with wild rice, garden salad with French or ranch dressing, buttery dinner rolls, baked and fried chicken, roast beef, lasagna, green beans, mashed and scallop potatoes, ice cream for the cake and tea, coffee or pop for beverages.

Pier ate very little. Her stomach was too nervous to swallow anything. She and Landis said very little to one another during dinner. Light music played as they ate. Just what she needed love songs, she was thinking? A few of Landis friends stopped over toward the end of the meal to say hello. Pier assumed he didn't have many friends. She said as much to him. She had turned her toward him in seat.

"I can see I don't know you really at all," she concluded.

"You're right. I don't have many friends. I just know a lot of people. There's a difference."

"I sit corrected," she teased.

She made the mistake of crossing her legs causing the split to open, revealing more leg than she wanted. Embarrassed, she quickly uncrossed them; hoping Landis didn't see or maybe she hoped he did.

Boy, did he see. Closing his eyes for a second, Landis wondered if there was any end to her legs. Glancing at her taking in her embarrassment, Landis pretended he hadn't notice. "Landis, the great pretender, that's me", he thought.

The servers brought out the big lavender and white frosted birthday cake and set it at Shannan's table. Her lips had a wry twist to them when she saw all twenty-seven candles. Everyone sang happy birthday again and the cake was served.

"Okay, everyone, I'll open only a few gifts and then we party," said Shannan twenty minutes later. She opened her parents' gift first. They were diamond earrings, necklace and a bracelet. She opened a few friends' gifts of perfume, bath and body, a purse and a beautiful gold watch from Landis. She oohed and aahed and thanked everyone for her gifts and called for the DJ with the music.

Elder and Mrs. Mortimer were making their way through the crowd to where Pier, Landis, Speedy, and Micah Rochelle were standing talking.

"Landis, I was hoping to see you earlier," said Mrs. Mortimer, lifting her cheek for his kiss. He shook hands with the elder.

"Me, too. Shannan invited quite a few people tonight. But without a doubt, I'll visit before I leave town."

"Spencer," said his father. "Make sure your sister gets home." They left along with a few other people.

Speedy looked at Landis, "Haven't I always took care of the brat?"

"I am not a brat. I'm a lady." She stuck her tongue out at him.

"See what I have to put up with. Okay, lady, when you're ready to leave, let me know. I'll ask Devin to take you. He's a little salty about Shannan changing his seat." At Pier's frowning look, Speedy threw his hands up. "I'm only kidding." He grinned at Landis. "Devin is in love with Pier. But he's wasting his time."

Landis nodded his head. "I see," he said quietly. He had opened his jacket and put his hand in his pants pocket.

Speedy had draped his arms around Micah Rochelle. "How long are we staying?"

"Not long," answered Micah. "Why don't y'all come over to our place when we leave? Mom's going to drop Spency off tomorrow afternoon."

"Sounds like a plan. We'll tell Shannan. She can meet us there," Landis said.

The DJ was playing a slow song.

"Come on, baby, let's dance," Speedy said. He pulls Micah Rochelle hands.

"Do you dance Pier?" Landis inquired.

"Not very good."

"There you are, Landis. I been looking for you," said Kayla. "Wanna dance?"

"Sorry, I was getting ready to dance with Pier. I'll get you the next one."

"No Landis," Pier interrupts placing her hand on his arm. "Why don't you dance with her and I promise to dance the very next song."

"Okay." He gazed at her with amusement. "You promise?"

Pier nodded as she headed back to their table. She sat down with a grateful sigh. She watched Landis holding Kayla in his arms as they moved slowly to the music. She grimaced. Kayla surely had to feel like she was in paradise. Pier envied her at that moment. But she knew she couldn't handle dancing slowly with

Landis. Tonight had been exuberating and unbearable all in one.

She twisted some hair around her fingers. Landis was out of her league and she knew it. He was older, handsome, sophisticated and probably madly in love with his girlfriend. Surely he was just being nice to his friend's *little* sister.

The music had stopped. Since the songs were Shannan's favorite songs, Pier was certain a fast song was next. She could survive dancing with Landis to fast music.

Landis walked with precise steps to where Pier was sitting. She glanced at him with subdued excitement as he approached. Their eyes met. She was sure she briefly saw desire in his eyes. It was like when first lighting a fire, the match touches the wood and the flames blaze, and then mellow down. He gave her one of his slow gentle smiles. He didn't say a word as he stretched his hand towards her.

Chapter Four

Faltering, she stood and clasped her hand in his. Since the dancing area was still crowded with people, Landis carefully guided Pier over near a corner area. The music had yet to start as he expertly turned her in his arms. Suddenly a popular R & B female recording artist melodious voice filled the room singing of her belief in love. Holding Pier close in his arms, Landis silently asked, Father in heaven, what am I going to do? I love her. Will I be able to walk away again? Groaning inward he knew he shouldn't have came.

Of course, from his expression, one wouldn't know the dilemma he was in as he held felt Pier tremble in his arms. Or perhaps it was he who was trembling. He didn't know. He didn't care. For right now, holding her was all that matter. Landis Renee Lovington, who didn't do anything without calculating the costs or risks, was throwing caution to the wind. He was aware that he was playing with fire, but right now, right here, getting burned didn't feel too bad.

The song was over way too soon. Neither moved. He stood

looking at her, she at him. He wanted to hold her-kiss her, tell her what he felt. But, as if awaken from a dream, Landis did a reality check, cleared his throat and kissed her on the forehead. At least he kissed her somewhere.

"That wasn't so bad now, was it?" With his hand in the middle of her back, Landis steered her from the dance area.

Before Pier could answer, Micah Rochelle called to them.

"Hey y'all." She and Speedy strolled over to them. "We're ready to go. Y'all still coming home with us or y'all wanna call it a night?"

Landis, grabbing Pier's hand, looked at his watch. "I'm game. It's only eleven o'clock; that's not too late."

He looked at Pier. She had a confused expression on her face, causing Landis to feel bad. He can't ever give in to his emotions again. Even an innocent like Pier had to know he wanted to kiss her-that he desired her.

"What about you, Pier? Do you wanna go?"

Pier shrugged her shoulders. "I'm okay with it as long as somebody gets me home."

"Little Pier, I will personally take you home. Let's find Shannan and see what's up with her," Landis said.

Shannan was staying until everyone left the party. She said she'd meet them at Speedy and Micah Rochelle's house. Kayla conveniently needed a ride home. Not wanting to but left with little choice, Landis offered to drop her off. Raising a brow in Pier's direction, she opted to ride with Speedy.

"We had a nice time tonight," Micah Rochelle said once they were settled in the car and headed home.

"Umm," said Speedy as he navigated the car into the traffic.

Pier said nothing. She stretched as far as her seat belt let her.

She enjoyed herself more than she thought. Landis was flirting, she was sure of it. *Oh grow up, Pier.* He was simply being nice to you. She closed her eyes. She didn't want tonight to end. Whether he was being nice or flirting, she wanted the night to last forever. To be near him again was exciting.

"Kayla is a trip. Her attitude is getting a little redundant", commented Micah Rochelle. "Shannan should be ashamed of herself for even introducing Landis to that *lil runner.*" It was clear to Pier, Micah didn't like Kayla and she agreed with Mic. "The last time he was here, she kept chasing behind him."

"Landis is a big boy. He can take of himself." Speedy took one hand off the wheel, grabbed her hand and kissed it. "Besides, he's seeing Jackie. If nothing else, he doesn't play around. He's a one woman's man." Speedy chuckled. "It was kind of funny seeing him try and get out of taking her home."

"How long has Landis been seeing Jackie?" Pier hoped her voice didn't sound as strange to them as it did to her.

"Oh, I think he said 'bout a year. Right, Speed?" He nodded in agreement. "We've never met her or nothing like that. It might turn out to be serious." She shrugged her shoulders. "Who knows?"

Pier's heart went flip-flop. Landis married. She would definitely have to move back to Atlanta. She couldn't stand seeing Kayla all over him. A wife! She would surely die.

The ride to their home was about fifteen minutes. Everyone went into the kitchen sitting area. Speedy took his suit coat and tie off and unbuttoned his shirt. Pier gave him her wrap and took off her shoes. Micah Rochelle decided to change clothes.

Speedy sat down on the couch with Pier when he returned. "Tired, sis?"

"Nope. I'm glad I stayed. I had a good time. I was going to leave with the parents. But I had fun with you *old people.*"

Speedy's smile diminished to a very serious look. "Can I ask you a question?"

"Yep. What?"

"Are you happy?" Throwing up his hands, "I mean in spite of the fun, you had a sad look tonight. Like you were unhappy."

She wanted to say, *"Yes, I'm sad. I'm in love with your best friend and have been for years. I know I can't be with him-and I can't move on with my life. Every man I date I compare him to Landis."*

Sighing she said, "I don't really know, Speedy. At times I'm very happy. I'm not depressed or anything, it's just that," she paused gathering her thoughts. "For instance, sometimes in church, I feel like I can stay there forever. I really, really love God. I want to be obedient to Him. But sometimes I wish I were more like Shannan. You know, out going; throwing caution to the wind kind of girl. And then when I dance and have fun like tonight, I get scared, I feel like Jesus might part open the sky and I'm hell bound. Isn't that dumb?"

"No, sis. Everybody feels that way at one time or another. It just means you don't want to do anything to disappoint the *Father.* The thing I'm learning is a relationship with God doesn't leave at the drop of a hat. We are free to serve Him. Dancing and having fun doesn't always make you a sinner. God knows your heart and you must be led by Him and not by too many religious rules. What may convict one person doesn't always convict another.

"As for Micah and I, dancing makes us feel good. It's just another part of expressing our love. Sometimes at home, I'll turn the radio on and grab her and cut a step or two. Now I grant you, I wouldn't hang out at nightclubs but I do like having fun with my wife and family. Although I'm not into partying, I also believe it's more to being a Christian than hanging out at restaurants."

Pier stared at her brother as if seeing him for the first time. He was talking to her as one adult to another. She was grateful. "You know, Handsome, this is the first time you talk to me as an adult."

He grinned. "Now don't let it go to your head." Then on a serious note, "I know I trip a lot, but you are such a trusting little thing, it gets kind of hard to look past that." He kissed her in the same spot as Landis. "I want you to be happy."

"Anybody want something to eat or drink?" Micah Rochelle asked, as she returned to the kitchen. She had changed into blue jeans and a black t-shirt.

Both Pier and Speedy said colas. "Make mine diet if you have it", Pier said.

Micah Rochelle was busy getting glasses and ice when the doorbell rang. Speedy went to answer it. Pier could hear Shannan and Landis voices. They must have arrived at the same time.

Shannan enters the room with her friend LaSean. Pier had met him before. He was a nice clean-cut, average height, average looking guy who seemed as though he genuinely like Shannan.

"Hello, ladies. How's it going?" LaSean smiled. Micah gestured for him to sit down. She set two six packs of pops and iced filled glasses on the table.

"Help yourself", she went back in the kitchen area.

"Hey, y'all. Thought I wasn't coming. Didn't ya?" Shannan and LaSean sat on the couch next to Pier.

"We knew you were coming Big Head", said Pier. Landis squeezed his muscular body on the other side of Pier. Pressing his thighs next to hers made her chant in her head 'I should have gone home.' Is it possible to sit this close to someone you were attracted to and not give it away? Or do or say something stupid?

Landis laid his arm on the back of the couch and leaned toward Pier. "You don't mind if I sit here?"

"If you don't mind me nearly sitting in your lap, I don't."

"Imagine that", he mused.

"Are you flirting?" Pier whispered quietly.

A look of surprise crossed Landis' face. Then he smiled. "If I were, you would know, little Pier." He gently smoothed her hair from her face, then pushed him up and joined Speedy at the kitchen table. LaSean joined them also.

Pier watched him walk. She liked his walk. A sexy manly walk. Her heart sank. It was as she assumed. That look of surprise told it all. He was just being nice. He hadn't been flirting with her. All of a sudden she was ready to go.

Shannan leaned over and said, Pier was 'too old' to still have crushes.

"I wish."

Landis and Speedy were laughingly telling LaSean about their childhood adventures. Shannan and Micah Rochelle joined in. "What about the time we snuck out the houses and stayed all night at the park", said Speedy.

"Yeah, and the police picked our butts up and took us home," added Landis. "Speedy and I got grounded for what seemed like forever. But they", he pointed to Shannan and Micah Rochelle, "said we made them go. So they got off the hook."

"How were we to know they would believe us?" said a grinning Shannan. "We had to do something. We were scared of the police."

"Yeah, we thought we were going to jail. Besides I was only

eleven", pouted Micah Rochelle.

"And I was twelve", said Shannan laughing. "You should have seen the look on Micah's face when the police stopped." By now, Shannan was laughing so hard she had to grab her side. "She threw her hands in the air, waving them back and forward." Shannan gasped for breath.

"I still don't care how you laugh. I was scared and I never did anything like that again." Micah Rochelle mockingly defended herself.

LaSean looked over to where Pier was sitting. "What about you, Pier? Did they get you into trouble too?"

Pier hid a yawn. She pushed herself up. As she walked, the split revealing leg and thigh made her feel more uncomfortable now than at the party. She pulled an extra chair up to the table.

"They were too busy trying to tell me what to do than to let me have fun." She fringed sadness. "I had to learn the wicked ways of the world all by myself."

"Yeah, right," retorted Speedy. "You better not know anything."

Both Shannan and Micah Rochelle simultaneously said at the same time, "Shut up, Spencer."

"What?"

Shannan sipped some pop. She turned to LaSean. "This poor girl has too many fathers." Setting the drink back down, "I couldn't take Dad breathing down my throat. Can you imagine two men watching what you do?" She shuddered.

"Shan, you're tripping. I'm watching out for my little sister. Shoot, I had to get permission from Papa Renee and Landis before even asking Micah to marry me."

"So you're saying Pier's future husband will have to get

permission from you and Dad?"

Speedy nodded his head yes. "And maybe Landis might want to check him out, too. This is little Pier we're talking about."

Landis had been sitting quietly listening to brother and sister arguing over Pier. This was nothing new. They have been this way ever since he and Micah Rochelle have known them. The difference now is Pier was too old for this. His eyes rested on her face. She didn't give away much. She sat looking as if they were talking about the weather.

"Speedy, thank God you had a boy", said Shannan. "I pity you, brother, if you ever have a daughter."

Landis knew where this was heading. They were too much alike. He and Micah argued growing up, but Speedy and Shannan's arguments had always been heated; although, they made up just as quickly. He once again looked at Pier who was looking at him. When she stared at him like this, it took everything in him not to--he shook his head. Can't go there.

"I think we should end this conversation before the usual happens. Besides Pier's not getting married now." He paused looked again at her. "Are you?"

Maybe the lateness of the hour caused Pier to suddenly feel boldness, but she raised her now water down pop to her lips. Taking a small sip, she gave him a wicked look before smiling demurely with wide innocent eyes. "Why, Landis, didn't you know? I'm saving myself for you."

Speedy, taking a swallow of his drink, choked. Landis knocked his drink over. LaSean stared, not knowing whether she was serious or not. Shannan and Micah Rochelle laughed.

Micah jumped up, grabbing paper towels to mop up Landis'

drink. "Did any get on you?"

Landis didn't answer. He didn't hear her. His mind went back about thirteen years ago when a little girl of about nine asked him if he was going to marry her because she 'couldn't marry Speedy or Daddy cause they were blood related.' Landis remembered even then he had a soft spot for Pier. He had grinned at her and said okay.

Now that her surprise affect was over, he once again grinned at her and said, "Okay."

Speedy coughed a few more seconds. "Are you trying to kill me?"

"No sir. Just trying to get your attention *daddy*."

"Well, you did that." He laughed. "Got ole Landis here too."

Pier's eyes met Landis'. He gave her his slow smile and nod.

Shannan stood up. "This was fun but it's getting late. Ready?" she asked LaSean.

LaSean got up, also. He politely said goodnight.

"Don't bother to see us out, y'all." She put her arm through LaSean's and they exited the kitchen.

Landis looked at his watch. "I guess it is time to go. It's one in the morning. Isn't it church tomorrow-today?" Turning to Pier. "I promised to take you home."

"Yep, you did. Thanks. Thadda save Speed a trip." She jumped up and put her shoes on. Speedy and Micah walked them to the door. Speedy got Pier's wrap out the closet and helped her put it on.

"Alright, man, catch you later. See you at church Pier."

Landis helped her in his black convertible. After starting the car, he asked her if she was comfortable.

"Yes. I'm fine. When are you leaving?"

"Tuesday morning," he said, backing out of the driveway and pulling into the street.

"Oh." She sounded disappointed.

"What's wrong, Little Pier? Hate to see me leave?"

"Truthfully yes. I liked spending this time with you." She yawned. "Sorry. I missed you when I was in Atlanta. I didn't know how much until seeing you tonight." It was late. Pier didn't care what she said. She probably won't see him again for a while.

"I had no idea you liked me like that. That's good to know, little Pier." He lifted her hand out of her lap and kissed it. Fifteen minutes later he pulled in her driveway and put the car in park. "I may not see you again before I leave. So I want you to take care of yourself. And if you're ever in Chicago, look me up. I'll take you to the zoo. I seem to remember you liked it."

"Landis, that was when I was a kid," she sighed. "You're right. I do still like the zoo."

"I'm stopping by Monday morning to visit with your mom. Will you be there?"

"I have to be at work at eight. So probably not." She turned completely around to face him. "Landis about my eighteenth birthday, I-"

"Pier, we agreed never to talk about it. It was an unfortunate incident. Let's forget about it."

"That's just it Landis, I can't. If you remember, you stopped talking to me after the incident. I blamed myself for what happen."

Landis cradled her face between his hands. "Baby! Don't ever let me hear you blame yourself for some jerk's problem. I could have killed him for ever touching you." Before she knew what was happening he bent and kissed her. Just as quickly he stopped.

"Take care of yourself, Little Pier."

"You, too, Land. I love you." She got out of the car quickly and hurriedly ran into the house.

He sat in shock after hearing 'I love you' escape from her lips. Did she mean it or was that once again the Mortimer's traditional typical *I love you* when ending a conversation. He put the car in reverse and backed out of the driveway. On the way to his parents' home, he thought about kissing her. He needed to resign to the fact that when it comes to Pier Janise Mortimer, he has no control. His only option is to stay away once again… But how can you stay away from forbidden fruit? Goodness, is this how Adam and Eve felt?

Landis felt tension all in his body as he pulled up in his parents' driveway. Sighing, he got out the car. After helplessly kissing Pier, he knew he had decisions once again to make. Either go to Elder and Speedy and confess his feeling for her or continue to stay away. It would be hard but he opted to stay away again.

Pier let the tears pour down her cheeks once she reached the haven of her bedroom. This was too much, she kept telling herself. Why did he kiss her? Why, Lord? Help me, Father, out of this mess. And to top it off, she let 'I LOVE YOU' slip from her lips. He must think of her as a fool.

"I don't care what anybody says. That was not a brotherly kiss." Not this time. Maybe she should just ask him. She picked up the phone. He should be there, it only take three minutes. No. It's too late to call his parents' home. Calm down, Pier, she told herself. She brushed her teeth, wrapped her hair and put on a gown. She knew sleep would be a long time coming. Landis. He'd always called her baby. This time when he said it, it was not like talking to a kid. She slid into bed and turned the light off. She'd wait for sleep.

It wasn't a long wait. As soon as her head hit the pillow, she was asleep.

Chapter Five

Although the wind was blowing, the sun was warm for May was Pier thoughts, as she headed to the parking lot after Sunday service. Church acquaintances, Alicia and Phenda, called out to her as she prepared to get in her car.

"Hey girl, hey girl, how you living?" asked Alicia.

"Good, or should I say large," answered a laughing Pier. "What's up with y'all? Service was good, huh?"

"You better believe it," said Phenda, swinging her micro braids out of her chocolate colored face.

"Hey, listen; we stopped you because in June we're going to *Chicago*. Heey. Wanna go?" asked Alicia bobbing her head.

Pier's stomach felt like it did a somersault. "Chicago? Why you guys wanna go to Chicago?"

"Alicia's grandmother lives there and it's her birthday. So we're going for her surprise party."

Landis parting words flashed in her mind, if she was ever in Chicago to look him up. "Sounds like a plan." Pier quickly agreed. "What are the exact dates so I can clear it with my parents? And where will we stay?"

"Let's plan for the first weekend in June," said Alicia. "Girl, we're staying in a hotel, with my grandmother's rules, we wouldn't have any fun staying under her roof."

"Oh, good, school's out too, I'll arrange my schedule." They laughed and talked for a few minutes then each went to their own car.

Pier was secretly excited about the trip. If the truth to be told, she was hoping Landis would not be out of town that weekend so she could visit him. Maybe even get to the bottom of her feelings for him. With no family around maybe they could talk freely, and maybe she'd have enough courage to tell him exactly how she felt.

It was about a week before her twenty-third birthday, and she was sitting in the kitchen eating dinner when the phone rang. Since her parents were out and she had her own line, she usually let the voice mail pick up their calls, but for some reason she answered.

"Hello?"

"Hello."

The old saying 'heart in your mouth' came to Pier, for hers was beating at a record speed. She felt her mouth go dry.

"Landis?" She placed her hand on her chest as if she could slow the beating.

"Yes, Pier. How you doing?"

"Great. And you?" She knew her dry mouth made her voice sound husky.

"Oh, I'm okay. So what have you been doing since I last saw you?"

"Working. School will soon be out. So we're all dancing around like an old Soul Train line."

Landis laughed which made her laughed.

"Please, baby, don't make me imagine you on Soul Train," he said with amusement.

"Is that so hard to imagine?"

"Not at all. Quite the opposite," his voice immediately sobered.

Pier was enjoying their conversation. She had no clue as to why he was calling but she was glad. Just hearing his voice made her evening.

"So tell me little Pier, why on earth are you home on a Saturday night. You should be out having some fun with your boyfriend," his voice was sounding a little strained.

"I know. You're sounding like Shannan. I had a date with my friend Devin but he had to cancel at the last minute." She didn't add that she was glad because she was tired of going out with anyone that wasn't him.

"Umm. I see."

"Were you calling my parents? Can I give them a message?"

"Oh, I couldn't be calling you?" he teased.

"Everyone calls me on my line," she teased right back. She was suddenly full of energy. She had moved from the chair to the counter, back to the chair.

"Well I don't have your number."

"I don't have yours either."

"We can remedy that now," he gave her his number.

She in return gave him hers. "Now you better call me, Landis."

"I will."

They talked for at least an hour. He talked about his work and the traveling it involve; his town home, friends, and living in Chicago. He didn't, however, talk about his girlfriend.

She talked about her job as a teacher's assistant and being a teacher next school year, how she's thinking of getting her own place, her friends. She didn't bother to mention about coming there in approximately three weeks.

They probably would have continued talking for hours had her parents not returned and he asked to speak to her father.

Her phone rang just as she finished showering causing her to rush to the phone leaving her breathless when answering.

"Pier?"

"Landis! What you doing checking to make sure I gave you the right number? Maybe I should call you."

"Anytime. You sound as though you've been jogging."

"Sorry. I was in the shower. What's up?"

There was absolutely silence on Landis end of the phone. "Hello, Landis? You still there?"

Landis cleared his throat. "I was calling you back because I'm going to be out of town on your birthday. I'm sending your gift to Micah Rochelle and she's instructed to give it to you on your big day. So if I don't talk to you on your day, I hope you have a happy twenty-three."

"Thanks, Landis. You don't have to send me a gift."

"I want to," he said softly. "I'm just sorry I won't be there to help you celebrate.

"You are too kind…"

Whatever else she was going to say, she paused because of a woman's voice in the background. That must be his girlfriend.

"Listen, Landis, I have to go; I'm dripping wet here. I'll talk to you later," she said in a taut voice. She was jealous.

Sounded like Landis stifled a groan. "Yes, Little Pier, me too. Good-bye." He hung up.

Pier was beside herself with jealousy. She knew she had no right to be. Be as it may, she was jealous. *Jealous!* Why did he call her back when his girlfriend was over anyway? Because, Pier, you are *his best friend's little sister* and don't you, missy, ever forget it.

Pier dried off and got ready for bed, punching the pillows with more force than necessary. She popped in her favorite gospel CD and went to sleep with Landis on her mind.

Pier birthday was a quiet affair compared to Shannan's. Just the way she liked it. Her family took her to a nice elegant restaurant where they ate dinner and gave her gifts. She'd invited her new friends: Phenda, Alicia and her long time friend Sherry, also, against better judgment, Devin and his twin brother, Daron. Their attire was dressy but not black tie. Pier wore a white spaghetti strap dress with gold earrings and the gold bracelet Landis gave her.

She opened each and every gift, which took a while. Her girlfriends gave her Victoria's Secret lotions, bath and shower gels and to her embarrassment underwear, which she didn't show. Devin gave her a beautiful red silk scarf. A gift card to Macy's from Speedy; red leather shoes from Micah, a red coach bag from Shannan. And from her parents keys to a red car.

"I take red's your favorite color," Daron said dryly.

Her family and Sherry said at the same time, "always."

Pier thanked everyone for her gifts and exclaimed over what a great day she was having. She and her friends were going to hang out for a while.

"Oh, Pier, before we leave we have one more gift," said Micah Rochelle. "It's from Landis. He's in Denver right now. I talked to him before he left and he wanted you to know he wishes he could be here to help celebrate your birthday." She reached under the table and pulled out a small white box with a red bow. She handed it to Pier.

Pier could feel all eyes on her as she accepts the gift and, with fingers that were all thumbs tried to open it. She took a deep breath and gently opens the box. Inside was a jewelry box. Inside it on black velvet background laid a gold chain with a diamond and ruby heart shaped pendant.

Everyone was in awe over the beauty of the jewelry.

"If it was anybody else I'd send it back," stated Speedy.

"Ah, he asked me if it was okay to get her this kind of gift," Elder told his son. "I told him sure, he was family."

Pier only heard a roaring in her ears. Her heart was thumping way over the rate it should. She was trying to compose herself so no one knew what this present meant. Every time she tried to forget him, something happened to overwhelm her with more love.

Shannan was watching her closely. "What do you think of Landis' gift, Bighead?"

Pier cleared her throat. "I think that was nice of him to re-member me on my birthday."

"Just remember to thank him, girl," said Alicia.

"I will."

At exactly eleven forty-five that night Landis called Pier. She was sitting crossed legged on her bed looking at his gift.

After exchanging pleasantries, he asked if she liked her gift.

"Oh, Landis, I couldn't believe you would buy me something so expensive. Speedy said if it were anyone else, he would give it back. And to think you asked my dad if it was okay. You are such a sweet man. Oh yeah, thanks."

"You still didn't say whether or not you like the gift."

"Are you crazy? Who wouldn't like a tight gift like this?"

"I gather tight means nice," Landis said dryly.

"Yes, and more."

"So where did you go after dinner?"

"We just hung out a while and then I came home."

"We?" He queried softly"

"Alicia, Sherry, you remember Sherry, umm Phenda, Devin and his brother, Daron. We went to the movies and a Christian Club. Don't ask! This was my first time going."

Landis was laughing at her. "Pier, Pier, Pier. What am I going to do with you?"

"You gotta love me," she said. The more she talks to Landis on the phone, the less nervous she became.

"Oh, yeah. That I do. But I gotta get off this phone. It's getting late and I have an early meeting tomorrow. I'm glad you enjoyed your birthday, Little Pier."

"Thanks, Landis. And thanks for the gift. 'Bye."

"You're welcome, baby, 'bye."

The first weekend in June finally arrived to sunshine blue skies. A great day for traveling. Phenda, Alicia and Pier left that morning, arriving early evening at a hotel on Lake Shore drive. They should have arrived sooner but they stopped at every shopping area and restaurant on the way.

Chicago was everything that the commercials advertised.

Since Pier had never been to Chicago, Alicia, the driver of the hour, drove downtown showing the Sears Towers and Michigan Avenue. Although Minneapolis' downtown was growing, it was small potatoes compared to Chicago's. Lake Michigan was lined with colorful boats and people.

After settling in the hotel, they headed out to Alicia's grandmother's birthday party, which happened to be a barbeque in her big back yard. Her family was very friendly and nice. They treated Pier like an old friend. The young men flirted, the old men wished they were young again, and the women were so sweet and easy going that Pier felt quite at home.

The grandmother was happy with her gifts and was pleasantly surprised to receive gifts from Pier and Phenda. Pier gave her a multi-colored scarf, and bath and body wash from Phenda.

Pier had a wonderful time, but her mind periodically drifts to Landis causing her heart to skip a beat in anticipation at the thought of seeing him. Then anxiety, causing her to not want to see him.

The three were tired and sleepy, but happy arriving back to their room.

"Tomorrow I'm going out with an old boyfriend," said Alicia. "Want to tag along?" She asked out of politeness, because she assumed Pier was going to spend time with Landis. They all agreed, after the birthday party, to do their own thing the rest of the trip.

Knowing they weren't committed to hang out with one another, Pier wasn't surprise to be left to her own means.

"I'm going out with your cousin Ritchie. I hope he's cool. I only agreed because he's your cousin," said Phenda.

"Oh, girl, Ritchie's okay, I guess," Alicia made a face. "You're probably going to the same place Steve and I are going." Turning her large brown eyes toward Pier, "So what are you going to do? You should come with us. I can pull up another cousin so you'll be with someone."

Laughingly, shaking her head, Pier declined. Gathering her toiletries, she headed for the bathroom.

"Ohh," yelled Phenda lying across the bed. "You are going to call your brother's in-law and hang out with him. Do something," she yelled even louder, "don't make us feel guilty tomorrow."

Laughing again, Pier closed the door in her face. Once the door was closed, Pier stopped laughing. In one mind she wanted to call Landis and ask if she could see him. But the other mind, the sensible mind, said do not call. She was so confused. And having no one to share this burden with was getting to be nerve wrecking. How she wished she could confide in Landis or her sister, Shannan. What a joke! *Oh, Landis, I want to see you but I am nervous because I have feelings for you. Oh no, Landis, not sisterly feelings, womanly feelings.* Exhaling Pier steps into the shower.

It was afternoon the next day when Phenda and Alicia left for their fun day. They asked again to go with them, but she again declined.

"I'm kinda assuming you will spend the day with the in-law", remarked Phenda. "You are surely not going to sit around in this big beautiful city doing nothing.

"Yeah," Alicia agreed. "We're not sure what time we will be back."

Pier wanted to tell them how she wished she had the courage now that she was here to spend some time alone with him but she was afraid of being rejected. She was clear that Landis cared for her. But is he attracted to her? How does he really see her? As a woman or his best friend's sister? A kid that he sat on his knee and played with…

"Pier? Hello?" Alicia called out.

Pier blanked. "Sorry. I was miles away. Listen, you all, go ahead with your plans. I may give Landis a call. Maybe go out with him and his girlfriend."

After they left, Pier showered and got dressed, all the while debating as to whether she should call Landis or not. Speedy probably called him and told him she was coming to town. So maybe, just maybe, Landis was expecting her to call.

Pier sat on the bed. She kept debating if she should call or should she wait until she was getting ready to leave. Then that way, she could see him only long enough to say hi and bye.

A walk around outside will clear her head. She pushed up off the bed and put her red spring coat on when she heard a knock at the door. No one was at the door when she opened it. Not thinking, she stepped out before realizing the door automatically locks.

Pulling the handle to no avail, she was locked out. Oh great, she thought. Now I have to sit around and wait until Phenda and Alicia get back. Looking at her watch, she realized it could be midnight tonight, over ten hours from now.

She went downstairs to the front desk and told them her dilemma. They sympathized with her and she felt dumb, but unless she could produce an ID they couldn't let her in, which made Pier feel even dumber.

She wanted to wring the woman's neck. At home they were so laid back about things like this. They probably would have accompanied her to the room, waited until she produced her ID and laughed with her about doing silly things.

But this was the big Windy City. They are too busy to be nice. They probably have heard every story. She got a 'go sit down and wait for your friends' look. How could Landis live here?

Landis! Now she had to call him. She searched her coat pockets hoping she had some change. She did. She had twenty dollars, three quarters, two dimes and three pennies.

Chapter Six

Landis and a couple of his friends from work were sitting in the living room watching the sports channel when his phone rang. He answered on the second ring. It was Pier on the other end of the line. The sound of her voice made his heart race and his mind go blank.

"Hi, Landis."

"Little Pier? What's up?" He rushed to turn the TV down, to the chagrin of his friends.

"Why did you turn it down?" His friend Keith wanted to know.

Landis gestured for him to be quiet.

"I'm in Chicago. I know my *father*, Speedy, probably called you and told you already."

Landis chuckled. "Yes he did."

"I hope I'm not bothering you. But I have a slight problem here at the hotel."

"What's wrong?" His voice immediately laced with concern. "What happened?"

"I-like a dummy, I'm locked out of the room and my friends, Alicia and Phenda, won't be back until later."

"What hotel? Did you let the front desk know?" He sat down on his couch.

"These people here are a trip. They said I need ID, which is in the room."

"I'll come and get you. What hotel?" he asked again.

"No, actually I'm right by a cab stand. I can jump in and be there quicker."

"Okay." He gave her the address. "You're sure?"

"Yes. The other problem," she began.

"Baby! There's another problem?" At his use of the word 'baby', he became the focus of his friends' attention.

"Oh, Land. I'm really embarrassed, but my purse is in the room and I may not have enough money to pay for the cab. Umm, can you help me out? I'll pay you back," she rushed on.

"Done deal. You're sure you don't want me to come and get you?"

"No. I'll be fine. Umm, I'm not interrupting anything, am I?"

"No way. I'll see you when you get here."

Landis hung up the phone. He stood up and saw the inquiring looks on Keith and Brian's faces. "That was my friend Speedy's kid sister," he volunteered. "She's on her way over." He hoped he sounded casual to them, because, in fact, he felt adrenaline flowing from head to toe.

Keith studied Landis face. "Is there a problem?"

Landis nodded. "She's locked out of her hotel room."

"How does she look?" Brian wanted to know with a shimmer of hope in his eyes.

"You're most definitely outta here."

"How old is she?" Brian continued. "I'm in between women."

Landis and Keith laughed at Brian. He was only a player in his own mind.

"She's too young for you, Brian." Brian was thirty-three.

"What about me?" Keith wanted to know. He was twenty-five.

Landis raised a brow at Keith. He was, what the women at work called, drop dead gorgeous.

"You may be a problem. Hands off guys, I promised Speedy I'd take care of his little sister."

"How little?" queried Keith.

Landis looked at Keith. He was a nice person. Landis met him when he started working at Monroe-Phillips Bank. Keith Carlton Monroe had been in college and worked at the bank during the summer. He had worked from janitor to personnel clerk. He didn't care where he worked because he knew when his dad retired, he would be CEO. He'd become good friends with Landis.

"Don't let me keep you," Landis said sarcastically.

"Not playing the heavy handed big brother now, are you man?" Brian wanted to know.

"Yes, I am. Anything happens to little Pier, Speedy will have my head on a platter."

They laughed as Landis paced the carpet.

"Hey man, why are you so nervous?" teased Brian.

"Well, this is her first time being here. I hope she's alright."

"She's fine, mother hen."

He stood at the door as Pier got out of the taxi. He waved as she walked up the driveway. She was quite stunning, he mused to himself. He again took in her height, the remembrance of her voluptuous figure now hidden under a long red spring coat, and the way she quickly smiled causing her honey brown eyes to reflect her hidden humor. She moved with such confidence for one so young. Landis liked that. The bottom line was Landis liked everything about Pier.

And the phone calls were exuberating. At first, she seemed uncomfortable talking to him, but gradually she relaxed and talked. Not only was she beautiful; she's also smart. After all, she graduated top in her high school. There were so many things he'd gotten to know about the adult Pier. So many things he still wanted to know. No, he better not go there. Why? Because she is Speedy's little sister, Lovington, try and remember that.

"Hi, Landis. I had enough cab fare," Pier said once standing on the small porch.

"Hey, Little Pier". Did he see a flash of annoyance cross her face? So little Pier no longer liked being called little. Landis knew he had to think of her as little or what? He shook his head, he couldn't think of her in any other way.

"Let's go into the living room. Right this way." He led her through the short hallway into his living room. Keith and Brian stood up as Landis and Pier entered. "Pier, meet Keith and Brian. Y'all meet Pier, my friend's *little sister.*"

"Hey, what's up Pier?" Keith took her hand.

Landis was watching Pier closely. She had no idea the effect she was having on them or on him.

Pier smiled and shook hands with both men.

"Make yourself at home," Landis said. "Want something to drink? I have coffee, iced tea, pop and water. Oh yeah, let me get your coat," he said as she took it off. Oh brother, she should have kept her coat on. She had on one of those red midrib t-shirt and a blue jean snug fitting skirt reaching above the knees. All three men's eyes traveled from her red flat shoes to her full shiny lips that were now smiling. She shook her head to the offer of a drink.

"Thanks, Landis. Sorry about having to come over like this. I know Speedy asked you to keep an eye on me. I never thought I would need it."

"Hey, it's okay. I hate you' being locked out of your hotel room. I should have came and gotten you instead of you taking a cab." He gestured for her to sit on the navy leather couch.

Brian and Keith hurried to sit on the sofa next to her. She started to cross her legs but decided against it.

"Alicia and Phenda will not be back until later tonight. I don't call them enough to know their cell numbers by memory." She looked embarrassed. Landis couldn't help watching her. Jumping to his feet, he went down the hall to the kitchen. He grabbed beers out the fridge and a cola for Pier. He returned back to the living room to see her smiling and talking with Brian. Landis cleared his throat.

"Here you go," he handed Brian and Keith another beer. "I brought you a cola anyway. Want a glass?" Pier said no. Sitting in the leather chair, Landis crossed his legs on the coffee table.

"I feel so dumb," Pier sighed. "I've lived in Atlanta for five years, no problems. The minute I visit Chicago, I do something stupid."

"Actually I don't think it was dumb," Keith said. He seemed to be fascinated with her legs. He couldn't take his eyes off them. Landis felt a surged of jealousy shoot through him. Where is this coming from? He'd never been jealous of anything or anyone in his life. But he's going to put them out.

"Listen, things like this happen. Don't sweat it," Brian was saying. He too kept glancing at her legs.

She smiled at him and stood up. They all stood up also. "Which way to the bathroom?"

Landis showed her the way. On his return, Brian and Keith were there sitting looking like the proverbial cat that caught the canary.

"Man, did you see her leg?" Keith exclaimed in a whisper as he threw his head back on the couch. "I'm definitely a legs man."

"She doesn't look like a little sister to me." Brian sighed.

Landis stood staring at these people he'd known for five years and wanted to rip their hearts out.

"You dudes are gonna have to go. You're making her nervous." Landis sounded curter than he should have.

"I was hoping you'd let me take her out and show her the sights," Keith was saying.

Suddenly, Landis felt older than his twenty-nine years. Before he could reply, Pier returned to the living room.

"Don't get up men. So what do you guys have planned for today?" She sat on the arm of the chair that Landis had vacated. "I'm sure you have something planned on a *Saturday*."

"I did promise to take you to the zoo," Landis said standing near the window.

She graced them with a giggle. She looked at Keith and Brian, "Would you believe he and my brother used to take me to the zoo? I've known Land, as far as I'm concern, my whole life but actually since I was four."

"Oh yeah," said Keith. He seemed Landis thought to himself,

to really be interested in her. "So technically he's like a big brother to you."

Landis, not being able to stand anymore of the conversation, interrupted before Pier could answer. "We're going to the zoo," he stated firmly.

Pier batted her eyes at him and said she looked forward to it.

Keith, realizing he didn't stand a chance with her guard dog, decided to take his leave. Brian followed.

"Okay man," Brian was saying, "we'll see you at work. Nice meeting you, Pier."

She smiled and waved.

Keith stood towering over her. "When do you leave? Maybe I can take you out or something."

"I leave Sunday." Coining what Landis said to her, "Look me up if you're ever in the Twin Cities. Land can give you the info."

Landis locked the door behind his friends. He heard Brian say Jackie may be in trouble. He rested his large frame on the door. Was he that obvious? Sighing he walked back into the living room. Pier was standing in front of his entertainment area. She looked up when he approached her. She seemed a bit ill at ease since Landis' friends left.

"I'll go and change clothes. Then we can leave. You do want to go to the zoo? You'll like the Lincoln Park."

"That will be fine."

Pier glanced through Landis' impressive collection of CDs as he ran upstairs. There were rap, jazz, R&B, and gospel. She saw a popular male recording artist and settled on his romantic tunes. She had a weakness for his music. She noticed the plants in the living room and wondered if a woman lived here. She noticed quite a bit of womanly touches in the living room. Well, what would you expect? Landis was good looking, too good-looking. He made Pier nervous. The last thing she wanted to do was spend the day with some hunk and tries to pretend he was like her brother. God forbid. Get a grip on yourself Pier, she murmured. You are a Christian. Now if only her hormones would realize this. I got to get out of here, she thought, before I make a fool of myself.

The sound of rattling keys and the front door opening brought Pier out of musing. A tall dark complexioned woman stood in the entrance. She was beautiful. Her hair was short and curly. Black jeans hugged her slender hips and she had on a white top. She could be a model. She probably was a model.

Suddenly Pier knew she played the wrong music. The woman mean mugged her.

"Hello. Who are you?" She asked, walking in like she owned the place. Maybe she did. Pier only knew what Landis told her family. The woman sat in the leather chair and crossed her legs.

"You're not Landis' brother-in-law's little sister, are you?"

"Yes, I am. My name is Pier." She didn't want to hold out her hand, knowing this woman wouldn't take it, but good manners made her hold it out anyway.

"You're not little. You're grown." Pier's theory was right; the woman ignored her hand.

Pier, not liking being snubbed retorted before she thought it through, "Yes, well that's a good thing from my point of view."

The woman continued to stare at her. Pier, not knowing what her hang up was, stared right back. And that's how Landis found them when he entered the living room.

"Sorry I took so long, Pier", Landis yelled coming down the

stairs. "I decided to take a shower. Hey, I thought you only listened to gosp..." He paused in mid sentence. "Jackie. What are you doing here? I thought you were going to head out of town this weekend for a photo shooting." He had changed into blue jeans, a red T-shirt and a pair of red and white gym shoes. He didn't seem too happy to see "Jackie".

"No, Rick canceled. I thought I would drop by to apologize for our argument last night," she sprang up out of the chair and tilted her head. "But I see you have moved on to better things." She proceeded to leave. Landis, raising his head heavenward blocks her passage. "Get out of my way, Landis." She shoveled him.

Pier was amazed how calm Landis was. He stood in the doorway, looking as if he could see right through Jackie.

"No," he said quietly. "I will not get out of the way. What's up with you? This *is* Speedy's little sister. And this is not the time for this discussion."

"Little! You call her little? When you said your boy's little sister was coming to town, for some reason the impression was given like she would be a thirteen year old or something. Not some grown woman. Now why is that?" she raised a perfectly arched brow.

As Pier stood feeling trapped, she happened to observe a look of guilt cross Landis' angry face. However he quickly masked it. Did he deliberately conceal her age? Maybe Jackie's acting heavy handed may be the reason.

"I have company," he said coldly. "We can talk about this later."

"Oh, I see." Her voice had taken a sarcastic tone. She folded her arms. "You want me to leave like a good little girl, while you entertain *little sister."*

Landis was looking at Jackie like she was insane.

An overwhelming feeling of tiredness hit Pier. She was tired of being talked about as if she wasn't in the room. Speedy and Shannan did it. Fine. They are family. But there was no way she would accept this from a complete stranger. Or Landis for that matter. There was no other way to leave except by the entrance where they were standing. Suddenly the music was too much. Pier turned it off. Dead silence filled the room and with it the atmosphere of anger and hurt slicing through. Pier didn't know what was going on. Somehow she seemed to be in the middle of a lovers' quarrel and she didn't like it one bit.

"Excuse me. I think I better leave." She didn't have a purse to grab, so she walked toward the two of them. Pausing at the door, she turned to Landis, "I'm sorry I caused a problem. I'll call you before I leave tomorrow." She brushed past him, opening what she hoped was the closet to retrieve her coat. It was. She grabbed her coat, observing Landis closing his eyes as in pain as she left.

"Now that I'm outside, I have nowhere to go. No money for that matter", she said aloud. She headed in the area the cab driver came. Behind her she heard a car speed off. She didn't bother to turn around.

"Pier", Landis called from behind. He grabbed her arm gently. "Hey, you're trying to get me killed. Do you know", he said steering her back to his home, "that Speedy would have my head. I could think of another word. But let's just go with head."

Once back in the living room, Landis sat next to her on the couch. "I am sorry about Jackie. We are going through a rough time right now." He waited for her response. When he didn't receive it, he suggested they still go to the zoo.

"Landis. I am not a child. I'm a grown woman. I know you are upset about your girlfriend. You should be in your car chasing after her, trying to make up, instead of attempting to entertain your *best friend's* sister."

Landis closed his eyes. Man, this was getting very complicated. How did agreeing to entertain someone, who was suppose to be like a sister to him, become so complicated? The parting words of Jackie still rang in his ears. She had said, "Landis, I'm not clear what's going on, but I know it's more than meets the eyes. Look, we have been arguing a lot lately. There is a lot going on, so maybe we should call it off for a while. I'll leave you with *LITTLE SISTER.*"

How was he to argue? Landis wanted to be alone with Pier. He loved her. He was willing to take whatever crumbs dropped his way. Even now, all he wanted was to look at her. Kiss her---

"Landis, did you hear me? I said I can go back to the hotel and wait in the lobby until Phenda and Alicia get in."

Landis stood up. He glanced down at Pier. "Look, little, ah, Pier, I have never said sorry so much in one day, but I am. You've had a rough day. Tomorrow you are leaving and now you are feeling stranded. Why, don't you want to spend a little time with me?" he was grinning like the old Landis she knew and loved.

"I didn't want to be any trouble. And look what happen, your girlfriend is mad."

"Jackie and I understand one another." Landis paced the floor. "I want to take you to the zoo. Its fun and I know you will like it." She ran her hand through her hair nervously. Landis observed this to be a habit of hers.

He cleared his throat. "Now this is what we're going to do. First, the zoo, secondly, we go eat and thirdly, we come back here and wait to call your friends. Finally, I'll take you to the hotel." He took her hand, raised a brow and asked if there were any questions.

She needed to get away for a few moments to sort out her thoughts. Pier stood. "Just one. May I go to the bathroom to freshen up?"

"Be quick about it." Landis walked over to the bay window. He didn't notice the trees, the flowers or the neighbor working in the yard. All he could think of was Pier and then there was Jackie. He slapped his hand on his forehead. "Landis Renee, you are playing with fire", he whispered aloud. If he had any sense at all he'd go to the hotel and demand they open the room for Pier and find Jackie. Then his life would be back to normal.

He didn't blame Jackie for what she said. It was his fault entirely. He had not been the same since Shannan's birthday when he saw Pier across a crowded room. What did that make him; attracted to someone he'd known technically since she was a baby?

Pier stood looking in the bathroom mirror. Since she didn't have it with her, she couldn't touch up her make up. She took a Kleenex and patted it on her face. The bathroom décor was navy and light blue. Once again a woman's touch. She paused and looked at the face in the mirror. "Do you know what you're doing"? No, of course not. The way things were going for her now; this may be the day Jesus returns. *Hell bound! That's where she seemed to be headed.* Pier knew the Word of God. She'd always practiced living accordingly.

"Help me, Lord", she closed her eyes. "This is not the path I should be going. Please help me not want him." This is indeed hard for *Iron Woman*, the name she was honored with back in Atlanta. She didn't do a lot of dating, but the few she did date couldn't get past a peck on the cheek, hence the name. So why is Landis so differently?

Pier walked out of the bathroom to find Landis at the front door waiting. He had her coat in his hands.

"You may not need this now", he stated as he helped her into her coat. "But maybe later. It can get cool at the zoo."

"Thanks."

"Ready?" He asked

"Ready."

He led her to the garage where his car was parked.

They arrived at the Lincoln Park Zoo geared up to have fun. It turned out to be a good idea. Landis treated Pier with the utmost respect. They drank soft drinks, ate popcorn and talked about everything from childhood to now. Landis was very easy to talk to. She laughed at Landis when he imitated the animals. She laughed. She laughed until her face hurt. Landis was quite funny. Every now and then, she would casually slip her arms through his or he would throw his arms around her and pull her to him. Then when realizing what they were doing, each would quickly remove his or her arm like they had touched fire.

They visited every animal except the Reptiles. She'd begged to bypass them. They had paused at the fence by the elephants. Pier stared at him. The tension was back. He was so handsome. A man's man, yet gentle as if crying wouldn't faze him. He was a lot like Speedy. She could see why they remained friends.

"Hungry?" he asked.

"Not really. You?"

"We could get some take out or go home, thaw out some

steaks and grill them."

"Okay. Steaks sound fine," she found herself saying. Pier had vowed to herself she was going to keep him out until Alicia and Phenda returned to the room. Let him take her to the hotel without stepping another foot in his home.

So why was she on her way to his place?

Chapter Seven

J ust like Chicago, the Windy City, the wind was blowing cool air. Landis let up the drop top of his car. He glanced at Pier. She looked deep in thought. They had a good time today, he thought. Pier's laughing made him laugh a lot. He'd enjoyed being himself with her.

Once they get back to his house, he'll feed her and get her back to her hotel room. He'll find a way to get that room open. Maybe the person on this shift would remember her and let the ID issue go. He had to do something. It seemed his control was dwindling.

Taking a rugged breath, he exhaled slowly. All he had to do was get through a couple more hours, then he'd breathe again.

Pier was thinking of the many times she'd judged her friends when they discussed how easy it was to find yourself in this very situation Pier was in now. She'd always prided herself in thinking when alone with a man and sexual tension was present, get out in a hurry.

Now here she was wishing the day would last. She wasn't as

naïve as she was at Shannon's party. She's well aware that Landis is feeling something. Her mission was to find out what.

Fifteen minutes later, they found themselves pulling into the driveway.

"You make the salad and I'll thaw and grill the steaks." He opened the kitchen door for her and headed for the grill. Pier opened the fridge to get the ingredients for the salad.

"Oh, good, you found everything", Landis said on returning to the kitchen. He opened the freezer and grabbed the steaks. "I'll just thaw these babies in the microwave and grill them. It shouldn't take long. You know, I was thinking maybe we should go to the hotel after we eat. Maybe the person that checked you in may be there and remember you." He saw Pier stiffen. Then relax.

"Yeah, sounds good." Pier continues to slice tomatoes.

"You don't drink, do you, Pier? He asked after getting a beer out of the fridge.

"No, I don't. But maybe I'll try a beer, too."

"No way. I'll get you another cola."

"Scared I'll get drunk?" She was flirting. She couldn't help herself.

"Now that's an idea. Then maybe I can have my way with you," he replied half playing.

"Then I'll tell my brother and he'd beat you up for taking advantage of his baby sister." Pier batted her eyes at him. They both burst out laughing- tension ebbing away.

During dinner, they talked some more about their work, hobbies and five-year life plan. Landis learned Pier still enjoyed swimming, reading and writing. She would start teaching kindergarten in September. Speedy always bragged about how smart she was.

"I know your favorite color is red. From our talking I've learned quite a bit about you but what else is there to you, little Pier? At her frown, "excuse me, Ms. Mortimer?"

"Well, let's see. You know, I love old movies because I used to watch AMC with my dad. I like all types of singers not really any favorites. My favorite kind of music is of course gospel but I like country music, R & B. Now," she leans forward, elbows resting on the table, "what is your favorite kind of music?"

"With the exception of hard core music, I pretty much listen to any kind," he grinned wickedly, humming the melody to the song they danced to at Shannan's birthday party.

She shook her head at him. "I don't understand you, Landis. She paused. "Now tell me about you and Jackie."

"What do you want to know?" He immediately shuddered.

"Are you two serious?" She nervously played with her napkin.

Landis lean back in his chair, lost in thought. "I don't know. I thought we had an understanding, but lately she's been acting kind of whack. She's a wonderful person. Of course with the way she was acting today, you couldn't tell. We go out together, have fun." He shrugged his shoulders. "I can't pinpoint it, you know what I mean, but something is different I'm always very upfront and clear with my-I-What about you? Are you serious about any-one? Devin perhaps?"

She sat up straight in her chair. "No, there is no one. Devin is a fun person to just hang out with. I'm---Landis, I..." taking a deep breath, Pier looked into his chocolate eyes. "I'm usually a straight forward type of person and from what I know and see, you are, too." Clearing her throat, voice trembling she contin-ued, "I'm not experienced with men and I need to know I'm not tripping. Are you attracted to me?"

Landis nearly fell out his seat. He wasn't expecting her to cut through the chase and ask the question they have been dancing around since Shannan's party. He shouldn't have let the conversation get this far. He leaned forward and touched her hand. He looked up at the ceiling. "Pier, what am I going to do with you." He looked at her intensely for what seem like forever but only a few seconds. Finally he sighed and leaned back again in his seat. He simply answered, "Yes, I am."

Closing her eyes, Pier definitely wasn't prepared for an answer like this. Hope? Yes. Prepared? Not in this lifetime. She expected him to lecture or be vague about it, but never to say *yes I am* to her.

"Baby", Landis called softly. "Look at me. Pier, open your eyes and look at me." He scooted his chair up close to hers. "I want you to open your eyes and listen." Landis held her small soft hands in his large ones as she open her honey colored eyes. "I have known I was in love with you since the night of your eighteenth birthday party. I fought it and took the promotion offered to me and left town. For five long years, I have fought this attraction, this feeling."

Pier's hands began to tremble. Landis squeezed them gently. "I love you, Pier!" He took a deep breath. "Why do you think I didn't attend your college graduation? I was afraid I would show my feelings. Embarrass myself. Betray Speedy and my friendship. There was a lot running through my mind five years ago and it has not stopped. On the night of Shannan's birthday, I didn't know if I was going or coming. It was hell."

Leaning back in his seat, Landis released her hands. "Listen to me sharing my feelings, taking for granted you feel something for me as well. How arrogant am I?"

"But Landis", Pier said earnestly, "I do feel something for you. I am in love with you and have been since I was sixteen when I used to email you. But I didn't know that was what it was until you returned home", she gave a dry laugh. "What I don't understand is why you left and didn't say anything. Six years is not that bad. Well, maybe when I was sixteen, but I was eighteen. I was legally an adult." Laughing wearily, she said, "Although my family doesn't see it and I let them. So it is my fault. But why didn't you say something?"

Sighing Landis leaned forward. "Because of Speedy. Speedy threw such a fit when Ace asked to date you." She widened her eyes. "I see you didn't know. But yeah, at the wedding he told me Ace told him he wanted to date you and Speedy freaked out; saying Ace was sick to want to date his little sister, and if any friend of his dated his sister, they were no longer a friend. Well I certainly wasn't going to say I had feelings for you." Rubbing his brow, Landis took another deep breath and exhaled. "I couldn't stay-I mean neither one of us let on to the other how we felt, I wasn't going to risk loosing my best friend for feelings that wasn't shared."

Smiling sadly, Pier shook her head, "Speedy is the best big brother ever, but he's such overkill some times. He put up such a stink about me going away to college and then he and Mic visited more than the parents. I love my brother but I wish you had said something Landis.

"I didn't want to go away but I was afraid you would return and I couldn't take seeing you, loving you as I did. I couldn't tell anyone how I felt about you because I knew they would say I was took young; it's just a school girl crush or needed to be ashamed of myself. So I left."

Raising her hand, Pier lovingly caresses his face. "So, Handsome, what do we do about it?"

As if in a dream, Landis basked in her caresses. Holding her hand to his face, not wanting the moment to pass, but knowing it must, Landis gave a deep sigh. "We do nothing. We must carry on as if this interlude never took place. You go home and get on with your life. And as impossible as it will be, I will try to do the same."

"But why?" Pier whimpered, the sound of the sea roaring in her ears.

Releasing her hand, Landis straightened up in his chair. "Why?" He looked at her with such longing and sadness. "Let's see. Well for starts Speedy would kill both of us. I don't care if he is a preacher. He'd come after me and the Lord would not be on his mind. Then there's your dad. He'd probably raise me from the dead just to kill me again." He shook his head. "Pier, it just won't work. Family is too important. What a mess! I wish I could pull myself out of myself and beat myself. I-Don't look at me like that, baby", he said half groaning.

Pier looked puzzled. "Like what?"

"You really don't know, do you? You have no idea how good you look right now. All day I've been kicking myself for wanting you. All I have wanted to do since you step into my home was carry you to my bed and make love to you, hold you. I have dreamed of this for years." He ran his hands over his face allowing his eyes to reveal all the passion he felt.

Pier was frightened of the emotional turmoil she was feeling right now. It's one thing to think about this all day and another to actually discuss it. Needing something to do, she quickly stood lifting the plates off the table, carrying them to the sink. Her hands shook so bad, she dropped one of the plates on the floor, breaking it.

"Oh Landis, I'm sorry. I'm--," with tears streaming down her cheeks she said, "scared. I have been all day. I have dreamt of this moment for what seems like forever. You confessing you love me and I you. Almost every night I wake up with your name on my lips. It is you that I want. I'm sorry." She hiccupped. "I thought I could move on and I have tried. God knows I've tried but ever since Shannan's birthday, I can't stop wanting you." Pier stood in front of him shaking and crying incoherently, repeating, "All I've ever wanted is you. I'm sorry."

So overwhelmed with emotions Landis staggered to his feet. Drawing her into his arms, he held her for while, stroking her hair as she cried into his red t-shirt. "Shh baby, don't cry. Please, Pier, don't cry." He started kissing her forehead, then her cheeks, finally her lips.

With her body pressed close to his, Landis deepened the kiss. Breathing hard, he gently pulled away. Looking into her passion filled eyes, he calmed himself. "I am the one sorry. You have nothing to be sorry about. I am older; I should know better. God help me-I need you, Pier. But baby this can't happen, not now. I-I can't take advantage of this situation. I can't betray our families' trust." He was talking more to himself than Pier. He closed his eyes briefly trying to get a grasp on his emotions.

Carefully holding her face in his large hands as he gazed into her tear drenched eyes, "I don't know how this happened", he murmured sorrowfully to her. "I had everything planned. There's too much at state to ever give in to our feelings again."

She pulled away, wiping her eyes with the back of her hand. "I know. I'm not usually a cry baby."

Moving to the counter Landis picked up the white cordless phone and gave it to her, "why don't we call your hotel and leave a message at the front desk for your friends to contact you at my number?"

Taking the phone, Pier nodded. She was confused. She was scared. She was in love. She dialed information for the hotel number. After being directly connected to the hotel, she left a message for Alicia to call her. Repeating the number Landis gave to the clerk, she thanked the lady and ends the call. Landis was watching her. She tried to smile but she couldn't. She was too emotionally drained. She had to do something.

At the same time, they both bent to pick up the broke plate. Their heads bumped. Landis rubbed her head and caressed her face. Before either could think about what was happening, he'd effortlessly picked her up and carried her up the stairs. He headed for his bedroom, paused, turned around and moved down the hall to one of his guest bedrooms.

Pier, with her arms looped around his neck closed her eyes. How could this be wrong? This was love. There weren't any answers. She didn't have any coherent thoughts except this is what she wanted and for once she was giving in to her feeling and not worried about tomorrow and what it would bring. She finally was taking Shannan's advice and living a little.

Landis laid her on the bed. After turning on the lamp, he pulled his T-shirt over his head. He lay down next to Pier. He gathered her in his strong arms. The feel of her hands on his chest was his undoing. "I am sorry, baby", he whispered softly, "but with you I can't think straight. I have no control. I have no will power." He rose up on an elbow and looked down at her by the soft glow of the lamp. He had never in life seen a woman more beautiful than the one he was staring at right now.

Pier laid a finger on his lips causing him to kiss her hand. "Landis, I love you so much. This cannot be wrong. Please Landis, make love to me. I know we can't be together, but give me this one night to remember." She lifted her lips to receive his.

Landis stood in the guest bedroom watching Pier sleep. He wanted to hate himself for what happened and in fact he did but looking at her, he could never regret loving her. No matter what the price he would pay. God forgive us, he whispers quietly. He will fix this.

He walked to his bedroom and slipped under the covers. He lay there thinking about what to do. Maybe he'd talk to Speedy and beg his forgiveness, and then there are the parents. His and hers.

There was also Jackie. What would he say to her? Although he'd never promised her anything-she didn't deserve this. He owed her some sort of explanation. He rolled on his stomach. What a mess. His eyes went to the clock on his nightstand table. Six A.M. He couldn't go back to sleep. Landis dragged himself out of bed. May as well take a shower, he decided.

After showering and getting dressed to go jogging, Landis looked in on Pier. She was still asleep. He headed down the stairs just as Jackie was coming in.

"Jackie." He hurried down the stairs.

"Hi, Baby. Miss me." She stood smiling like yesterday never took place and Landis had never felt more like a jerk.

"Can we go into the living room? Umm, Pier is upstairs sleep and I..." She cut him off with a 'she's what'.

"Why is she here, Landis?" She stalked off into the living room.

"Excuse me?" He asked coldly.

"I asked why is *little Pier* here." Jackie was speaking very slowly as if he was hard of understanding.

"I let her stay, that's why. Last time I checked, this was my home." He knew he shouldn't vent his frustrations out on her. The phrase 'what a mess' kept replaying in his head. Taking a deep breath he said, "She got locked out of her room." It is funny how hollow the story sounded now. "It's the truth," he barked out at her look of disbelief.

"Yeah right. Why don't I go have a little talk with little Pier?"

Pier woke up a little confused as to her whereabouts. As she glanced around the room seeing her clothes scattered, everything came tumbling back to her mind. She was here in Landis' home- in Landis' bed. She smiled until she thought about the mess they both cosigned to. God help them, this was definitely wrong.

She heard Landis speaking quietly in the stillness of the morning. She was just debating how she was ever going to face him when she heard a woman's voice shrieking. Jackie? She wasn't sure. She couldn't make it out. Finally the woman screamed, "so if I went upstairs right now, I'll find her in the guest room. Well, let me pass, Landis, let me pass. Why are you trying to stop me?"

"You're crazy. You know that? Crazy. Why are you tripping like this?"

Pier, with her heart in her mouth, sprinted out of bed. She grabbed her skirt and threw it in the chair. Thinking, she quickly put her underwear and t-shirt on. Glancing around the room it looked okay. Oh my God! The bed! She ran and straightened the bed out. She made it look like one person had lain there instead of -- she won't think about that. Not now. Good thing, too, because the door burst open and an enraged Jackie walked in.

Quick thinking she grabbed the pillow Landis laid his head on and put in front of her. "Landis, close your eyes. What's going on? Jackie? I heard arguing, is it a problem my being here?" To hear her calm voice, one wouldn't know that adrenaline was flowing through her body and that she was holding the pillow tightly because she was shaking.

Landis, standing stiffly behind Jackie said, "Sorry, Pier. We are having another embarrassing argument. There are towels in the bathroom closet. Come down, when you are dressed." He gave a strained smile. "I won't tell Speedy I saw you half naked. Apologize, and let's go Jackie." He turned and walked out of the room.

"I am embarrassed, Pier. I'm so sorry."

Feeling extremely guilty, Pier tried to smile. "I understand. I would do the same," she said as Jackie followed behind Landis.

She barely made it to the bathroom before the tears streamed down her face. They flowed as one with the shower spray as she bathed. She didn't care that her hair was getting wet or how it would look. She didn't care about anything except getting back to the safety of home. She was a fool. Nothing but a fool and *a sinner*. The tears continued to flow like a waterfall as she dressed.

Pier's feet felt like lead as she proceeded down the stairs. If she fell down to the bottom of the stairs, she wouldn't feel any pain. She heard voices in the kitchen so she headed in that area. They were discussing… Jackie's pregnancy.

Oh, God, this couldn't be happening!

Jackie's pregnant.

NOOO. THIS CAN'T BE HAPPENING!

As she walked in, Landis was standing looking out the kitchen window. Jackie was at the table drinking tea. She had tears in her eyes.

"Hello again, guys." Landis turns around not making eye contact with her.

"Can I get you some breakfast Pier?" he asked quietly. When had he stopped saying little? After last night how could he call her little anything?

"No. I'm fine. I don't usually do breakfast. But I would like to use your phone."

He gestured toward the white phone on the wall. "If you need some privacy, you can use the one in the living room or my bedroom."

The thought of being in his bedroom, and she was sure Jackie shared that bedroom as well, was too much to stomach right now. "This one's fine. I just want to talk to Phenda or Alicia." She picked up the phone and dialed the room.

"Hello," said a sleepy voice.

"Hi Alicia, its Pier."

"Pier? Where are you? I know you left a message at the front desk saying you'd be at the in-law's house. Are you still there?"

Pier made a poor attempt at laughing. "Girl yes. What time did you guys get in? Do you see my purse there? I hope the maid or someone didn't steal anything." She knew she was rambling but she couldn't help it.

"Yes, your purse is still here. I wouldn't know if anything's missing. Exactly what happened, Pier?"

"I was dressed and ready to go out when I thought I heard

a knock at the door. I opened it and stepped out, letting it slam behind me."

"I don't believe you, girl. What were you thinking? Did you ask them to let you in?"

"I wasn't thinking apparently. Anyway I'll fill you in on the rest when I get there. Can you be downstairs with some money?" Out the corner of her eye she saw Landis shaking his head trying to get her attention. Alicia said she'd be there. "Okay. I see you then." Pier hangs up.

"Pier," Landis said softly, "I'll be more than happy to give you a ride to the hotel. I refuse to let you take a cab."

She put on a bright smile for Jackie's sake. "That's okay, *daddy*, a cab will be fine." Picking up the phone, she asked for a number. Jackie gave it to her. Glad to see the back of her probably.

Landis stood there, rooted to the window. His whole life was falling apart. *PREGNANT*. How could this have happened? Well, he knew how it happened. He felt so numb. And Pier. She must have heard them arguing and made the room presentable. Pier, looking so brave when he knew she had to be hurting on the inside. He shouldda, wouldda, couldda. Whatever. Too late now! If he had stayed in bed with her like he wanted to, it would be a bigger mess. Jackie would have caught them and left, and he would never have known anything about the baby. He'd never again give any woman a key to his house unless he was married. MARRIED! What was he going to do? Marry Jackie for the baby's sake? Does she deserve to be with someone only there for the baby? Pregnant! A baby! His baby! Pregnancy must be the reason why she's been acting crazy lately.

"And how long will that be", he heard Pier ask. "Fifteen to

thirty minutes? Okay. Thanks. She hung up the phone. She took her time turning around. "How accurate are your cabs."

"Living on the north side, they come quickly. It will be about that time," Jackie answered. Great, thought Landis, now she wanted to talk. Lord, what a mess. "Sit down." Jackie was saying. Pier's leaving; she could afford to be generous.

"No, I better get my coat." She turned to look at Landis. Her eyes no longer held humor. Yesterday she was an innocent young lady, laughing and having fun. He did this to her. She attempted a smile at him as she headed out of the kitchen. Her hair was damp from the shower. She had no make up on and she'd never looked more beautiful. He smiled back at her.

He noticed Jackie was watching them so he looked away. Landis and Jackie sat in complete silence. A few minutes later, a horn sounded hollow in the early morning.

"That was quick", said Jackie.

Pier stuck her head back in the kitchen. "The cab's here. I better go."

"I'll walk you to the cab", Landis said with firmness.

"Okay." She looked at Jackie. "Nice meeting you."

"You too".

Landis helped her put her coat on. He squeezed her shoulders. "You all right, Pier?"

"Fine", she said stiffly. "Thanks."

They walked down the driveway. Pier had a far away look. "Pier, she told me she's pregnant."

"I heard y'all talking. Makes sense. The anger. The tears. It reminded me of when I visited Micah Rochelle in her first trimester"

Landis stood awkwardly by the cab. "At least let me pay for

the cab." He reached in his pocket.

"Landis, please don't. I have my own money."

"I know I took advantage of you. Your innocence, your trust. Your brother-my friend's trust. There are no words to describe how sorry I am for this morning. But Pier, I can never regret last night." He kissed her cheek. She got in the cab.

Landis stood watching her ride off. Out of his life. Forever. Well, at least he didn't have to worry about confronting Speedy because there is no budding relationship for him and Pier.

Unknown to him, Jackie was watching him watch Pier. Unknown to him Jackie, saw his expression.

Pier cried all the way to the hotel. The cab driver continually asked her if she was okay. She assured him she was fine, but the tears continued like a waterfall. Phena and Alicia were waiting with the money. Pier gave the driver a two dollars tip and wished him a great day.

"Are you okay, Pier? You look like you've been crying," asked Alicia.

"I'm fine. Just got my feelings hurt." She didn't elaborate any further.

"What happened?" Phena always was noisy.

"As you know, I end up staying at my *brother's in-law's place* and this morning his girl came over and they fought, and deep down I feel like I'm at fault." It pained her to relate the story but why not. Practice makes perfect.

"And go on," eagerly Phena waited.

Pier sighed as they got in the elevator, heading for their room. "I don't know, Phena. I rather not talk about it."

On entering the room, Alicia said she would be jealous of any woman with him. "I mean I've seen your brother's friend. Talk about a movie star smile."

Pier walked over to the window. She could see a lake, sail boats and people enjoying the Sunday morning.

"Actually, I think he could be a movie star with that body", said Phena as she sat on the bed with a dreamy look in her eyes.

Turning around, Pier said quietly, "He is handsome and very kind. A woman couldn't have a better man."

"Oh yeah," said Alicia giving Phena a knowingly look.

"Okay, ladies, it's almost check out time. I'll change my clothes and pack, and we are outta here."

The drive home wasn't as bad as Pier thought it would be. She was learning to be good at pretending. They laughed and talked about the trip. A whole weekend to do nothing but hang out. Alicia met some man. She had fun with her relatives. Pier liked them, too. But as she now knew her primary purpose was to come and see Landis. Well, she got what she wanted and more. "I too, Landis, can never be regretful," she whispered softly to herself as she looked out the window. Tears welled in her eyes. She wiped them before her friends observed them.

As the car stopped in front of her house, Pier unfolded herself out of the car, grabbed her luggage and waved to her friends. "Thanks, y'all, for the trip. See you at Bible study." She sprinted up the stairs.

"Hey, hon. did you have a good trip? I wasn't clear what you girls were going to Chicago for," said her mom. Pier had just entered the back door. Her mom was sitting at the kitchen table reading her Bible. "Hungry?"

"Hi, Mama," Pier put her luggage down and hugged her. "We went to Alicia's grandmother's birthday party. We were just a group of girls hanging out. I like Alicia family. No big deal." She sat down at the table. She looked around. "Where's Dad?"

"Oh, he went ahead to night service. I didn't feel much like going tonight. Guess I'm getting old, huh?"

Pier laughed the first genuine laugh all day. Looking at her mom, you couldn't tell she'd turned fifty-six this year. She looked at least ten years younger. "Mama, you will never get old." She rose to her feet. "I'm a little tired. I think I'll go to bed now. Good night."

"Good night, my dear." Pier picked up her luggage and headed up the back stairs. "Oh, Pier, I almost forgot. Landis called. I told him you'd call him back. So, you saw him while you were there?"

Pier froze right where she was, her mind racing. Landis called. Why? I can't do this. I can't talk to him. Not tonight. "Yes, ma'am. He took me to the zoo." Her mom laughed as Pier expected. "He no doubt is wondering if I arrived safely." She must be careful, too much explanation will cause people to wonder, especially her mom. *I'm getting paranoid.* Pier threw her bags in the over-stuffed red chair in her room and threw herself on the bed and cried until sleep came.

Pier woke up for some unknown reason. She lay still for a minute. It was the ringing of her telephone. Leaning over, she turned on the bed light, eyes immediately going to the clock as she answered the phone. Ten o'clock. She'd only been asleep for a couple of hours.

"Hello."

"Hi, Pier, it's me. Landis."

Her heart literally stopped. "Hi," a little more breathless than she wanted.

"I called your mom again. She assured me she told you I called. I figured you didn't want to talk, but I had to talk to you."

"What do you need to talk to me about?" she asked softly, resting her head on the pillows.

"I promise not to call or bother you again. I just had to know if you were okay."

"I'm fine, really."

"I'm glad." With hesitation in his voice he said, "I can be there in a heart beat if you need me."

"Landis", her throat clogged with the urge to cry; she cleared her throat, "you are an honorable man but it isn't necessary for you to be concern for me. I'm fine, really."

"Baby, I never thought, even in my wildest dreams I would be in this kind of situation."

"There is no situation, you said we couldn't be and now you have a baby on the way, so there is no situation for us." The fountain of tears streamed freely down her cheeks. She laid her head back on the pillow and smothered a sob."

"Oh, Baby, please don't cry."

"We could never be." She paused, he was silent, and "I want you to know I do not regret our night together. I will never regret loving you, Landis. But, I can't handle talking to you. I'm sorry but I can't take this. Goodbye." She hung the phone up. It rang again but she ignored it. She put the pillow over her head. No more. No more, she sobbed uncontrollably. God, I'm sorry! Lord! Help me! Please help! Pleeease!

Chapter Eight

Landis put the cordless phone down. Tears filled his eyes. This was all happening so fast. In the heat of the moment, he found himself in bed with the love of his life and the next thing he knew, Jackie dropped this bombshell. She's pregnant. PREGNANT. *PREGNANT.* It rang so final in his head. There was only one thing to do-marry her. Yeah, marry her. He cared about Jackie. They got along good together, same interests and same hobbies. Isn't that what was marriage all about? This was the first time in years he couldn't pick up the phone and call his friend, Speedy. He couldn't even call his parents on this one. Landis closed his eyes. He was lying on the pillow Pier laid on, in the bed she slept in. The lightest scent of the fragrance she wore was still in the air. He drifted off to sleep.

The alarm clock brought him out of his sound sleep. He jumped up out of bed and headed for the shower. His thoughts once again went back to Pier. He prayed to God she was fine. And Lord, he prayed silently, forgive me for taking advantage of her. It was funny how you know whom to call when in trouble, he mused to himself. He got out of the shower and got dressed for work.

Landis couldn't work. He couldn't concentrate. He had no appetite at lunch. By two o'clock, he gave up and decided to go home. Grabbing his suit jacket and brief case, he walked to his administrative assistant's office.

"Latrisha, I think I'm coming down with the flu or something. I'll be home if needed."

The phone was ringing as he walked into the house. Putting down his brief case, he looked on the caller ID. He saw it was Speedy's number.

"Hello."

"Whuz up, Landis?"

"Hey, Speedy. Playing hooky from school bro?" He walked in the living room. He noticed Jackie's scarf on the couch. Since it wasn't here when he left this morning, it meant she'd been here. Boy, did he need his keys. What is he thinking; he's supposed to ask her to marry him.

"Summer school hasn't started yet. But what about you? Hardly working as usual. I guess the rich don't work."

Landis forced a laugh. He wanted to know had Speedy talked to Pier. How was she? He only said, "What's up?"

"Nothing, man. I just wanted to thank you for looking out for little Pier."

"You know, man, Pier's not so little anymore," Landis stated tightly.

Speedy laughed. "Don't tell me you had a little problem with Jackie about my sister." He laughed again. He knew Landis too well.

"Go ahead and laugh. It wasn't funny when it happened."

"What happened?"

"As you said she had a problem about Pier coming over. Seems Pier doesn't look little to anyone except you man. She thought, little meant twelve or thirteen or something."

"That is bad, but I know you handled it. I'm sure Pier will tell me all about it on Saturday when she comes over for our monthly. You know our monthly get together. I wish Shannan would make time to come over. Now that girl is a trip."

"Shannan will always be Shannan. She will come around. Imagine what Jackie would have done if it had been Shannan."

Speedy laughed. "And Shannan would have given her a hard time. Honestly I didn't think you and Jackie would be together this long. Especially since you've told me how she's been tripping lately."

Landis blurted out "she's pregnant" before he knew it. Speedy's silence was expected. As kids, they always talk about not having children outside of marriage. They saw what unwed pregnancies did to a lot of their friends. Baby mama drama. That's one of the reasons Speedy never really messed around. When he and Micah Rochelle realized they were in love, they got married. And it's a good marriage. They are happy and he couldn't have picked a better mate for his sister.

"PREGNANT!" Speedy finally said. "Wow! What are you going to do?"

"Marry her," he stated flatly. "What other choice do I have? You know our parents. You know how we are."

"Yeah, I know. Well, bro, I don't know what to say, except to do the right thing. Pray, man, pray. Ask God to help. Stop trying to fix everything and pray. Man, I hate this is happening."

Landis leaned back on the couch. "You hate this. Just imagine how I feel."

"Let me ask you this. What are your feelings for her, Landis? A couple of months ago, the way you talked, I thought maybe it was only a matter of time before you asked her to marry you."

That was before your sister came on the scene, before I felt hope again, he thought. "When something like this happens, you feel trapped and the thing you think you wanted, you run from it."

"Yeah well. I don't know what to say. Why don't the two of you come home for the fourth of July?"

"I don't know. Man, I don't know."

"That will give the family a chance to meet her before you spring on them marriage."

"Speedy, I hardly talk about women in my life to my parents. If I bring Jackie home and tell my mom I want to marry her, my mother will know immediately she's pregnant."

"Landis, you know I never pushed you about getting saved and serving God. But this is something only He can help you with. So you know I'll be praying for you."

"Yes, my friend, I know. You're a good friend to have."

"Don't ever forget it. Gotta go, I'm taking Spency to the park. Remember what I said about the fourth.'"

They hung up.

The rest of the week went smoothly for Landis. He woke up on Saturday, glad for the weekend. He didn't have much planned. Jackie had been out of town, so today would be the first time since Sunday he would see her.

He'd ask her to marry him tonight. If she accepted, they can go to Vegas or something. Then he'll tell his family and voila, done deal.

NO! He will not think of Pier. He hoped she would move on

with her life. Liar!

⊷《❮》》⊷

This was the first Saturday, since Pier started having once a month meals with her brother and his family, that she dreaded going. And like a big joke on her, she walked in and who's on the phone. Landis. Now she wished she had come up with an excuse not to come.

She waved to Speedy who was as always frying chicken. Micah Rochelle went upstairs to check on Spency, who had a late nap. Her heart was pounding in her chest. She used to wonder about Landis when they would talk on the phone with him and laugh. Now she knew first hand who Landis was. The man she loved. The man who was going to marry another woman. The man who was lost to her forever.

Spencer turns to look at her. "Yep, that's little Pier." He was saying to Landis. "Hey, girl you gotta work today. Start peeling those." He pointed at the bag of potatoes.

Pier slid her jean-clad curvy body into the chair at the kitchen table, preparing to peel potatoes. Micah Rochelle walked in with Spency and he ran to his Aunt Lil Pier. She picked him up, talking to him when Speedy called her. She looked his way.

"Landis says hi," said Speedy"

Her hands trembled slightly as she put Spency in his chair and picked up a potato.

"Tell him hi," She wanted to grab that phone and tell him how much she loved him.

"Oh," said Speedy, handing her the phone. "He wants to talk to you," He had on another apron that read, *"Behind every successful man is a pushy woman. Thanks Dear."* She had no choice but to talk.

"Hello."

"I'm sorry," Landis said without greeting her. "I had to hear your voice and see how you were. I know I promised not to bother you again."

Pier quickly turned her back to Speedy and Micah Rochelle to face the window. The afternoon sun was shining on part of their lawn, making it look lighter than the rest of the grass. She took a deep breath.

"Hi, Landis, I'm doing great, and you?"

"Go in the living room, I need to talk. What am I saying that wouldn't work? Listen, Pier, I need to talk to you about something. Can I call--," Jackie's voice in the background.

"Well, that won't be necessary, Landis. No need. Oh, you want to talk to Micah." She handed the phone to her sister-in-law. She rushed out of the room. She had to get away. She was jealous. Jealous of knowing Jackie was with him, that he could probably be happy with her-and the baby. Once in the bathroom, she closed her eyes and let the tears run freely. She had long given up trying to stop them.

Spencer Trace Mortimer had spent years watching out for his little sister. And he knew something was wrong. She was trying to hide it, but he knew. He also knew that it had something to do with Chicago. Maybe Landis could enlighten him. He'd call him later. He watched her as she came back in the room. She looked like she'd been crying. What is going on? He'd get to the bottom of this.

Landis got off the phone with Micah Rochelle. Jackie's timing was bad. She'd just walked in while he was talking to Pier, which caused Pier to get off the phone. He sighed. He won't call or talk to her again. Some things are best left alone. Who was he kidding? He could no more leave Pier alone as grass can grow without sun and rain.

He watched Jackie as she walked in the living room.

"Hi. That was my sister and her husband."

"*Little* Pier's brother?"

"Jackie. Don't start", he pleaded wearily.

"Look," she sat on the couch next to him, "I know."

"Know?" he raised a brow.

"About you and *little Pier*," she answered sarcastically.

"I'm not going through this again with you."

"Landis, I know you slept with her. I know you have a thing for her. I saw how you looked at her that Saturday by the cab." She held her hand up. "No, let me talk, please. I came by on Monday to pick up my things. You haven't even noticed my stuff is gone."

"No I haven't notice."

"And the reason you haven't noticed is because you don't sleep in the bed you shared with me anymore." She sat back on the couch. "Landis, we are not headed anywhere. We haven't been for a long time. Actually, things really down sided when you returned from your parent's house last spring. Now I at least know why."

"I don't know what to say", said Landis. He rested his head in his hands. "I'm sorry is about all I can think of."

"I know. I'm sorry too. I care about you, Landis. I think we should end this now, and go our separate ways."

Landis sat forward in confusion. "I don't understand. What

about the baby?"

Jackie had such a painful expression. She wiped the tears streaming down her face. "I was thinking about terminating the pregnancy."

"What?" He raised his large tall frame so swiftly it caused Jackie to fall back on the couch. He stood looking down at her. "You're what? Thinking? Thinking? You're not thinking. You're pregnant. So you want an abortion. I have no say so in this matter?" He was talking through clenched teeth. Landis was angry. He was mad. He was frustrated.

Jackie started to cry harder. "I'm sorry, Landis. So sorry." She was sobbing uncontrollably. " It's just lousy timing on my part. I'm at the height of my career. Maybe in a few years."

"Shut up," he shouted. He rarely shouted, especially at women. "Just shut up. YOUR CAREER! YOUR RELATIONSHIP! YOU WANT TO ABORT MY BABY BECAUSE IT DOESN'T FIT IN WITH YOUR CAREER! YOU MAKE ME SICK!" He was so angry he was trembling. He grabbed her but immediately let her go. He had to pull himself together. He wanted to curse her out. "When is this supposed to happen," he asked. "Or do I have a right to know? Why bother to tell me you're pregnant."

"I wanted to work things out. But Saturday when I saw how gentle and protective of her you were, I was jealous. I realized that's what I want." She looked at him with red-rimmed eyes. "Do you understand?"

Landis sat back down next to her. He was more calmed now. He rested his hands on his knees. "Help me understand. I'm not quite following you. First you say it's the timing. Then you say it's your career. Now you're saying you feel jealous. Jackie, I was planning to ask you to marry me tonight." He leaned back on the couch. "We could have worked it out. We still can." Please Father let this be the truth, he silently prayed. Let me convince Jackie to marry me and please let me forget Pier once and for all.

"The truth is I don't want a baby. I don't want to be a mother. Maybe in a couple of years, but not now."

"Okay, why don't you have the baby and give it to me. I'll take full custody and raise it. You can visit. The bottom line is I want this baby. Please Jackie don't destroy this child. I know I don't go to church anymore, but I still believe in the Bible."

She jumped up. "No. I'm not having it. Sorry, but I can't do it." She retrieved her purse from the coffee table. She reached in her purse and grabbed his keys and laid them on the table. "I don't know what else to say. I'm sorry. You're a good man. I hope you find the happiness you deserve." She walked out the front door.

Landis sat on the couch, staring at nothing. He felt so numb. He felt hopeless. He had just lost a child. A child he would never see. He couldn't cry. You have to have feelings to cry. Nothing could make him feel. Not even thoughts of Pier. Pier. It began to happen; yeah, he was feeling again. Feeling pain. Rubbing his hand over his brow. This was more familiar. This he was use to. This pain he could endure. He heard Speedy's voice saying, 'This is something only God can help you with.' "Our Father who art in heaven-," he started the only prayer he remembered as a child.

Chapter Nine

Four weeks! Four long weeks since Pier's disastrous weekend in Chicago. Disastrous? Maybe the word was a tad too strong. Maybe the weekend per se wasn't disastrous, just the outcome. Like knowing the man you love is indeed attracted to you-doesn't think of you as a child-slept with you. But you will never ever be with him because he's marrying another woman. *A pregnant woman!* Disastrous!

He'd tried to call her several times but she wouldn't talk to him. Jackie was pregnant. He had a responsibility to her. Their brief affair was over before it began. More like a one night stand.

Her mind had continually been occupied with thoughts of Landis, causing her to cry all the time. She couldn't eat or sleep. She was depressed. She missed him.

Around her family she pretended everything was fine. She had, however, noticed how her mother was always watching her. Strolling past the mirror in the hallway, she paused to take a good look at herself. Her eyes were tired and puffy. And she'd lost weight. Continuing to her bedroom, where she seemed to be hibernating, she threw herself on the bed.

Landis. Will she ever stop thinking about him?

Wow! She thought. How condescending she must have sounded to her friends when they talked about sneaking around sleeping with their boyfriends and still trying to live saved. That, as much as they loved God, it was hard.

Pier in her best preachy voice would tell them they must trust God and not put themselves in situations that would lead them to lose control. How they were still her friends, she would never know.

The advice was the truth, and good advice, but it was said without experience. Now that she knew what it was like to lose control of a situation, maybe, going forward, she should keep her opinions to herself.

Landis. It was kind of hard to regret being with someone you love. Surely God understood that. Landis. If only she could talk to him. Hear his voice.

Lately, the monthly Saturday had become every other Saturday. Shannan came one Saturday. Landis called and everyone but Pier talked to him. She told Speedy to tell him hi and made a grand effort of playing with Spency. Shannan looked puzzled but didn't say anything. Maybe she's finally being accepted as an adult.

She was still lying on her bed when her phone rang. It was Landis. The distressed sound in his voice made her not hang up.

"Pier! Please Baby, don't hang up." His voice was hoarse as if he has been crying. Surely not strong Landis, whom according to everyone can handle any situation, any problem.

"Hi, Landis. How are you?" Her voice cracked on the last word.

"Missing you, Pier. Please I need to see you. I could fly there and we could talk at the airport."

"I'm sorry that's not a good idea. Listen Landis, I love you. But I can't see you anymore." I will not cry, I will not cry, she repeated to herself.

"Please, Pier. I love you too. I've been trying not to call. I don't have the strength I had five years ago. I need you in my life. Without you, I'm empty. Please Baby. I can hardly eat, sleep, or work."

"And what about Jackie and the baby?"

"Jackie and I are finished. We've been finished. She got an abortion."

"A what? Oh Landis. That's awful. I know you're upset."

"I'm devastated. To know you have a child on the way, and bam, you loose it in the next breath." He sighed. "This made me think a lot about us. I need you, Pier. Please baby let's meet and talk."

"Let's sneak around you mean." She twisted a few strings of hair around her index finger.

"No. I don't know. When it comes to you, I'm so unsure. I know Speedy and Elder would kill me. I'm older, Baby. I should know better."

"Landis, I'm twenty-three, an adult. This has nothing to do with my dad or Speedy."

"It has everything to do with them. But I'll figure out something. All I know is if Speedy knew that I slept with his little sister, it would be the end of our friendship. Then there's Micah Rochelle. She's right smack dab in the middle."

It was Pier's turn to sigh. "You're right. There's too much at stake. So I guess we sneak around."

"Man, oh man," Landis said. "I feel like I'm taking advantage of you."

"No, you're not. I couldn't talk to you knowing you were with Jackie. Now that she's out of the picture, as far as I'm concerned, we can be together." She pauses, "Land, I'm yours for as long as you want me," she whispered.

Landis groaned. "I want you forever. Let's get together. Fly some place; any place, for the weekend, where we don't know anyone. We don't have to sleep together. I only want to see you. Maybe hold you a little."

"Okay. Where?" Pier asked excitedly. She sat up in bed. She hadn't felt this energetic in a long time.

"Just be at the airport Saturday morning. I'll call you with the exact time and arrangements. Will there be a problem getting away?"

"Oh, I'll get away."

Friday evening after service, Pier told her parents she was going away for the weekend. She expected the third degree, but after moping around for weeks, her parents were so happy to see her chirpy they didn't bother to drill her.

Eight o'clock Saturday morning, Pier was at the airport standing at the counter receiving her tickets to Las Vegas of all places. She and Landis agreed to meet at the baggage claim once they reached their designation.

It was the longest three and a half hours in her life. Finally stepping off the plane heading for the baggage claims, there he was, standing tall and distinguish and grinning at her as she made her way toward him. She ran the distance. Landis lifted her up in his arms and swung her around. They kissed.

"Hi Baby. Man, it's good to see you." He kissed her again.

"Hi, Handsome. I'm glad to see you, too."

They stood grinning for a few minutes. Finally he grabbed her hand. "Let's go. I have big plans for us." He stopped, turned her around to face him. Looking at her, he cupped her face in his hands. "I love you with all my heart, Pier."

"And I love you, Landis." She felt like she finally knew where she belonged. She would never feel out of place ever again.

Sunday evening rolled around too fast. Landis felt as if they had just stepped off the plane when it was time to get back on it and head their separate ways. It was going to be hard letting her go. They did, however, make some good plans.

At the top of the list, the plan was that in two weeks he was flying to the Twin Cities and they would talk with their families. The rest of the plans depended on how the discussion with the families went.

Pier's flight was first. Landis arranged it that way. He didn't want her standing around alone. When they called her flight number, he walked her to the ramp leading to the plane.

"Remember, I love you." He held her close. "I'll call you tonight."

"'Kay. I'll see you in two weeks." She looked a little scared to Landis.

"Baby, we did the right thing. Now go while I'm able to let you." He gently pushed her through the door. Lord, he silently prayed, as he watched her leave, let everything work out for us.

Pier was feeling queasy and a little light-headed as she stepped off the plane. When she got home, Shannan was there visiting the parents; they all were laughing and talking as she entered the family room.

"Hey, Bighead," Shannan said.

"Hey, Bighead," Pier said. She kissed her dad on the forehead, her mom on the cheek.

"Have fun?" asks Mrs. Mortimer.

"Yes." She felt light-headed again. "Although I feel a little sick. I think I'll go and lie down."

Shannan and her mother looked at one another as Pier left the room.

"Our baby is all grown up, Ella," Elder stated matter of factly.

"Yes, Spencer, she is," was the returned reply.

"I think I run upstairs before I head out of here."

Shannan stood and left the room. She entered Pier's room after a light tap on the door. Pier was in her bathroom throwing up.

"You okay, Sis?" she yelled.

"Yeah. I think it's something I ate." Pier entered the bedroom.

"You're different. Talk to me Sis." Shannan sat in the over-stuffed chair. She had on black pants and a lavender blouse, looking elegant as always.

Pier sighed tiredly. She stretched out on her bed. "I'm still the same."

"Nope. You're different. As if you're in love or something." She snapped her fingers. "That's it. You've met someone. Maybe while in Chicago."

Pier didn't say anything. Shannan stood up, threw her hands in the air.

"Okay, you will tell me when you're ready. I gotta go. I won't make you tell now since you're not feeling good. But," she pointed a finger, "You better tell all."

Nodding Pier jumped up and rushed to the bathroom. The phone rang. Shannan picked it up.

"Hel-lo," she sang into the receiver.

"Hi baby, I'm still at the airport. I had to hear your voice before I grab a cab home."

Shannan was quiet. She was shocked. This was Landis at the other end. Everything rolled into place. She remembered the phone call she had with him a few months ago. It was after Pier returned from Chicago, that she became withdrawn. She wouldn't talk to him at Speedy's.

Oh boy! This is too deep she thought to herself. Before she could decide what to do Pier walked back into the bedroom looking limp. Maybe mama's theory is true. But, Landis? Oh boy!

"Some guy is on the phone for you Pier." She handed her the phone, pretending not to know who it is. "I gotta go. See you later."

As Shannan hurried down the stairs, she kept thinking if Speedy found out about this he was going to kill Landis. Maybe she'd just keep this piece of information to herself until she figured out what to do.

"Hello," Landis was saying when Pier put the phone to her ear.

"Hi, Handsome. I thought you were calling me tonight."

"I couldn't wait. Who answered the phone? Please, God, say it wasn't Shannan.

"Yep, it was Shannan, but she didn't recognize you."

"Thank heaven for that. Are you okay?"

Pier lay back down. "I'm fine." She didn't mention she was feeling sick. She didn't want him to worry.

"Good. Good. Listen, baby, I've gotta go. Until tonight my love."

"Until tonight my love," she repeated softly.

———⫷⦿⫸———

Pier rolled over in bed. The clock showed seven a.m. It had been almost a week and she was still feeling sick. If possible, worse. Her stomach felt nauseous. Now she couldn't get out of bed. Her head felt like it was exploding over and over. She felt tired. Her mother half heartily suggested maybe it was a bug, and stated if she didn't feel any better by Monday, she was going to the doctor.

She laid still willing the room to stop spinning. It usually took getting out of bed for the spinning to occur. She felt so weak. She couldn't eat. Every time she swallowed anything, she would vomit. If only she could keep something down.

Pier decided to stay in bed all day today.

She must have slept some because she woke with a start to the knocking and opening of her door. It was her mom.

"Pier, are you alright? I was going out but you're looking worse. Are you okay?"

"I don't know, Mama, I feel so sick. I can't keep anything down. My head feels like little Spency is bouncing up and down in it"

Ella felt her daughter's forehead. "You don't seem to have a fever." She sat on the bed. "Are you having any other symptoms?" Pier was too sick to clearly understand her mom.

"No. I just don't feel like getting out of bed."

Her mom patted her hand. "Just sleep and maybe later you can eat some soup."

The thought of food made her gag. "Excuse me, Mama." She

leaps out of bed and ran to her bathroom and threw up again. Her mom came in behind her. Ella grabbed a towel and wet it. She put it on Pier's forehead and helped her back into bed.

"Lay down now, and I'll stay in to keep an eye on you."

"Thanks, Mummy", she murmured her child hood name for her mom.

Her mom stayed with her until she drifted off to sleep again. Ella looked very worried. She knew what was wrong. She had suspected it for a couple of weeks. Lack of appetite, the cravings, tired and sleepy all the time. Yes, Ella sighed, she knew what was wrong. She just couldn't believe it.

She picked up the telephone dialing Shannan's number. No answer. She tried her cellular phone, no answer.

"Where is that girl?" she muttered. Well, she couldn't share this information with Spencer Sr. Not until she was sure. Maybe Speedy could help. He was a little milder than his father.

———◉———

Spencer was sitting on the sofa, in the kitchen sitting area, watching the television. He and Micah had put their son to bed. It had been a long week. Thank God it's Friday. Micah sauntered into the room. She sat next to him. She nested her head in his neck.

"A long day, Baby?" she asked.

"A long day and week. I'm really tired. You?"

She kissed him "Let's go to bed."

"Sounds like a good idea. Well, I'm no longer tired." The phone rang. Speedy grimaced as he answered.

"Hello."

"Speedy." The voice on the other end sounded sad instead of its usual chirpier sound.

"Mama? Mama, what's wrong?" Micah raised her head as if being caught. She did this all the time. Sometime Speedy teased her saying they can't see us.

"We have a big situation here and I know it's late, but can you come right over?" Speedy didn't feel like moving but he knew his mom. She wasn't the type of parent to bug her kids. When she called it's definitely an emergency.

"Is everything okay with Dad?" He hunched his shoulders at Micah Rochelle, who was raising an inquiry brow.

"He's fine. He's at all night prayer. That's why I need you to come now. Is that okay, son?"

"Mama, you're making me nervous. What's going on?"

His mother sighed. She rarely sighed. "It's Pier. She's sick. Now get over here boy."

Speedy stood up. "I'll be there in twelve minutes. 'Bye."

Micah stood up also. She asked what happened. "Shall I get a baby sitter?"

"No. I'll run over and see what's going on. She said Pier is sick. She sounded real upset."

"Maybe I do need to get a babysitter if Mama Ella sound that bad." She ran her hands on the back of her shorts. "Look, Baby, I'm a nurse maybe I can help."

Speedy hugged his wife. "Umm, no, you stay home. I should be back in about an hour. Wait up for me. We can finish our *conversation* then." He raised a brow.

Spencer made it to his mom's in ten minutes. She was peeping out the window. She opened the door before he could pull in the driveway. He walked in the foyer asking what's wrong. His mom was crying. He didn't like to see his mom cry unless she was praising the Lord.

"Mama, what is it?" He led her into the living room.

"It's Pier. I wanted to keep this from your Dad until I knew for sure. But I think she's pregnant."

"What?" That was the last thing he expected to come out of his mother's mouth. "How can she be pregnant? With who? Who?" He began to pace the floor. "Doesn't matter. Who ever got my sister pregnant? I'll beat him to death."

"Now, boy I don't need you acting like that. I thought you were more level headed. Your father will be enough for me to handle." She started crying. He pulled his mom into his arms. In all of his life he had never seen his mom like this. God help the man that messed with his little sister.

"Where is Pier?"

"Upstairs sick. Speedy, she is throwing up. She's been sick all week. She's been acting funny ever since she went to Chicago. You don't think anything happen? Maybe she was raped or something. I don't know. Jesus. Jesus. Help, Lord." Ella started to pray.

Holding his mom again, Speedy decided he'd call Landis later and see if he introduced her to some guy there. He knew Pier was acting differently. But pregnant! No, not his little sister. Speedy calmed himself down. His mother had said think. She thinks she's pregnant.

"I'll go look in on her." He took the stairs two at a time. He knocked lightly on the door, and then opened it. Pier was asleep. The light from her bed lamp, probably left on by his mother, revealed how pale her face was. Her beautiful black hair, that she refused to cut, lay limp on the pillow. She looked very ill. But what make his mom think she was pregnant? He wondered. Pier stirred.

He didn't know she was dating anyone. He continued looking at her. A sad smile broke across his face. Little Pier had always been so different. He and Shannan never knew what to do with her. They were noisy; she was quiet. They argued, she made peace, they had lots of friends, and she had only a few. Not one time did their parents have to go to school because of some mischief Pier was in. She was the only one that stayed in church. He came back but Shannan still didn't go.

He rubbed his hand over his bald faded head.

Pier opened and closed her eyes. She rose as to get up but lay down again. Speedy could see she was very sick. She turned her head his way. He could see in the dim light her eyes had a glazed look to them.

"Hi, Landis," she whispered, not really focusing, "what are you doing here. I'm sorry Handsome, I didn't tell you I was sick whenever you called because I didn't want to worry you. But Land, I've been feeling sick since I came back from our weekend trip. I think maybe I should go to the doctor." She closed her eyes.

Speedy didn't move, he stood as though he was glued to the floor. A red hue washed over his fawn colored skin. Landis? Weekend trip? His mind started to race. Images began to pop up. How Landis kept watching her at Shannan's birthday bash. How he coincidently called on the very Saturdays Pier was there, especially after Pier returned from Chicago. How she rushed out of the room and came back looking like she'd been crying. Now it was all falling into place.

"This *mark* has slept with my sister. He is a dead man," he stated in a lethal quiet voice. His usually warm brown eyes suddenly acquired an icy gloss to them. Anyone who knew him knew to get out of his way.

Pier opened her eyes again. She saw her brother looking mad. What was he mad about? She wondered. Mom was worried and called him. She knew that was the reason.

"Hi, Speedy," she whispered. "Mom called you. Didn't she? I told her I'm okay. Is dad home yet? I know she said he went to prayer. What's wrong with you?" She raised her head up and the room began to spin. Her head started to hurt again. "Oh God," she moaned. "Why did I rise up?" She started to blank out. "Speedy, help me. I feel so sick." She fainted.

Speedy leapt over to the bed. He swept his sister and blanket up into his arms and carried her downstairs. "Mama," he hollered. "She's fainted. I'm taking her to the emergency room. You stay here."

"Boy, you're crazy. I'm going right with you. I was afraid something like this would happen," clucking loudly. "She must be pregnant."

Pier stirred as Speedy laid her in the car. "Pregnant. Who's pregnant? Where are we going? I got my gown on, Speedy! Speedy!"

"Don't talk, sis, you're sick and I'm taking you to the hospital." She drifted back to sleep. Speedy looked at his mother. "Who do you think the father could be?"

"I don't know. The only boy I've seen her with is Devin."

"Well, I got an idea." He reached in his pants pocket for his cell phone. While driving he speed dialed a number. The phone rang.

"Lovington."

"Landis." He said in a cold controlled voice, his expression hardened and wintry.

"Speedy, Hey, man, what up?" Landis sounded happy to hear from his friend.

"You up, man." He answered angrily. "I'm on my way to the hospital with my sister." Silence. "She is very sick. She might be pregnant," Speedy said very slowly.

"What?" Exclaimed Landis. "Sick? Pier? Pregnant?" If Speedy weren't so angry, he would have heard the panic in Landis voice.

"Did I say Pier?" Speedy asked coldly. "I have two sisters. Why is it that you immediately think Pier? TWO SISTERS! I don't believe this. YOU ARE THE SON--THE ONE WHO GOT MY LITTLE SISTER PREGNANT!" He yelled in the phone. Taking a deep breath to get a grip on his emotions, he stated with morgue quietness, "YOU, MY FRIEND, ARE A DEAD MAN WALKING." The car swirled.

"Get off the phone, Spencer! You gonna kill us, boy," Mrs. Mortimer cried out sternly. She was in disbelief over the accusations Speedy was lashing out at Landis. Landis would never do this. He would never get her baby pregnant.

"I gonna hurt you, boy, you hear me. You're dead. You're dead. I trusted you. We trusted you. You betrayed us." His voice trembled. The icy brown chips melted to liquid tears. He ended the call by turning the phone off and throwing it down, barely misses hitting his mom with it.

Ella continued shaking her head in disbelief. Landis? Impossible! She looked at her son. "Speedy, you've got to calm down. You must be mistaken. Landis wouldn't dream of doing anything like that. Why he loves Pier like she's his sister."

Speedy shook his head in the darkness. "When I went upstairs to her room. She thought I was Landis. She started talking about getting sick after the trip they took."

"Trip? What trip?" Ella Mortimer gasped. "Good Lord! She took a trip last week. Spence and I didn't even question her because she had been moping around. So we just assumed she was going with those girls again."

"You know what, Mama?" He sniffled. "I knew something was wrong. He called the house a few times since she came back from Chicago and one time when he had talked to Pier she rushed out of the room. When she came back her eyes were red and swollen." Speedy's voice had quieted down. He talked calmly.

"Would you believe I was going to call Landis a couple of weeks ago and ask him did he have any idea what was going on with her? Did Pier meet one of his friends? Did she confide in him or something? I knew it was a man. I just didn't know he was the man. The pervert! Taking advantage of my sister."

Mrs. Mortimer knew her children well enough to know saying something now would only stir this boy up. So she said nothing. Pier stirred a little. "Maybe I need to be in the back with her, Speedy."

"No, Ma'am, we're almost at the hospital."

A few minutes later they pulled up in the emergency area. Gently Speedy lifted his sister out of the back seat and quickly carried her inside the hospital, with his mom struggling to keep up.

"I need a doctor here," he boomed at the nurse in the admitting area. She looked up from writing and saw a limp Pier.

Immediately moving into action, "Call back and let them know we're coming," she told the nurse sitting at desk. "Right this way, sir." Speedy followed and placed Pier on the examining bed. Two doctors rushed in. They skillfully set about working. They were yelling pulse, blood pressure. What happened?

His mother calmly answered all their questions. "I'm thinking she's pregnant." Mrs. Mortimer stated. At their inquiring look, she explained the lack of appetite, the craving and the nauseous.

"Besides," she ended. "With all my pregnancies, I behave in the same manner."

Spencer looked at his mom and never felt so much love for her. He also gave information like her name, address and telephone number to the nurse.

Thank you, Mr. Mortimer, only one can sit with your wife. Would you like to or your mother?"

"She's my sister."

"In that case, you'll have to wait in the waiting room."

Speedy walked through the automatic doors and headed for the waiting area. He paced the floor for a few minutes, and then reached into the pocket of his jeans looking for his cell phone. Remembering he threw it in the car, he grabbed the phone on the wall. He dialed his home number.

"Hello," Micah Rochelle asked sleepily.

"Yeah. It's me. I'm at the hospital with mama and Pier."

"What happened," she asked more alert.

"I went to her room after mama said she was sick, and she passed out."

"Did you call an ambulance?"

"No. We drove her here." He sniffled. "I'm tripping, your brother Micah. Your brother, my brother, my friend." He was crying.

"Landis?" she was puzzled. "Baby what does my brother have to do with---?

He cut her off. "Micah Rochelle, did you know that your brother had the hots for my sister."

"Spencer, you are confusing me. What do Shannan and Landis have to do with Pier being at the hospital?"

"You're not hearing me. He has the hots for Pier. He slept with her. Call him. Ask him. Ask him what happened in Chicago. How I trusted my *best friend to take care of my sister and he took care of her alright, by sleeping with her. ASK HIM!*" He was shouting.

"I don't believe you. And stop yelling at me. I know she had to spend the night at his home, but my brother wouldn't harm a hair on her head, more over get Pier pregnant."

"She what?" Speedy realized he was at the hospital and quieted down. "Look I'm --I don't want to know. Not now. I'm sorry, baby. I'm upset." He took a deep breath. "I gotta go. Need to call Shannan."

"I'm on my way to the hospital." She hung up.

Speedy was left holding the telephone, with a shocked look. His head was spinning. Why would she spend the night with Landis? And why is he disgusted? But most of all, why is it that three hours ago, this piece of information would have made him appreciate his boy. Now it made him want to hurt Landis like he himself was hurting.

He dialed Shannan's cell number.

"Hello," she answered.

"Hey sis, I'm at the hospital with Mama and Pier."

"Why? What's wrong? I just got in and saw Mama's number on my caller ID. I was going to call her since she didn't leave a message. What's wrong? Is it mama? Pier?"

"Landis is what's wrong."

She gasps. "He's in town? He's sick?"

"It's Pier. Mama seems to think she's pregnant."

"Yeah, I know. She kinda suspected it for a couple of weeks

and after Pier came back from her trip a week ago sick, Mama was sure she was pregnant. Oh boy! Landis!" Shannan knew now was not the time to share she knew they were seeing each other in the boyfriend-girlfriend capacity.

"Shannan, God as my witness, I'm gonna kill him. Wait a minute. You knew Landis and Pier was seeing one another?"

"Listen, I'm on my way to the hospital."

"Yeah, well, you better stop at the church and let dad know we're here." He ended the call.

———— ≫«(◉)»≪ ————

Landis was in his bedroom with his garment bag open, wildly throwing clothes in it. If he forgot anything he'd buy it once he got there. He didn't care. He had to get to Pier.

He had sat in shocked silence after talking to Speedy. He tried to call back but the cell phone had been turned off. Pregnant! Pier! His baby! He paused and sat on his bed. Was she sick because she was loosing the baby? Oh Lord, please not another child lost. How could he have been so careless? Taking a deep breath, he made a fist and hit it in his other hand. He couldn't remember if they'd use any protection the first time. It all happened so fast.

Maybe he should call Micah Rochelle and see if she was still talking to him. He would probably act the same way if the situation were reversed. Micah was three years younger than him and he was protective of his sister. Just imagine six years

The ringing of the phone interrupted his thoughts.

"Lovington," he barked impatiently into the phone.

"Landis, hello"

"Micah. I was just getting ready to call you. Is Pier alright?"

"Is it true," she ignored his question with one of her own, "that Pier could be pregnant by you?"

"Look, I'm on my way out the door. I'll be there in a couple of hours. Is Pier okay?" He asked the question again, slowly, as if talking to a child.

"You're coming here? Have you lost your mind? What little sense you have, that is. Speedy is hopping mad and so will the rest of the family be when they find out what he's accusing you of. Is it true?" she yelled.

"What hospital is she in and why aren't you there?" He asked not answering her question.

"You know, Landis, I hate when you get stubborn like this. You hear me talking to you. Would you please tell me you did not have sex with little Pier?"

He winced at her bluntness in saying sex. "Look, you're holding me up. I'll find the hospital. I gotta go." He hung up.

Immediately the phone rang again. Sighing, Landis picked it up.

"It must be true. Why else would you run here," Micah whispered sadly. "She's at St. Peter's hospital. Landis, if you come here, you come at your own risk. I'm standing with my husband on this matter."

"I wouldn't want it any other way," Landis stated quietly. He laid the receiver on its hook. The blowing of the cab's horn had him racing out the door. He was so glad he could get a flight out to Minneapolis/St. Paul airport at such short notice.

Speedy was pacing back and forth when Shannan and their Father entered the waiting room.

"Son," Spencer Sr. grabbed him. "Have you heard anything yet? Has your mother been out?"

"Dad, they are still back there. Mama came out twenty minutes ago and said they were running tests."

"What brought this on?" Elder Mortimer's voice was slightly deeper than his son's. "Your mother said the flu a couple days ago. You think it developed into pneumonia?"

Shannan said to Speedy, "I didn't fill Dad in on much." Speedy getting the message, she didn't tell about the suspected pregnancy.

"Mom will be out to fill us in."

Micah Rochelle walked into the waiting room with her parents trailing behind. "I called mom, and she and dad insisted on coming," she whispered to Speedy.

"Micah, my dad hasn't a clue to what's going on," he whispered back. "Who's with Spency?"

"Dennis and Shell." Dennis and Michelle were neighbors and friends of theirs.

"What's this about little Pier being pregnant?" Louise Lovington demanded.

Elder Mortimer went very still. "Excuse me, Louise, what did you say?"

"I--I," she stammered, "I understand there's a possibility that your daughter may be pregnant by our son. So we decided to come and see how she and the baby are doing."

Renee Lovington, taking in the situation, asked his wife to be quiet.

"Which son?" Elder hissed. Knowing very well they only had

one. He stood up. "Not Landis. Spencer, do you know what your mother-in-law is talking about?" His tone mild but firm.

Speedy at a lost for words, hunched his shoulders. His eyes went to Shannan. She was sitting cool and calm as if everyone was talking about the Minnesota Twins. She was watching him, taking into account his anger, his sadness, and his feelings of betrayal. She shook her head and smiled sadly.

"Now, Spencer," Renee was saying in his usual calm voice, "Ella will be out in a little while and she can fill us in on what's going on. I know my son wouldn't dream of having an affair with little Pier."

"He better not, Renee. He better not."

"He should be here soon," Louise volunteered.

"He's what?" Speedy, who had been staring at the aquarium, turned to face the Lovingtons. "Has he lost his mind? He's crazy. If I could just get my hands around his neck," he snarled. He broke off from what he was saying when his mother entered the waiting room.

"Spencer, I've had enough of your ranting and raving. Ain't nobody doing anything." She turned and looked at her husband and raised her hand up at him. "And don't you start." She went over to Louise Lovington and sat next to her. Everyone else moved closer to hear what she was saying.

"They are talking about keeping Pier in the hospital for a couple of days. She's severely dehydrated. They gave her some medicine, compazine or something. Anyway she had an awful reaction to it."

"Ella, what's this about a baby, and how is Landis, of all people, involved?" Elder Mortimer demanded to know.

Mrs. Mortimer closed her eyes as if to wipe away the day's

event. "Yes, Spen, she's about six or seven weeks," she spoke quietly almost a whisper. Her face seemed to age before them. "They have an IV in her arm that she must wear for a while." She started to cry. Elder Mortimer, who had been standing, sat his tall frame down and gathered his wife in his arms, rocking her back and forth. All anger left him. He could never be angry when his wife cried.

On the other hand, Speedy's anger has been rekindled. "Did she say who the father is?"

"Boy, she's too sick right now. She doesn't know she's pregnant, I don't think."

"Ella," Louise called. "What are we going to do?"

"Y'all can do whatever. I know what I'm going to do," said Speedy.

"Shut up, Speedy. It's getting kind of old," Shannan complained. "Be worried about your sister."

A nurse came out. "Mrs. Mortimer?" Ella stood up. "Your daughter is in her room. Private as you requested. She's asleep. Probably will not wake up until morning. There's a waiting room on that floor."

Mrs. Mortimer thanked the nurse. She turned to the Lovingtons. "I guess y'all can go home. I'll call you tomorrow."

"No offense Ella," Renee said gently. "But if Landis is on his way to the hospital, we'll wait for him. We need to get to the bottom of this. You understand?" His wife, Louise, nodded in agreement.

"We understand," Elder spoke for both of them.

Chapter Ten

Landis gave a weary sigh as he pulled the rental car into the hospital parking lot. He rested his head on the steering wheel. He didn't know what to expect when he got in there. The old saying 'when it rains, it pours' ranged in his head. He thought the day he left Minnesota was the most painful thing he'd ever done. But it was nothing compared to the last few weeks of his life. Jackie made it clear that she didn't want to be bothered. Not that he was calling her for anything other than about the abortion. She'd said everything was fine.

Now Pier was sick.

"Please, God, let Pier be okay. And if it is a baby, please let her live," he prayed.

His day today had been going south before Speedy called. There were numerous appointments to deal with. His secretary was on vacation. The temp couldn't type. He had to fire a young man; that was always hard. Landis had given him plenty of warnings.

And to top it all off, Keith stopped in his office, teasing him about giving Pier a call. Landis took it serious and had warned him against it. Keith laughed, said he knew Landis had more than brotherly love for her.

"Brian said I was tripping, so I let it go. But your attitude has been kinda whack so I went with my hunch. What's the deal? Why y'all not together?"

Landis shrugged his shoulders. "It's a long story. Am I that obvious?"

Keith grinned. "More than you know." At Landis' frown, he said, "Will it make you feel better if I said you put up a good front?" He raised himself out of his seat across from Landis. He leaned, palms down, in front of a seated Landis. "If I were you, I wouldn't let anything or anyone keep me from the woman I want. I'll go get her." He straightened up and headed for the door. He turned and leered. "Maybe I will." He left.

Landis sat there staring into space, trying to come up with a plan. He'd decided to call Speedy and set up a time to visit and talk with him. The whole nine yards. Then this happened. He shook his head.

Taking a deep breath, he unfolded himself out of the car and headed for the emergency area. He followed the arrows to his destination. When he walked in, everyone was there but Spency. He closed his eyes and hoped he would wake up from this nightmare.

Speedy happened to look toward the entrance area just as Landis walked in. He jumped to his feet not caring that people were watching. He rushed his wiry body into Landis and slammed him against the wall. Just as he raised his fist to punch him, both fathers rushed to grab Speedy to pull him off. He was only able to get a half punch to the mouth before they succeeded.

"Man, thatta teach you to go screwing around with some-body's little sister."

"Watch your mouth boy," Elder scolded.

"You mean you gonna just let him get your daughter pregnant and stroll in here as if nothin' wrong." He jerked away, walking back to the aquarium.

Landis stood, mouth bleeding, as he carefully watched every-one. His father and Elder Mortimer, who have been friends just as long as he and Speedy, had a devastated, look about them, Mrs. Mortimer's, once his confidante, eyes held a wounded look. His mother and sister looked at him with disbelief or was that disgust on Micah Rochelle's face? Shannan, although her expression was sad, had an 'I didn't think you had it in you' look. She held his gaze, for what seemed minutes but was only seconds finally gave a smile. A smile so like Pier's, he hadn't noticed before. Then she winked. That gave him hope until he held Speedy's gaze.

"Speedy, calm yourself down," he heard Elder Mortimer say-ing. "Get all the facts before you beat him." Mrs. Mortimer shook her head at the men in her life.

Renee Lovington walked toward his son. "Landis, what is going on here? Your being here must hold some truth to this here story." His southern accent thickened, always a sign he was angry.

Shannan handed him damp paper towels for his mouth. He hadn't seen her leave the room.

Wiping his mouth, he fastens his gazed at his father. "Pop, I'm sorry, but I love her."

Speedy's cold angry eyes, mingled with hurt and disappointment, rest fully on Landis. The assault from his eyes hurt more than the punch. Landis slowly turned back to Mrs. Mortimer.

"Is she alright? May I see her?" he asked inaudibly.

"Stay away from my sister," Speedy stated with frightening finality. They had already drawn more than enough attention. This outburst brought about more people staring. The hospital security guard paused, waiting to see if he was needed.

Deciding to ignore Speedy, Landis asked again to see Pier. His eyes never wavered from Elder Mortimer's, his voice extremely quiet. He stood tall and lethal, waiting now like a panther ready to pounce.

Speedy, in his right mind, would remember when Landis, in this move, you step aside and grant him whatever he wanted.

Landis, in his right mind, would also recognize when Speedy hollered and yelled, he can be reasoned with, but whenever he's quiet he's equally dangerous. They rarely fought but when they did, they were like iron sharpening iron. Now they were like two dangerous animals ready to fight.

Micah and Shannan, both recognizing what was going on, leaped to their feet to prevent what was coming.

"Baby, do not even think of doing or saying anything you'll regret." Micah Rochelle had her hand on him as if she could stop him.

By the time Shannan reach Landis, her father was already standing in front of him, demanding to know if he was the father. His stern look once frightened Landis the boy, but Landis the man stared back saying nothing. He wouldn't say anything until he'd seen Pier.

Ella Mortimer, tired of the nonsense, beckons for Landis to come with her. "Young man, you have some explaining to do. But it can wait. She's on the third floor in room 302. We were just getting ready to go up when you came in. She won't probably wake up 'til morning."

Everyone else trailed behind Ella and Landis. They got on the elevator. No one said a word. Landis got off the elevator and walked hurriedly to room 302.

Unaware of the surrounding, the family or the questioning looks, he walked into the room. Pier lay on the pillow pale and limp. She had on a hospital gown, an IV in her arm and a monitor; the white covers neatly pull up to her waist.

Landis swerved toward Ella. "What's wrong with her," he whispered. "Why is she ill?"

"She is severely dehydrated. She's suffering from a severe morning sickness called Hyperemesis gravidarum that can last as long as a few months or until the baby's delivered."

Landis said nothing. His mind was racing; His ears roared; his heart felt as if a juicer was squeezing it. She really is pregnant. Taking a deep breath he walked over closer to the bed, pulled up a chair and sat down.

Speedy was ready to pull him up and kick him out, but what Landis did next made all the anger in everyone evaporates.

Gently lifting Pier's hand and placing it in his, Landis buried his face in them and cried brokenly. He raised his head and looked toward heaven. Lord, please hear my prayer. Don't let anything happen to Pier or this baby, he prayed silently.

"Landis," his mother called. "Son, you must talk with us. We are waiting to hear your side of the story." She was whispering by the time she reached the bed.

Landis turned his tear stained face to his mother. She saw the helplessness in his eyes. He looked so alone. From the time her son walked, he exerted independence never needing anyone. Louise never knew what to do with him. Now every instinct told her to grab her son and support him in whatever had happen. She put her arms around him sighing as he held on to her as if his life dependent on it.

"We are here for you, Land, don't ever forget it." She kissed his forehead. "Don't ever forget it," she repeated. "Shall we stay or we talk tomorrow?"

"Tomorrow, Mom. I'm staying until she wakes up." He turned his attention back to Pier.

"I'll stay with Landis," Shannan volunteered. "You guys can go home and I'll call as soon as she wakes up."

"Spencer, I'll get in touch with you later," Renee said.

Elder nodded his head as Renee and Louise exited the room.

Micah Rochelle was watching her husband. She knew he didn't want to leave. But right now he and Landis didn't need to be in the same building together, much less the same room. She had to convince him to go. "Speedy, I think we should leave also. There is really nothing we can do. She's fine now. This is more common than you think." Speedy looked ready to argue. "Please baby, let's go home."

Speedy stubbornly shook his head. "I'm staying. Everything is cool. I'm ah right. It's all good."

Micah threw her hands up. "I'll stay too. Let's go in the waiting area."

Shannan observed her parents. They looked tired and she knew they needed to be home. "Dad, please take Mama home, you guys need to get some rest. I'll call first thing in the morning. Like Mic said, she is fine now. We know what is wrong and all that."

Elder Mortimer knew his wife needed to be home, so he agreed. "Shan call as soon as she wakes up. No matter what time."

"Yes sir."

They all walked out, leaving Landis still holding Pier's hand. Speedy paused, looking back watching Landis. At Micah Rochelle's prompting, he continued out the door.

Landis sat staring at Pier, wishing she would wake up. He needed to hear her voice, to know she was okay, to take her home and take care of her for the rest of their lives.

Around six in the morning Speedy stuck his head in to check on Pier. Landis had his eyes closed. Speedy proceeded into the room. Pier stirred. He moved to the bed on the opposite side of Landis.

Pier stirred, trying to open her eyes. She didn't know where she was. Her throat was sore and her stomach felt like someone had scraped the insides out. Finally, eyes open, she looked around the room, which caused her head to hurt, so she immediately closed them. Opening them again she remembered, this is a hospital, she was sick. Speedy had come over and took her to the hospital. Her eyes focused, she saw Speedy standing over her watching her. LORD! I hope I'm not dying, she thought to herself.

She mustered up a smile. "Hi, Handsome," she whispered.

Speedy eyes filled with tears as his mind immediately remembered years ago when Pier had learned what the word handsome meant, she decided he and their father fitted the bill. She also knew that particular endearment got her off the hook the rare times when she was in trouble.

"Little Pier. You're trying to give us a heart attack."

Landis woke to the sound of voices. Seeing Pier awake, he instantly leaned forward.

Pier eyes followed the direction of Speedy's. She gasped. "Landis. What are you doing here?" Her hands began to shake. She looked at Speedy. "Oh, my God! What's wrong with me?"

"You're dehydrated," Landis answered for Speedy. "You're going to be okay, Baby."

Speedy angrily looked from Landis to Pier. Seeing Landis eyes filled with-- *love?* He exhaled. He was still angry and hurt, but clearly, they seem to have feelings for one another.

Sighing, Speedy cleared his throat. "I'm going to let Micah Rochelle and Shannan know you're awake."

"Speedy, what is it you're not telling me? Why would Mic and Shan be here? And where are Mama and Dad."

Landis picked up her hand and kissed it.

"Dude, you're pushing it," Speedy spattered out.

Landis didn't say a word. He continued to hold Pier's hand. He looked at Speedy. "I can imagine how you feel, but I won't talk about it until she and I have talked."

Pier was watching both men and detected the under currents in their voices. What happened? She wondered. She turned to Landis, as Speedy walked awkwardly out of the room. "Landis, what is going on?"

Landis, seeing how excited she was getting, gathered her in his arms. "Calm down Baby, everything is going to be fine." His voice was gentle and comforting.

"The only thing that could make my brother behave this way would be if he knew about us." Her voice was soft and frightened. "Landis," she whispered desperately, "please tell me-my-no one knows about us."

Landis sat on the bed looking at Pier. A couple of hours ago, the nurse had removed the monitor but she still had the IV in her arm. Being careful of the IV, he pulled her toward him and placed a kiss on her forehead.

Unfortunately at that moment, Speedy, Micah and Shannan walked in and Speedy saw red.

"Get away from my sister." Speedy's tone was as cold and hard as granite. He was not happy to see his best friend holding and kissing his little sister.

"Speedy." Both Shannan and Micah called out simultaneously.

Pier broke out of Landis' arms and rested her head against the pillow. She knew from everyone's expression that they were aware of the nature of her and Landis relationship. Suddenly feeling tired and overwhelmed, she began to cry.

"Pier. Baby, don't cry. I can't take it when you cry. Please calm down." Landis lifted her face with his hands. Her tear filled eyes looked like liquid pools of honey. Not caring who was in the room or what they thought, Landis only concern was to reassure the woman he loved and the mother of his child.

"Remember, Baby, what we agreed. No regrets."

Pier closed her eyes. She couldn't open them. Not when her brother, sister and sister-in-law knew about them. She felt drained. She wanted to go back to sleep.

"Pier," Shannan called gently. She walked over to her bed. Placing her hand on Landis' shoulder she leaned over him to see her sister. "Open your eyes, Big Head. I'm not clear on what's going on but the two of you have my support."

Pier opened her eyes. She gave a watery smile to her sister.

"Hey Big Head," she attempted another smile. "I don't know what to say."

"You don't have to say anything, sis, you are a grown woman," said Micah Rochelle. "Not to us that is." She grinned teasingly.

Speedy, who had been pacing the floor, suddenly stopped. He walked over to Pier. "The parents will be here in a few. Shan called them."

"Only because I promised I would," she explained. Sensing they needed some time alone before their parents came, Shannan suggested they should leave. "I'll be back later to see you." She turned to her brother. "You coming?" Throwing her arms around Landis' neck, Shannan whispered in his ear to call her, before dramatically leaving.

The nurse came in to check on her patient as Shannan left. "Hello Pier," she said in a cheerful greeting. "How are you doing now?" She checked the IV, her temp and blood pressure. The name LaDonna Palmer was on the nametag.

"Okay, I guess."

"Well, you sure gave your family a scare," LaDonna said smiling.

Landis moved and stood next to Micah Rochelle. Speedy hastily walked near the window. Just standing close to Landis made him sick.

"I go off duty at seven. Is there anything else you need?"

Pier shook her head. LaDonna left. Landis was quickly at Pier's side again. She felt a little tired. She closed her eyes and immediately drifted off to sleep.

"I guess we better go Micah. Mama and dad will be here in a few. We can visit her later." Speedy headed out the room.

Micah Rochelle hadn't talked to her brother since their phone conversation. She looked at him sitting by Pier. She knew her brother. Only deep feelings of love would cause him to do something so uncharacteristic. She walked hesitantly to him and kissed his cheek. "I love you, Land."

He held on to her words like a lifeline, knowing what it cost his sister to openly support him. "Love you too, sis." He turned back to Pier, watching her. Waiting for her to wake up again.

Minutes later, Elder and Mrs. Mortimer sauntered in. Mrs. Mortimer looked much better. The rest was just what she needed.

"Shannan said she was awake," said Elder.

Landis vacated the chair for Mrs. Mortimer. "She was. She went back to sleep. Did you see Speedy? They just left." He was a little nervous. For some reason today his nerves of steel were gone. He felt wise enough to put some distance between he and Elder. He moved to the windows, which covered an entire wall.

Mrs. Mortimer sat down and was caressing Pier's hands. She glanced up at Landis. "Did she seem okay, son?"

"Yes, ma'am. A little upset, but okay."

She sighed, "Thank the good Lord. I thought it would be a problem getting in so early in the morning, but having ministers licenses helped."

Pier stirred to the sound of far away voices. She tried to wake up but her eyelids felt like they had been sealed shut with cement. Gradually the voices sounded closer. Her parents were here. She forced her eyes open to find her mother sitting in the chair Landis was in. Fear caused her to close her eyes again. What if her parents knew about her and Landis? How could she face them? When she opened her eyes again, she couldn't help noticing the sadness in her mother's eyes.

Where was Landis? Had he left? She searched the room spotting him staring out the window. He had a defeated look that broke her heart. Her eyes immediately came back to the end of the bed where her father stood his large frame gazing intensely at her.

"Hello, hon," her mother said gently. "How are you feeling this morning?"

"Hi, Mama. Sorry I gave you such a scare. Landis says I'm dehydrated."

Mrs. Mortimer nodded her head.

"Well, young lady, what do you have to say for yourself?" her father asked gruffly.

Before she could say anything Landis step forward. "Uh sir, after Pier and I talk, we will give you all the answers you need."

By now Pier's mind was racing. Say for yourself? After we talk? What on earth was going on?

Mrs. Mortimer glanced at Landis. She knew what he was trying to do, protect Pier from knowing about the baby. "Landis, as soon as the doctor comes in, he will tell her. Don't you think it will be better coming from us?"

Realization enlightened his face. He nodded his head in agreement.

Pier's heart was pounding. Why all the secrecy? What will the doctor tell her? Looking at her father and remembering what he just said, a thought came to her. No! She couldn't be pregnant.

"Pier. Hon, you gave us quite a scare last night. As well as being dehydrated, you are pregnant." The hurt and pain etched on Ella's face.

Pier closed her eyes, willing the floor to open and swallow her up. Just her luck, it didn't.

"Pier, open your eyes," Elder demanded. "I want to know who the father is. Landis here ain't saying anything. Now, young lady, open your eyes and talk to us."

"Elder. Sir, I--" Landis began, but stopped when elder held his hand up.

"Young man, you are in a lot of trouble with me, so your best bet is to be quiet." He spoke in a still quiet authoritarian voice-which no one usually would dare go against.

"Spencer, we can discuss this later. What's important is our daughter get out of this hospital and get home where we can take care of her."

"I disagree. I want to know what's his," he waved his hands toward Landis, "intention is toward my daughter, my baby." Elder was getting agitated.

Pier, eyes still closed, said nothing. Pregnant! Played over and over in her mind. I'm pregnant. But I had my cycle. There must be a mistake. I couldn't be pregnant. And why not? She asked herself. "If you have sex, there's always the chance of getting pregnant," her mother had said years ago when sharing the facts of life with Pier. "Absentee is the best protection."

"Pier, you gotta talk to us sooner or later. Now is my preference," said her dad.

Landis felt totally helpless, watching Elder badger Pier. He could see the dampness on the pillow from where the tears ran. He moved from the window to Pier's bed. No one will talk to her like that, not if he could help it. The worse case scenario, Elder hit him.

"Elder Mortimer, Sir, with all due respect, I can't allow-

"Can't allow," Elder Mortimer's eyebrows raised high. "Landis, boy, have you lost your mind? HAVE YOU LOST YOUR MIND?

Who do you think you are to tell me you can't allow?"

"Now, Spencer," Ella Mortimer interrupted, "calm yourself down. We are going to discuss this like Christian adults."

"Ella, this boy done lost his mind."

"No sir, I haven't lost my mind. I willfully admit I am the father of this baby. I just wanted to talk to Pier before we talked with our family. That was the plan."

Elder moved toward Landis. Ella stood up. Pier cried.

Landis threw his hands up in surrender. "Before you kill me, sir, there's one thing I need to know, and one thing you need to know." Elder stops. "I need to know if you have the faith to raise the dead. And you need to know I won't allow you to talk to Pier like this because she is my wife and my responsibility."

Landis waited for whatever Elder intended to say or do to him. He was astonished when nothing happen.

Pier's eyes flew open in shock. Her father didn't say a word, just stared in shock. Her mother looked shocked also. Poor Landis. Poor me. Poor Daddy and Mama. Poor everybody. By now, her pillow was drench as the tears freely streamed down her face. She had disappointed and shamed her parents.

"Mama," she whispered, her throat clogged with unleashed tears.

"Yeah, hon."

Refusing to look at Landis or her father. "I'm sorry you had to find out like this but the truth is I love Landis. I've always loved him. Only him."

Landis stared at his wife with unconcealed love. "And I love her, only her."

Before he could continue, the doctor walked in. "Well, I see you have visitors, Pier. I'm Doctor Bradley. I was on duty when they brought you in last night. How are you feeling today?"

Dr. Bradley was a tall blond nerdy-looking man with the kindest smile Pier had ever seen.

"I'm doing okay, I think," Pier answered softly.

Noticing the tears, he sat down and took her hand. "You'll probably be a little emotional for awhile. Not to worry; you'll be as good as new in no time at all."

Landis and Elder stepped out into the hallway while the doctor examined Pier.

Elder stared long and hard at Landis. He seemed to be weighing him out.

"Well. Married. This is definitely a mess you're in. We had no idea how you and Pier felt. So you love my baby girl?"

"Yes, sir, I do. I loved her as a child, and then I fell in love with her as a woman." Landis leaned against the wall with relief. If Elder asked that question maybe his life was preserved from the Mortimer men.

Speaking of which, he'd go over to Speedy's and duke it out with him, sighing wearily, that is, after he showered and got some sleep.

"How long have y'all been married?"

Pulling himself from the wall Landis gave Elder eye contact. "We got married last weekend."

Nodding his head, Elder leaned a little closer to Landis.

"So that means you got my daughter pregnant, and then sneaked off to marry her."

"No sir. I had no idea she was pregnant when I married her. I found out last night, like everyone else. I married her because I love her and wanted to be with her."

Ella opened the door, interrupting their conversation. "You

can come in now." He went back to her chair.

"I told this young lady she can go home tomorrow with restrictions," Dr. Bradley was saying to Landis. "She will have the pic line," he gestures toward the IV, "for two to three days as we explained last night. The nurse will show her how to set it up at home. A nurse will come out on Tuesday and take it out if she's doing better."

He patted Pier's hand. "You'll get your appetite back before you know it. No stress. Oh and no sex for now."

A red hue mingled with Pier's honey skin at that remark. Nothing could make her look at her dad or mama for that matter. She did however, steal a quick glance at Landis and saw he took it all in stride.

As Dr. Bradley headed out the door, he told them he would look in on her later this evening.

"You need to get some rest, hon. Come along, Spence. We will check on her later," Mrs. Mortimer said.

A reluctant Elder agreed. "We'll finish our conversation tomorrow at my house after church." He nodded and left the room.

Leaning over to kiss her daughter, Mrs. Mortimer said, "Give your dad time. He'll come around. Not to worry, everything will be okay." She left.

Landis reclaimed his seat. "Do you want me to leave?" Pier shook her head.

"I never expected my parents to find out about our marriage like this. Was my brother real mad at you?"

"Yes. He'll probably kill me sooner or later."

"Landis, don't kid like that. I am so sorry you and he are having this problem."

"Baby, you know what?" He continued before she could say anything. "As I said in Vegas, I moved to Chicago because I loved you. When I found out you were sick, everything else seemed unimportant. All the years of loving you is what mattered. I realize I should have been stronger, and trusting. I should have told your brother how I felt and dealt with it."

"I should have been more like the Christian I thought I was," Pier whispered.

He leaned toward her, "Baby, you are the most loving and kindest person I know. There is no better Christian than you. We made mistakes, but God does forgive and he will forgive us. Now let's be together and a united front."

"Oh, Landis, I love you so much. Now we can be together."

"I love you, too, sweetheart." He kissed her gently on the lips.

"I'm okay. Go home and get some rest." With Landis by her side, she could handle anything or anyone.

"I am. I'm going to the parents now to shower and sleep." He didn't tell her about later popping up on Speedy, hoping for the chance to talk, fight or whatever.

He picked up her hand and kissed the palm. "I'll see you later. Go to sleep and dream about us. We're going to be a family if I die trying. I love you, baby."

A little of the old Pier popped up. "But Landis, if you die then we won't be a family." She grinned slightly. One final kiss on the forehead and an "I love you" and he was gone.

Watching the door close behind him, with tears once again in her eyes, Pier said softly, "I love you, too, Handsome."

Landis was grateful his parents were gone when he got home. He was too weary and couldn't handle any more confrontations. Rubbing a weary hand over his face, he headed for the shower. He was beginning to think the proverbial black cloud was hanging over him. This year has been awful. Well, not too awful. He had Pier in his life: his wife and a baby on the way. He still grieved the loss of the baby with Jackie. But he had Pier.

Pier. All the pain and heartache were obsolete now that he had her love and support.

He dried himself off, put on boxers and t-shirt and got into bed. Black clouds no way. He couldn't let it get him down. When you get lemons, make lemonade had always been his motto. There was no way he was changing his MO now, he declared as he drifted off to sleep.

Landis woke up a few hours later, lying in bed and hoping the past day had been a dream. Upon looking around his old room, he knew he was dreaming to even think it was a dream. Pier. It was out in the open now. Together he knew they would survive this. She was his wife and that's all that mattered.

With that thought, he dressed in some black Karseeme LaMarr jeans and t-shirt and headed to Speedy's house. He didn't bother calling in case Speedy would tell him not to come.

Micah Rochelle saw him pull up in the driveway. She opened the door with Spency hugging her jean-clad leg.

"Hi, brother," she greeted him. "He's in the family room downstairs." She acted like she'd been waiting for him. Knowing her, she probably has been.

"Hi, sis." He scooped Spency up in his arms. "How's uncle's little man doing?" He hugged him tight and tickled him a bit before putting him down.

"Ay unal nandis."

"I'll take Spency to the park. No need for him to hear all the shouting." She laughed a little.

Landis smiled ironically. No doubt there will be shouting. Well he is prepared for whatever. He hopes he hadn't lost his friend and brother. But, no matter how mad anybody got, it was he and Pier.

"He's all yours. I give you guys an hour and then I come back and comfort whoever is not standing." She giggled. She seemed at peace with this situation, Landis thought.

She turned around upon reaching the end of the driveway. "Landis," she called before he entered the house. "Try to see his point of view." Waving, she proceeded down the street.

Taking a deep breath, he entered the small foyer and continued downstairs. Spencer was sitting on the sofa with the remote in his hand channel surfing. He had on blue jeans and an old Chicago Bulls t-shirt Landis had given him.

He looked up at Landis' entrance, then back at the television.

"What's up, Speed?" Landis strived for casualness in his voice.

"Nothing much." He didn't take his eyes off the T.V. He seemed fascinated with a rerun of an old seventy's lawyer show.

Landis cleared his throat. "I left the hospital earlier. Pier will be home tomorrow."

Speedy nodded his head. "I know." His parents must have told him. Did they tell him also about the marriage?

Landis, usually a patient man, was losing it big time. "Hey man, I'm here to talk about this situation. I don't want to lose you as my friend."

Speedy's light brown eyes blazed. He leaped up from the sofa. "You shouldda thought of that before you messed with my sister," he shouted. "My kid sister. My baby sister."

"Alright. I know," Landis shouted back. "Now what? You're going to fight me? What?" He threw up his hands.

"This is whack and you know it. I never slept with your sister until we got married. As much as we wanted to, I didn't. Wanna know why? Because I respected her and I was glad my *best friend* approved of me marrying his sister." Speedy was pacing like a caged animal.

"Why? Why did you sleep with her? And got her pregnant on top of everything."

Landis, expecting a fight, was surprised at Speedy for not trying to punch him.

"I don't know. It just happened." He rubbed his brow as if to rub away the pain. "I don't know."

Speedy stopped pacing. He stared at Landis. "What? You crazy or something? She's too young for you, dude."

His eyes focusing on Speedy, he spoke carefully. "She is not a kid anymore. She is twenty-three. She's a woman. A desirable woman. A sexy woman. A funny and loving *woman*. And I love her." He was prepared for the assault. He continued when nothing happened. "I've fought it long enough. I left town to be away from her. Too young I kept telling myself. Speedy will kill me like he wanted to do to Ace but not anymore, bro. Understand me, brother. Nothing is going to keep me from her. Not you. Not your dad. Nothing! *You got it.*"

Speedy flinched as if Landis had physically hit him. He looked like a balloon that'd lost its air. "Why didn't you tell me, man? Why did I have to find out like this?" Totally drained, he sank on the sofa.

Landis' heart was breaking as his mind searched for the right answers. He at least owed him that. "What was I suppose to say? 'Hey man. I want your sister. Oh no, not Shannan. The little one. Pier.' God knows I tried to resist. Honestly I did, Speed. But it just happened. Before I knew, it was happening. I lost it. I won't have anybody blaming her. I take full responsibility."

"And I blame you totally and completely."

They were silent for a moment. Speedy rubbed his face wearily. He had circles around his eyes. He sighed. "I just wished you hadda told me. I just wish I knew."

"Remember your wedding-how you snapped out about Ace wanting to date Pier?" At Speedy's nod, Landis continued, "well, I was fighting my feelings for Pier and I was going to ask her to go to the movies or something as a date. If she looked like Shannan would have looked, like I asked her to commit incest, then I would have been heartbroken but I would have left it alone.

"But if she showed interest, I was going to talk to your parents and you to see if it was okay to date her. I would have waited for her to finish college. Everything."

Taking a deep breath and exhaling Landis continued, "But it never happened. You know why, man?" Speedy shook his head. "Because at the wedding you said, any friend that talked to your baby sister was no longer a friend. I couldn't risk that, especially not knowing how Pier felt. So I fixed it as usual by leaving. So there you have the story."

Shaking his head Speedy said again. "Man, I wished you had risked it and told me. I wished you had told me." Exhaling Speedy said, "anyway for what it's worth, I know my sister. If she wasn't consenting, it wouldn't have happened." He puts his head in his hands. "Lord, what a mess. And what about Jackie. She's pregnant too. Man, you screwed up big time. Boy when you plant, you plant. And what about safe sex?"

I always practice safe sex even with Jackie. I took care of everything and," hunching his shoulders, "absentee is the only guarantee."

Landis finally sat down next to Speedy, heave a long sigh. "Jackie got an abortion," he stated flatly.

"You're lying."

"Mmm Yep. Said the timing was off or some junk like that."

"You're lying," Speedy said again.

"What a mess," Landis repeated. "I wish I were. I shouldn't have messed with her or anyone. I just wanted to forget Pier. But I couldn't."

"Yeah. Well, we Mortimers are hard to forget." Speedy half grinned.

"Well, Lovingtons ain't so bad either," Landis said with a faint smile.

"I understand Dad came down hard on you. Mama said you held your own. Should I say good job?" Speedy asked mockingly.

"How about waiting until it's over first? I know your dad; he will not be letting me off easy."

"Better you than me."

"Uhmm, Speedy, I got something else to tell you."

Speedy's body went taut. "Yeah, what?"

Landis cleared his throat. "Well we got married in Vegas last weekend."

"What?" Speedy quickly leapt to his feet.

Landis exhaled noisily. "Man, I need her. I love her. I couldn't allow her to go against everything she believed in just to sneak around to be with me." He stood also. It was his turn to pace the carpet.

"Please let me explain," he said as Speedy sat back down on the sofa. "The weekend she came to Chicago, I purposed in my heart to treat her like my little sister. I took her to the zoo and everything.

"Let me back up a bit. She got locked out of the hotel she was staying at. Her friends were gone and she called me. That's when we went to the zoo."

Landis paused. He sat back down on the sofa. He looked Speedy directly in the eyes. "I resisted the feeling. I was just congratulating myself when at dinner, she asked me if I was attracted to her and," feeling and looking uncomfortable, "one thing led to another."

"So you're saying you lost control and slept with my sister." Speedy's shoulders began to shake. He was laughing.

"Something funny, bro?"

"Dude, you never lose control over anything and my," he laughs, "little sister causes you to lose control. I must be losing my mind because this is getting funny."

"Maybe you're in delayed shock," Landis suggested sarcastically.

Speedy was still grinning. "So you decided to marry her."

"Yes. What so interesting is she loved me back then and I was too afraid to say anything."

"So you left. I always wondered why you left so abruptly."

"Yeah. Well, it's been pure hell for me all these years. But I win. I now have a wife and a baby on the way. I am happy."

They both sat and grinned at one another and that's how Micah Rochelle found them when she and Spency came down the stairs. "So neither is standing. So I guess I have to comfort both of you." She wedged between both. Spency bounced on his daddy's knee.

At Speedy's inquiring look Landis said, "She said she'll comfort whoever's not standing." He stood up. "I'm outta here. Back to the hospital to be with my love." He was testing Speedy's reactions.

Had Landis not been watching for a reaction, he would have missed the slight flinching.

Sitting Spency down, Speedy stood up also. Hesitantly both men hugged one another. "Tell little Pier I'll see her tomorrow at the house."

"Okay. Don't bother to walk me to the door." He headed for the stairs.

Spency, running around like he was an airplane, yelled bye to his uncle.

Micah cuddled up next to her husband after he sat back down. "It's going to be okay?"

Closing his eyes, Speedy nodded. "It'll take some time, but what can you do?"

"I mean, sweetie, your friendship."

"It'll take some time but he's determined to be my friend." He laughed.

Micah Rochelle sighed. It felt good to hear that laugh. It felt good to know love conquers all. "And you're determined to be his friend."

She had been very upset with her brother. He went about it all wrong. He should have never slept with Pier. He should have talked to Speedy and Elder to get their input or permission. Micah Rochelle sighed again. All water under the bridge now.

Chapter Eleven

P ier felt much better. She was ready to go home. Her parents and Landis' parents had stopped by to visit.

After inquiring how she felt, the men gathered in the corner near the windows and quietly talked.

The mothers looked ill at ease, but after a few minutes they launched into a discussion about being a grandmother together for the second time.

Pier's dinner tray arrived at the same time Shannan did.

The parents left, stating they would see her tomorrow.

She was glad to see her sister, but she wished Landis were there.

Shannan insisted on feeding Pier her dinner. She fussed so she made Pier tired.

"I guess you know I'm pregnant?" Pier finally asked.

Not missing a beat Shannan said, "Yes."

"I'm sorry. I know I've disappointed everyone." Her eyes welled up with tears.

"Stop it Big Head." Shannan hugged her little sister. "You

have nothing to be sorry about in my book. Everybody falls sometimes. You've got to live your own life." She sniffled and she grabbed tissue off the table for her and Pier. Wiping her nose, she continued, "Besides, Landis is a good catch. I still can't believe y'all married."

"He wanted to get married. So off to Las Vegas we went."

"I'm glad for you Big Head."

"Shannan, can I share a secret with you?"

"This is a first," Shannan said with surprise. Knowing Speedy had always been the one to share Pier's secrets.

"Sometimes I'm a little scared. You know he had a girlfriend named Jackie? She's a model. She's beautiful."

"So are you, Pier. More than you know." Shannan sat on the bed. "Hey listen. I've known Landis a long time. I never have seen him act this way. He has always been the level headed one.

"For him to marry you must means he loves you. We wouldn't have known you slept together first if you weren't pregnant." She grinned wickedly. She cocked her head and raised a perfectly arched brow.

Pier knowing her sister's mind giggled. "I won't tell you anything. You can't make me either."

"C'mon Big Head tell me." She pretends to choke Pier.

Landis entered the room to a lot of giggling.

"It's good to see my baby feeling better."

His presence made Pier's mind race. And when he talked like that, it made her heart soar. He was unbelievably handsome. He was like a breath of fresh air.

Shannan couldn't believe the love she was witnessing with these two. How were they able to hide it, she wondered? Unable to resist, Shannan asked, "Which baby."

She had to give it to Landis. He didn't miss a beat. "Both," he stated.

"Hi, trouble maker." He leaned over to kiss Shannan's neck like he's done for years, hesitated and kissed her cheek.

"Oh, no more kisses on the neck," she mocked. Turning to Pier. "I like it when he kisses my neck. Please permit him to continue."

Pier shook her head in embarrassment. Landis leaned over and kissed her cheek.

"Hi Baby. Miss me."

Pier said yes.

"Isn't this cute? She's his baby and misses him." Shannan made scissors movement with her hand. "Cut it out." She grinned at Pier's embarrassment.

"Hey, listen. I have a confession to make. I kinda suspected at Speedy and Mic's wedding, Pier was attracted to you."

Landis and Pier stared in surprise.

"Hey, you two, I'm not stupid. As often as she could, Pier was hanging with you and Speedy. Then it was just you and Pier. I know the signs especially when, at the wedding, she avoided you like the plagues of Egypt. Now I asked myself why. I took it to be a school girl crush."

"Shan, you never said a word," said Pier.

"Well, I knew you were young and I wasn't quite sure how Landis felt. So I decided to test my theory. I bought the dress so Landis could see you as an adult and not our little sister."

Landis grinned. "And what a dress it was."

"What can I say? I have superb taste."

"I fell in love with Landis during the times we e-mailed one another."

Shannan laughed slyly. "I forgot about the e-mails. All I know is when Landis saw you in that dress, and couldn't take his eyes off you, and then you guys were flirting with each other at the house that night, I kinda thought it might be serious. I had no idea how you were going to handle it, but I was rooting for you."

"Shan you don't know the half of it." Landis lifted Pier hand and kissed her palm. Looking back at Shannan he grinned. "It feels good to touch her and not worry about getting your head ripped off from the Mortimer men.

"That night was the second hardest night of my life. The first was when she came to Chicago. But on the night of your party, man, I did everything to stay away and everything to stay."

Pier closed her eyes in remembrance. "I just know I was so nervous. I wasn't sure if he was flirting or being nice to your little sister. Then when he dropped me off at home, he kissed me. Nothing passionate, but not brotherly either. I was confused because he was running hot and cold."

"Always hot from now on, baby."

"Cut it out, you two. This is something. And to think no one had a clue." Shannan looked thoughtful. "I, also, confess I knew who you were when you called last weekend. I pretended I didn't until I could figure out how to handle Speedy. To see you alive and well is a good thing."

Shannan stood and hugged them both.

"So y'all married and expecting a baby. I'm feeling a little old here. I guess I can deal with it. I wish you both the best."

"Now all we have to do is win over the parents and it will be all good," said Pier.

Shannan said she had to leave and she would see them later.

Landis sat again in the chair next to her bed. "Shannan is so noisy. Wouldn't you agree?"

"Always has been," agreed Pier. "But you gotta love her."

"Speaking of love, have I told you I love you?"

When he talked like this, Pier felt as if she could bust. And she felt as though her heart would stop beating and she would die of pure happiness. I could get way to use to this, she thought to herself.

"It must have been too long 'cause I can't remember."

"Pier Janise Mortimer Lovington, I love you. Thank you for taking me out my misery and marrying me."

"No, thank you Handsome." She had a thoughtful look as she fidgeted with the sheets.

Landis watching her closely asked what was wrong.

"Jackie. I know you have feelings for her."

"Baby! I love you. Only you. Always you. I admit I cared for Jackie but *I love you.*"

"And I love you, Landis. Very much. I guess I'm a little jealous and insecure when I think about you being with other women."

Landis leaned across the bed. Careful of the IV, he held Pier in his arms.

"This is a new beginning for us. I am sorry about the other women. But you are the only one for me until the day I die."

"I love you," Pier whispered.

"Ditto.

He held her close for a few minutes. "I'll be here first thing in the morning to take you home. I know your parents will be here also. Look, sweetheart, they're going to have to just get used to us."

"I know," she said. Wow, I have to get used to us. Do you know how many times I've dreamt of us being together?"

"Do you know how many sleepless nights I had wishing we were together?"

"We have a lot of making up to do," Pier said.

"Yeah, I know. Tell me, Pier, how do you feel about being pregnant?"

"Other than being so sick, I'm pretty happy about it. I didn't know because everything was normal or so I thought. How do you feel about it?"

"You have made me the happiest man on earth. I hope we're having a girl."

"Landis, you're supposed to want a son."

"Maybe next time. This time I want a girl and I hope she looks just like you."

Eyes filled with love, Pier smiles and yawned.

"You're tired. Go to sleep. I'll be here when you wake up."

"No, Landis. You need to get some rest yourself. I want you to go home now. Let's both get some sleep."

"I'm okay. I'll just stay for a little while. Go to sleep."

Heeding his commandment she closed her eyes and fell immediately asleep.

Later Speedy opened the hospital door to the same scene he left, Landis sitting in the chair watching Pier while she slept. His eyes got a little misty. His friend loved his sister. He guessed he'd get over it. Beyond the shock, it was not so bad. He'd always wanted Landis to have the kind of love he and Micah Rochelle had; that's why they'd pushed Shannan off on him. No one dreamed little Pier could pull the strings of his friend's heart.

Speedy, had to admit, when thinking about it, he visualized Landis always being in control, even with the woman he would love. Now he found it funny Pier could make him lose control like that. If it were someone else, he would probably laugh himself silly.

"Stuck on you," Speedy sang quietly to Landis.

"Speedy! I thought we wouldn't see you until tomorrow," Landis whispered.

Shannan called and insisted I come get you and make sure you go home. I see she still knows you," he whispered back.

"I guess she does."

"Is she still doing okay?" he gestured at Pier.

"Yeah, just a little tired. The IV is helping her keep her food down."

"Good. Well, Landis, are you ready to go home? You know how Shannan likes to get her way."

Pier woke to see her brother and Landis having a seemingly decent conversation.

"Hi Handsome."

"Hi, little Pier. And before anybody says anything, she will always be little Pier to me. I'm her big handsome brother and she's little Pier." He stood daring the two of them to disagree.

Pier and Landis had twin smiles. "I don't care." They both said at the same time.

"Good, we're in agreement. Now, Landis, I want to apologize for my behavior the other night. Can you forgive me for hitting you?"

Pier looked shocked. "Exactly what happened with the two of you?"

"Nothing to complain about," Landis said. "Speedy, I forgive you only if you forgive me for not telling you how I felt about Pier."

"Done deal," said Speedy. Landis stood up and they hugged.

Pier started to cry. She was the cause of two best friends fighting. Lord, she hated being a cry baby.

Landis moved quickly to the bed. "Baby, what's wrong?"

"I caused best friends to fight. What if there was no reconciliation? Then what?"

"Listen to me, Pier. Speedy and I have fought for years. Nothing this serious but we fought. We will always be friends and brothers no matter what."

"Little Pier, don't upset yourself and the baby. Landis is right. Listen to him."

She hiccupped. "I just don't want the two of you not to be friends because of me."

Speedy looked at Landis and grimaced. "Get used to this, Mic did this during the whole pregnancy."

Landis nodded his head. Looking as if to get permission from Speedy, he hesitantly gathered Pier in his arms. "Baby, Speedy and I will never not be friends. We have fought over so many things; like the time we were at the court and Speedy, hyper as usual, accepted the challenge some dude threw out and wanted to bet on the game we were playing."

Speedy sitting on the other side of the bed, casually throwing his arms around the two of them, interrupted, "and old tight wad here didn't want to bet."

"He betted but didn't have any money…"

"…On me," finished Speedy. Both burst out laughing.

Pier closed her eyes briefly, glad they were laughing.

"Anyway, we started arguing right there in the middle of the game."

"After we finished arguing, Landis ended up betting on the game anyway because old boy challenged him."

"Who won the game?" She asked.

"We did. Landis doesn't lose when it comes to money. That's why he's rich."

"Comfortable," protested Landis modestly.

Pier closed her eyes and fell asleep with two of her favorite men holding her in the tiny hospital bed.

Shannan and Micah Rochelle entered the room. They looked at each other misty eyed, glad everything back to normal, each walking over to their brother and throwing their arms around him. It felt like old times. Brothers and sisters hanging out with little Pier in the middle needing them to take care of her. And as always nobody minded.

The next morning was a hot sticky July. Landis had agreed to meet Mrs. Mortimer at the hospital to take the patient home.

The patient was waiting patiently with instructions in her hand for them. She'd improved so rapidly the doctor decided to take the pic line out and see how she fared by herself.

Mrs. Mortimer was the first to arrive. She greeted her daughter warmly. She gave Pier the carry-all with her clothes in it. Pier carefully went to the bathroom to put on her things. She returned and gratefully lay back down on the bed.

Mrs. Mortimer was out of view when Landis strolled into the room, causing him to bolding bend down and gives Pier a passionate kiss.

"How are my babies today?" He demanded to know.

"Landis," Pier whispered through clenched teeth, "my mom is right over there." She nodded her head in the direction of the corner near the windows.

Embarrassment engulfed his handsome face. "Good morning,

Ma'am. Nice day isn't it?"

Ella threw her head back laughing. Shaking it she said, "You, young man, need a spanking."

He grinned. "So sorry, Mrs. Mortimer. Didn't see you."

"Well, you better behave yourself."

"Yes, ma'am."

The nurse came in with a wheelchair. "All set to go, Pier?"

"Yes, with pleasure. I mean y'all have been great, but I'm longing for my own bed."

The nurse laughed. "Believe me, we are not offended by our patients wanting to go home."

Landis quickly helped Pier into the wheelchair and pushed her out the door; not caring if he was supposed to or not. Mrs. Mortimer and the nurse trailed behind him.

After securing Pier into the car, Landis trailed the women home. Once there, ignoring her protests that she could walk, he lifted her out of the car asking Mrs. Mortimer where to take her.

"Let's take her to her bedroom for now."

Landis took the stairs two at a time, holding Pier in his broad muscular arms as if she were the weight of a newborn baby. He froze as Mrs. Mortimer pulled down the white and red comforter on the four-posted bed with red pillows. This is where it all began. His love for Pier as a woman.

Landis gently laid Pier down and exited the room so Mrs. Mortimer could help her get undressed and in bed.

"Mama, I'm fine. Really I am. You and Landis keep fussing over me like this I'm going to be very spoiled."

"You're already spoiled and that husband of yours is going to spoil you even more given the chance." Mrs. Mortimer helped her put on her pajamas and tucked her into bed.

She stood her small frame over the bed, sighing, she sat down. Staring at her daughter, she began to talk.

"Your dad has called everyone over for dinner and a meeting this evening. I hope when he's done, we feel all the tension is gone."

"Well, I can't say I wasn't expecting it." Looking at her mother, Pier noticed she looked exhausted. Guilt exploded in her heart at the pain she'd caused her family.

"Mama, please forgive me for causing you all this pain and embarrassment."

"I must admit, hon, you scared me, sick and all, but everything worked out fine. Now I'm going downstairs and get started on dinner. Louise and Micah Rochelle are bringing a dish. Shannan, her non-cooking self, is bringing drinks." She leaned over and kisses Pier's forehead. "Get some rest. Landis' probably lurking around here somewhere."

Landis was indeed lurking around.

"I hope it's alright for me to come in the forbidden room," he said on entering, remembering the strict rules Elder had about boys being in the girls rooms and girls being in Speedy's room.

Mrs. Mortimer was smoothing her hands over her blue printed dress. She paused and waved her hand at him. "Only if you leave the door open so when Elder tiptoe in, he won't catch too much," she said with such a deadpan expression, Landis didn't know quite how to take it. She looked at Pier and they burst out laughing at his uncertain look. She left the room.

Landis sat in the red overstuffed chair. He felt ridiculous sitting there and from the expression on Pier's face, he looked it.

"You can sit on the bed, Landis. I don't think Daddy will

shoot you. After all, we are married."

"It's not your father I'm worried about," he said getting up and sitting on the bed. "It's me. I can't sit close to you and not want to hold and kiss you." He kissed her nose. He could feel her heart beating fast. He closed his eyes.

"Should I get my rifle, Speedy? He says they're married, but I don't know, I didn't see any license." Elder asked, both men standing in the doorway. Both looked identical in suits. One dark complexioned and the other light. Landis stiffened and opened his eyes.

"Only if you have one, Dad." He laughed. "Landis, my man, you always seem to get caught with your, umm, pants down. Figure of speech."

Landis was now watching Elder, checking to make sure his life wasn't over. He could see it flashing. Since Speedy was laughing; maybe he'd still live. Forget that Speedy laughs at everything. Honesty is the best policy or something like that.

He reached into his pants pocket and pulled out the marriage license. "I brought it just for you, Elder."

Elder Mortimer pulled his reading glasses out as he received the paper. He read it, nodding his head. "We'll talk later." A smile broke across his handsome rugged face.

"Your parents will be over soon. Let's go downstairs and wait for them in my study. Spencer, carry your sister."

Landis wanted to protest, but he didn't.

Speedy swept her up in his arms and pretended to toss her to Landis, which petrified him. "Dude you got it bad." He headed out of the room laughing.

"Hi, Handsome." Pier said to her daddy as Speedy zoomed her past.

"Baby Girl. Doing okay?"

"Yes. Don't need the IV," she yelled back.

Landis and Elder remained in Pier's bedroom.

"So where will you live? You taking my girl to Chicago?"

Shaking his head. "Monroe-Philips opening a branch in St. Paul. So I'll move back here. I turned them down last year because I couldn't live here. Good thing because last year I would have been vice-president of loans, same as now. But now they want me to be vice-president of the branch."

Elder chuckled, patting his big hand on Landis' back. "That's good son, I knew you were destined to be very successful."

Landis gave Elder a startled look. "Thanks, Elder."

"You're welcome. Let's go get Speedy out the kitchen, and into my study to wait for your daddy."

Elder glanced around Pier's bedroom taking in the red and white décor, and exhaled. "You have your work cut out with this red. Why couldn't it be blue like her mother?"

Landis laughed as they headed downstairs. All these years and Elder was still able to surprise him with his humor. You never knew what to expect, preaching or jokes.

Pier was waiting at the bottom of the stairs. Landis rushed down and lifted her up in his arms.

"Landis you can put me down. I'm fine," she said drily. "Besides we don't want to push it with old handsome here."

Elder winked and kept walking.

Landis carried her into the kitchen and carefully sat her down at the kitchen table. He twirled around to the onlookers. His mother, Mrs. Mortimer, Micah Rochelle, Shannan, and Speedy were all standing looking amused.

"Why is she walking around like this?" he demanded. "Didn't

she just get out of the hospital?"

"Shut up, Landis, and stop hovering," Shannan retorted. "Give the girl some breathing space. Speedy, get him out of here."

"I told y'all he's got it bad. Come on, Landis, let's go to the study." He turned to his wife. "Make sure they cook my chicken right."

Landis and Pier were looking at each other with so much love it sizzled the entire kitchen.

Then she gave him that smile. The one where her honey colored eyes melt with humor and made him catch his breath. The smile that made him …

Speedy coughed. "Umm, hello? We are still here, Dude."

Landis grinned. "Hi, sis," he kissed Micah. "Great day isn't it." He bent and playfully bit Shannan on her neck as he and Speedy laughingly went out of the room.

"That big head bit me on my neck. Did you tell him he could kiss my neck again Pier?" Shannan teased.

"Old habits die hard," Pier mocked.

"How are you doing, Pier?" Louise Lovington asked.

"I'm doing okay. I don't feel sick. But this will be my first meal without the help of the IV."

"You let us know if you need to lie down," said her mom.

"Yes, ma'am."

"The women prepare the food and men sit and talk. Isn't this a little backwards here?" Shannan complained. She couldn't cook and she hated trying. "Even Speedy's big headed self got out of cooking. And look at Pier; least she could do is peel a potato while she's sitting there."

"It won't work now, Shannan, like it didn't when you were a child. Leave Pier alone and peel the potatoes," Mrs. Mortimer fussed. "Besides we'll get them Labor Day. Agreed?"

"Agreed," everyone but Pier said.

"I wonder what they are talking about," said Micah Rochelle as she fried the chicken.

"This marriage," said Mrs. Lovington.

Pier sighed. Here we go, here we go, and here we go.

Landis sat in the hunter green wing back chair and sighed as well. He knew it was coming. Let's do it, he thought. They had talked about everything else.

"Well, Renee, I saw the license. They are without a doubt married. Show your daddy them license, boy."

Landis reached again in his pocket and showed his dad the license.

Renee studied the paper with calm precision. "Yep, they married alright. Now son, what is your next step? Where you gonna live?"

Before Landis could answer Elder interrupted. "Maybe it will be better with Pier sick and all that they stay here." He glanced at Landis. "Her bedroom has its own bathroom. It's plenty of space in the house."

Renee nodded his head. "Yeah, that might be best. But what about his job in Chicago?"

"Oh, he's being transferred back here. Go head, boy, don't just sit there, tell your daddy about that new job."

Speedy sat on the burgundy leather couch with his hand over his mouth laughing.

Landis rubbed his hand over his brow. He cleared his throat. "Pop, I was telling Elder that I'll be moving back. The bank has opened a new branch in St. Paul-"

"Yeah," Elder interrupted again, "he's gonna be some big time vice president of the whole bank. Not some department."

Renee and Elder patted each other on the back. "Well, son, this just great. I'm proud of you."

"Me, too," Speedy said. The fathers looked at him like he was an alien.

"What? You want me to leave the room?"

"Yeah, go fry some chicken," said Elder teasingly. He and Renee laughed.

Rubbing a hand over a face so much like Landis, Renee began to speak, "Landis has been avoiding me these last couple of days. I didn't push it because I wanted to give him some space."

"Sorry, Pop, that wasn't my intention."

"I know, son. What I want to say is I'm not happy in the way you and Pier went about this, but I am glad you had enough sense to marry her."

Speedy stood. "Maybe I will go check on the chicken." He exited the room.

"You're a chicken," Landis yelled after him. Speedy made chicken sounds.

Landis raised himself up and walked to the window. He stared at the back yard. A yard he played in countless times.

Turning to his father. "I know I messed up big time, Pop, I'm sorry."

Renee Lovington tilted his head accepting Landis' apology.

"You see, son," Elder was saying, "You are a good person. We know all about your charity contributions. You tithe because that's how you were raised. But how often do you go to church? And what about serving God?"

Landis sat back down. "You're right, Elder. I only go to church every now and then. Mostly when I'm visiting here. But I don't have a problem with going. I'll go every Sunday."

"You better get it together or else. Little Pier loves church but most importantly she loves God."

They talked about being a father until Speedy returned, stating dinner was ready. The men made their way out the door. Speedy held Landis back a little.

"Can I talk to you for a sec?"

"What's up?" Landis asked.

"Tonight is my night to expound on a passage in the Bible and I want you to be there to hear me. I go up about eight. I have fifteen to thirty minutes to talk."

"I'll be there, bro. It's funny but this will be my first time hearing you speak."

Speedy grinned. "Don't make it your last."

Chapter Twelve

Dinner was noisy as always when these two families got together. Spency sat between his aunts and was being spoiled.

Pier was happy to see all the unpleasantness almost over. She started to feel a little queasy but didn't say anything. She wanted to wait until after the meeting.

They all retired to the living room and talked about the Landis and Pier situation. Most of the time they talked like Landis and Pier weren't in the room.

Their mothers, feeling cheated of a wedding, decided they should get married again. Speedy and Micah Rochelle were talking about being an aunt and uncle. Shannan was teasing about her second time being an aunt.

Pier, finally having enough, stood up and declared she was not getting married while she was pregnant.

The room fell quiet for the first time in thirty minutes.

"Landis and I haven't decided. Maybe next year after the baby is born."

"If that's what you want hon, its fine," said Ella.

"Yes, it is. I mean I don't want to get married and have people counting the months when this baby comes. Next year we can get married in church. But for now it's nobody's business."

Everyone nodded their heads in agreement.

Her father cleared his throat.

"Renee and I decided to have this meeting to give everyone a chance to express their feelings about this marriage and the upcoming baby. Because after tonight, we don't want anyone saying anything about it."

"Now is the chance to speak," Renee added.

"I'm cool about it," said Shannan.

"Me, too," said Micah Rochelle.

"Me, too," parroted Spency.

Everyone laughed.

All eyes turns to Speedy. He threw up his hands. "It's all good. I'm okay with it."

Louise Lovington looked at her watch. "What I'm not clear on is when this all began. I think I'm more shocked about this relationship than anybody."

"It began with the e-mails for me. I would e-mail Landis and he would e-mail me back. He would call and check on me, laugh at my jokes. I measured every boyfriend I had up against him and they always came out lacking.

"I didn't know for sure until the night of my birthday. When Landis rescued me from that friend of Shannan. When I realized I was in love with Landis and knew y'all would think I was too young and I didn't know how he felt, I decided go away to college in Atlanta."

"I'm confused," said Shannan. What friend?"

"I think his name was Maddog or something," explained Landis. "It was that same night when I knew I was in love with her. When Maddog followed her up to her room."

"What?" asked a shocked Speedy.

"Yeah. I'll never know what made me go to the bathroom upstairs. I heard Pier say 'leave me alone' and I lost it on that dude. I couldn't blame him for being attracted to her."

"Why didn't you tell me? You're full of secrets."

"I handled it, bro. Besides I gave Pier my word I wouldn't say anything. When I walked into her bedroom and he had his hands on her trying to kiss her, I knew I was capable of murder. I lost it."

Looking down on the sofa at Pier, Landis continued, "I lost it even more after I dealt with him and tried to comfort you. I kissed you. Remember?" She nodded. "I knew that I wanted to love and cherish you the rest of my life."

"Oh Landis," she whispered.

Without thinking, he pulled her in his arms.

"I love you, Pier."

"I love you, Landis."

"And I'm getting sick," said Speedy.

Everyone laughed.

Landis sat on the third row right behind Elder Mortimer and his father at True Foundation Christian Center. Service had begun by the time Shannan, who stayed with Pier, kicked him out. He did not want to leave his wife. *His wife*. Landis grinned. He liked the sound of that.

His wife. He is a married man with a baby on the way. Scary but wonderful.

Reverend Wright stood up and moved to the microphone after the praise team finished their song.

"Praise the Lord, saints," Reverend Wright said in his deep gruff voice.

Landis as well as the people in the congregation reply, "Praise the Lord."

Smiling, Reverend Wright said, "Now y'all know tonight is Minister Spencer Mortimer, Jr.'s night to bring forth the sermon. Are you ready to hear the word?"

The congregation stood up and clapped.

"Okay, sit down. Before he comes up I want to recognize and praise God for Brother Landis Lovington being here tonight. God bless you, Brother Landis."

Landis, knowing the drill, stood up smiling and waving to the congregation which consist of about two hundred people.

"Okay, okay. Now you stand up and give a good God bless you to Minister Spencer Mortimer. Let's clap our hands and give the brother some encouragement," said Reverend Wright.

Landis observed Elder Mortimer's expression of fatherly pride as Speedy walked to the podium.

Speedy had his Bible and notebook. At that moment he looked just like a preacher. Like Landis's dad and Elder looked. It sank in; he really was a minister.

He looked right at Landis and smiled. Landis smiled back and gave a 'thumbs up'.

"Good evening, everybody. Praise the Lord," said Speedy. "It is truly an honor and privilege to be before you tonight. I give all honor to God, who is the head of my life. To my pastor, Reverend Wright, my dad, Elder Mortimer, my mom, my family and my in-laws. This is the first time my very best friend, Landis, has heard me bring the message." Speedy smiled. "After he hears me, I hope this won't be the last."

Everyone gave the expected laugh.

Speedy looked around the room. "Let us pray." He led the prayer asking God to give him wisdom to say what God wanted and to be truthful in the task at hand.

"Let's go into the word of God. If you will turn your Bibles to James, the fifth chapter and twelfth verse." Speedy read:

"But above all things, my brethren, swear not, neither by heaven, neither by the earth, neither by any other oath: but let your yea be yea; and your nay, nay; lest ye fall into condemnation."

Speedy cleared his throat. "Now turn your Bible to 1st Corinthians, chapter ten and the twelfth verse.

"Wherefore let him that thinketh he standeth take heed lest he fall."

"There are many ways you could go with these scriptures but what I want to emphasize on are the words 'lest ye fall'.

"When I read the verses, I hear that I'm to be a man of my word. If I say yes then it's yes; if I say no then it's no; lest I fall into judgment. Lest my judging brings judgment to me, when I think I got it all together take heed lest I fall. Lest he fall, repeat that with me." The congregation obediently repeated the words.

"I want y'all to know this weekend was one of the hardest times of my life. I realized that for years I have projected myself to be a man of action. Whether good or bad, you could count on action from me. I was and had always been quick tempered, opinionated and very protective of my sisters. Even after giving my life to the Lord, I still had the same persona.

"But never in a million years did I think I was unapproachable. Until this weekend."

The entire church was quiet. The usual soft music that sometimes played when the message is going forward was silent. Speedy had the people's attention with his sincerity.

"Lest ye fall. When I hear this, it sounds like a warning; we say to our small children, don't stand on the table lest you fall and hurt yourself; as a teenager, my parents would say, 'don't forget the time boy, lest you miss your curfew,' and of course I missed my curfew a few times," Speedy smirked. Everyone laughed.

"Seriously, y'all, God give us instructions and warnings for our good. The truth is we need Him and we need each other. When we think we got it all together, when we try to fix it ourselves, usually is when we mess up. And that's what I realized this weekend. I won't go into details, but I will say this, sometimes our mouth and opinions can prevent our loved ones from finding true happiness because of their love for us, they sacrifice their happiness for us. In this I was sorry…"

Landis felt a piercing in his heart as Speedy was speaking. Speedy was right. He was so busy trying to second guess Speedy and handle his love for Pier by himself. So busy trying to do the right thing until when he and Pier did get together he lost it and everything started tumbling down like a house of cards. They fell.

Hindsight is something else. If only he had told someone, he could have gotten a better insight on the situation and handled things differently. Thank God everything worked out. Thank you, Lord! He silently prayed.

"…Lest ye fall," Speedy was saying. "We don't have to fall.

Let's examine ourselves tonight and see where we lack, and give it over to Him; the great I AM."

Landis had spent his whole life in church and never had he heard a sermon like this one. It was simple and truthful, and it stirred something in Landis that he had never felt before. Maybe because he could relate to what Speedy was saying. Maybe because he fell.

Speedy closed his Bible and came down the three stairs, microphone in hand.

"Now is an important time to make a decision. If you don't have a personal relationship with God and want to make a commitment to Him, come now. If you do have a relationship with Him and want to improve it, come now."

Of its own accord, Landis felt his legs and feet make what felt like a long journey down to the front of the church where others were already gathering, to dedicate his life to the Lord.

Pier and Shannan were sitting at the dining room table playing cards when their parents, Speedy, Spency, Micah Rochelle and Landis returned.

"Hi," everyone greeted them.

"Hey, how did it go for the preacher man?" Shannan asked.

"Good. Real good," Elder answered. "The boy preached. It was very good. Lest he fall," Elder nodded his head and rest his hand on Speedy's shoulder. "Good job, son."

Landis walked over to Pier and took a chair next to her. Everyone followed suit and took a seat at the table.

"How are you feeling?"

"Doing good. Missed you." Pier, smiling, caressed his face. He grabbed her hand and kissed it.

"Kiss, kiss, kiss. That's all y'all do. Excuse me, all we see y'all do," Shannan said as she waves her hand at them.

"Shannan leave them along, they're in love," scolded Ella Mortimer.

"Just teasing, Mama. So Landis what you think of your boy preaching."

Landis twisted his head to look at Shannan. "I think he was awesome. The message was truthful. It made me get up and go to the altar."

Shannan smiled, then frowns, causing everyone to laugh. Her running days were numbered and everyone, including her, knew it.

Speedy, looking at his watch pulled himself up. He rested his hand on Micah Rochelle's hand. "I guess we better get home, Sweets."

Micah Rochelle stood up. "Ready when you are, Sweets."

Landis stood also.

Pier looked unhappy. She didn't want him to leave. She wanted him to stay with her. He was, after all, her husband.

"And where do you think you're going?" Elder and Ella asked simultaneously.

Pier saw Landis' handsome face flush with embarrassment.

"I was going to head back to my parents' house."

Ella made clicking noises. "You'll do no such thing, boy. Your place is right here with your wife. Now go to your room."

"Yeah. And remember what the doctor said," Elder couldn't help teasing him.

Pier and Landis both looked uncomfortable.

Landis had just showered and was standing in Pier's bedroom

with a towel draped around his waist, Pier was under the covers, when Ella and Shannan knocked and walked in. They have done this Pier's entire life and neither she nor they have ever given it a second thought until now.

"Oops," said Ella stepping back. She cleared her throat. "Sorry, old habits take some time to get rid of."

Landis' large frame stood stone still. He didn't know what to say. Finally he smiled politely as Ella left the room. Shannan was a different matter.

"Wow, Landis. Looking kind of good in that towel," she teased.

"Come on, Shannan," she said from the hallway. "I'll see you in the morning, Son. Goodnight."

"Goodnight," he parroted.

He glanced at the bed and the covers were moving. Pier was laughing.

"Oh you think that was funny."

"Yes, I do. I should have locked the door. Sorry," she said between catching her breath.

They were sitting eating breakfast. That is Pier was trying to swallow the food without throwing up. Elder and Ella had their breakfast earlier and were gone.

"I have to leave this morning so I can go to work. If I could get the time off I would, you know that, don't you?"

Pier laid her fork down. She angles her head sideways. "I know, Handsome." She grabbed a few strings of her hair.

"I'll call you everyday until I come back Thursday."

"I'll count the days until your return."

"I love you."

"Kiss me, Landis."

He obliged her. They heard a throat being cleared. They turned toward the door. Speedy stood in the kitchen doorway.

"Excuse the interruption, I'm on my way to work, Landis, you straight getting to the airport?"

Landis nodded his head. "I need to run to the parents' house to grab my bag; then I'm outta here."

Pier was feeling a little queasy, got up and put her plate in the dishwasher.

"I think I'll go lay down for a little while." She hugged Landis then Speedy. "Don't get too busy until you forget to call, Handsome."

He gave her one more kiss. "Never. I better go get my things."

"'Kay. Have a safe trip." She went upstairs.

"I'll call you the moment I get to the house," he yelled. He didn't say home because home was now where she was.

"Missing her already?" asked Speedy. "Somebody got it bad."

Landis grinned. "Yeah, I do. But look who's talking. You and Micah still act like newlyweds."

Speedy gave a satisfied smile. "Something for you to look forward to."

"Can't wait." A worried look crossed his face. "Do you think she'll be alright?"

"Oh, yeah. Although Micah wasn't that bad, she did give me some scares a few mornings."

"Man, I am tripping. I never expected to ever be with her and now we gonna have a baby."

"Yep. Me either. One day you're going to have to finish telling the story about dude following Pier."

Landis agreed. "Not much to tell, it was Bulldog, he had to be about eighteen, braids in his hair and gold in his mouth."

"That thug," Speedy exclaimed. "He was the nicest one out of the bunch, or so I thought. I guess I slipped on my judgment of character."

"Not really, he was kind of nice. That's why I didn't call the police on him. Pier was testing the waters that night. She was innocently flirting," Landis laughs, "I think every male but you suffered."

"Oh, I suffered. I had to watch every male eye my little sister. I kept asking myself where did the breasts come from."

Landis laughed. He wondered the same thing himself for days afterward.

"Well, I handled things. End of story."

He would never in his life forget the look of terror in her eyes. Or the way that thug had his hands on her face trying to get a kiss. Landis had seen red. He grabbed that little punk before he knew what hit him.

Pier didn't scream, thank God, because somebody would have heard and it would have been worse for her. She did, however, look scared. Of him or Bulldog, he couldn't tell. Landis threw him up against the wall and choked him before either knew it.

"I had no idea this was happening. Why didn't you say something?" asked Speedy.

"I handled it", Landis repeated. "Besides I'd be visiting you in jail."

"Alright, Landis, I'm off to work. Catch you this weekend. How long do you think it will be before you move here completely?"

"A few months."

"You sure gonna make the airlines happy. Glad my brother-in-law twice over is rich." Speedy left out the back door.

Landis peeped in on Pier before he left. She was sound asleep. He didn't wake her.

His mother was home when he stopped by to get his bag.

"Hi, son. How's married life?" she teasingly asked.

"The best, mom. The best."

"I'm very happy for you. I know I've said it before but I am happy for you."

"Thanks mom," he Kisses her forehead. "Where is Pops?"

"Store."

"I'm kinda in a hurry, Mom, I gotta go to work. I just stopped by to get my bag. I can change when I get home."

He ran upstairs and grabbed his garment bag and went back downstairs. He talked a few minutes with his mother and then left.

Pier woke up feeling sick to the stomach again. She lay in bed. She was not about to get up. She would lie there until her mom returned.

She slept all morning and most of the afternoon. Landis called as soon as he got home. They talked for a few minutes then Landis ended the call because he had to get ready for work.

Shannan came by around three in the afternoon. Pier had never felt so loved in all her life. To think she always thought she was a bother to them.

"Hey, Big Head," said Shannan. "Why you still in bed? You doing okay?"

"No Shan. I feel sick again," Pier moaned out.

"What? Did you call the hospital? The doctor? Where is Landis?"

"He went back to Chicago to work. I was waiting for Mama."

"Girl, you can't be sick and not tell us. You know me, I'm always looking for a reason to call in. Let me call the hospital."

She picked up the phone and dialed information.

"The number on my discharge papers, Shan."

Shannan made a face. "Too late, they're connecting me. Hello," she paused. "We brought my sister in on Friday evening, her name is Pier Mortimer." She waited. "Yes, that's right. She's feeling sick again. Yes. Yes. Okay, we'll see you in one hour." She put the receiver back in its cradle.

"Okay, Big Head, I gotta take you back to the hospital. I better call mama and let her know so she can tell Speedy and Mic. So come on, let your big sister help you get dress."

Chapter Thirteen

Landis walked into the door of his 'temporarily' home exhausted and tired from the weekend events. He was missing Pier already; his plan is to work late every night this week so he could leave early Thursday. He wanted to be in Minnesota before the rush hour. After setting his garment bag at the door, he grabbed the mail. As he sat on the leather couch, he listened to his messages as he sorted through the mail.

"Hey, Man, what's up with your pager and cell phone? I've been trying to reach you all day," said Keith. "Give me a holler when you get in." He had called Saturday.

"Hi Landis, this is Jackie."

Landis froze. He closed his eyes. Why is she calling? What now?

"I-I was calling to say hello and see how you're doing. You don't have to call back. You know how I feel about people calling and don't leave a message. So take care of yourself."

She hung up. Landis stood and walked to the window. He wondered why Jackie was calling. Should he call her back or just leave it? He was hurt about her aborting his baby but he didn't hate her. He decided to leave well enough alone. He wouldn't call her. He had Pier and the baby to think about.

As he got dressed for work, Landis thought about Jackie again. He regretted her getting hurt. She was good woman. He wished Jackie the best.

Once seated at his desk, he called and talked to Pier, visualizing everything about her. She was fine. Everything was fine. Life was fine. Fine was a fine word. Boy, will he be glad to see her Thursday.

At six o'clock that evening, Landis was still at work in his office with sleeves rolled up deep in paper work.

"What's up Landis? Why didn't you call me back?" Keith asked as he entered the office.

"Sorry, Man. I had a lot to do. I was out of town this past weekend. Now I'm trying to catch up on some work and rearrange appointments so I can leave by noon on Thursday."

Keith sat down in the chair in front of the desk. "Went to Minnesota?"

"Yep. And guess what?" before Keith could guess, Landis continued, "Everything is out about Pier and me. And," he pauses, "we got married two weeks ago in Vegas."

"Oh, yeah?" he didn't look a bit surprise. "You didn't need my advice? Huh." Keith grinned. He leaned over and shook Landis' hand. "Congratulations, dude, that's great."

"Thanks, Man. And the other thing is I found out this weekend is my Baby's pregnant."

The expression on Keith's face was priceless, Landis decided. He leans back in his chair and grinned his heart out.

"What? You are a sneaking you know what. I gather the baby

is yours."

"And who else would dare touch my woman," Landis demanded.

"I would have loved a go at it," Keith said dreamily but at Landis expression he said, "I'm only kidding. How did Speedy take it? I mean that was the reason you hesitated, right."

Landis briefly explained his events of the weekend. Keith was laughing so hard after he had finished until he wanted to hit him.

His cellular phone rang.

"Yes, Lovington here."

"Hi Land. This Shannan.

"Shannan! Is Pier okay?" He asked.

"Well, if you promise to not fly off the handle, I'll tell you."

By now Landis was sitting up in his seat with alarm written all over his face.

Keith was looking concerned for his friend.

"Don't play with me," he said sternly. "Is Pier alright? And I want to know now."

"I should have listened to Pier and not call. She's back in the hospital. Only for a little while," Shannan added quickly.

"What happened? Never mind, I'm on my way." He put the phone down and jumps up gathering his papers.

"Landis. I know you didn't hang up on me." Pier heard her sister say.

"Hello. Hello. Landis I hear you there. Pick the phone--
"Hello?"

"Landis?" Shannan waited, tapping her fingers on the chair as she listened. "Oh, yeah, I remembered him talking about you the last time we visited."

Pier could tell by Shannan voice it was a man, but whom?

"Listen, Keith, Pier wants to talk to him and reassure him she's fine. Whatever you do, don't let him come or my little sister will kill me because she told me not to call."

Shannan handed the phone to Pier.

Pier put the phone to her ear and heard Landis yelling.

"Man, calm down and talk to Pier. Here."

"Hello," Landis whispered into the phone.

"Hi, Handsome."

"Baby, are you okay? Why are you in the hospital?"

"Calm yourself down, Hunk. I'm fine. I am sitting in this room watching TV with the IV in my arm. I just need to keep the pic line as planned."

"The pic line?"

"Yes. I keep dehydrating, so they decided to give me the pic line after all. Oh, that's right, you and Dad left out of the room. It just some kind of IV, for fluids, to keep me from dehydrating."

"I hate you are going through this, Baby."

"No, Landis, it's not as bad as you think."

Shannan was gesturing with her hand. "Hold on a minute." Pier put her hand over the phone piece. "What?"

"Ask him what his friend look like."

"Landis, I'm back. Why don't you invite Keith for a visit so Shannan can see what he looks like?"

"Okay."

"Listen, Handsome, I'm all done here so I'm going home. Call me as soon as you get in. 'Bye. I love you."

"Love you too, Baby." He ended the call. He grinned at Keith.

"Man, I've never seen you this hyper. You've got it bad."

"Sorry. I am getting a little crazy. By the way, Pier said to invite you for a visit. Something about her sister seeing what you look like."

Keith raised a brow. "Tell me what her sister look like. Didn't you use to date her?"

"No. Nothing like that. Shannan's like a sister. I did take her on prom because she broke up with her boyfriend the day before the prom. But never dated as in boy-girl date."

"What does she look like? As good as Pier?"

"They're sisters, they look about the same."

"You know I'm a leg man," he reminded Landis.

They both laughed.

"For the last time, Shannan, he is quite handsome and sweet. I liked him on sight. He even flirted with me. But I was all eyes for Landis," Pier was saying as they left for home.

"I'm due for a change. I hope he comes."

"He will."

Pier looked down on her left arm at the pic line. "I hate this thing already."

"It will be okay. Don't worry," said Shannan.

During the next couple of days, Pier felt better but she knew it was because of the fluids she had put in her body. If she went a day without the liquid, she knew she would get nauseous. The doctor said it would probably be another two weeks before they let her eat independently of the pic line.

Thursday finally arrived. The day was hot and humid and Pier was tired of being stuck in the house. Landis was due home any time now and she wanted everything to be perfect for their weekend together.

Landis' parents had insisted on having a small dinner party to celebrate the newly married couple on Saturday. Having the party cancelled Speedy's once a month Saturday. But it also gave Keith Monroe a chance to come to Minnesota.

"This is one of the happiest days I can remember, to see my son marry such a beautiful woman and love her like all Lovington men are known to do. We love with passion and respect and honor. We cherish our women and take care of them. We never let a day go by that we don't love them more than the day before." He turned to Elder, "Spencer, as you know, I am pleased with Speedy as my son. He has done well by my Micah Rochelle, and now I am pleased with little Pier.

"Although Louise and I don't say much, we want the Mortimer family to know we are pleased and honored to have you as our family. We have grown to love your children as ours and you, Spencer, are my brother.

"We were business partners. I remember the day we met and you offered me a chance to make money. Thanks be unto God for accepting. Thirty years ago when Louise and I moved here from Louisiana, we only dreamed of having good friends. Now we are sharing grandchildren together. So I toast to my new daughter, Pier Janise, who has always had our love and to my son, may I be the earthly father that says 'well done'." He wiped his eyes and sat down.

Speedy stood. He smiled at everyone. "I've always wanted my best friend to have the love we both saw in our parents. The love I have with my wife. I am glad that he found it with my little sister." He laughed. "It's kind of hard imagining little Pier all grown up. I thought of this day when she turned eighteen and I dreaded it. She was my baby. No man was good enough for her. But today I stand looking at the greatest man for her. May they be as happy as our parents are and as we are," he bent and kissed the hand of Micah Rochelle.

Chapter Fourteen

Landis had checked into the hotel on Lake Shore Drive and was now on his way to the closing of his townhouse. He decided to drive instead of flying. The weather for November wasn't so bad. He was thinking of getting rid of the convertible and getting a Lincoln Navigator truck. Maybe he'd just have both.

He smiled to himself thinking about Pier last night. She just didn't look pregnant. Her small round stomach was barely noticeable. She could eat a little better now that she was five months. He couldn't wait to get back home.

The ringing of his cell phone juggles him out of his thoughts.

"Yes. Lovington."

"Hi, Landis. I'm glad you didn't change your cell number yet."

The voice was so unexpected, he swirled his car a little. Taking control and ignoring the horns blaring at him, Landis took the next exit.

"Jackie?" He pulled on a side street.

"Yes. How are you, Landis?"

"I'm doing good. How about you?" They sounded like strangers instead of a couple who once practically lived together.

"Okay. It could be better. I heard through the grapevine you're moving back home."

"Yes, I am. I'm only here now to close on the townhouse."

"I'm glad for you." She was silent briefly. Then said, "I know you're wondering why I'm calling."

"It did cross my mind," Landis said impatiently, unbuckling the seat belt.

"Umm, I need to talk to you. Can we meet?"

"I'm not sure that's a good idea." He didn't want to hurt her feelings, but they didn't have anything to talk about.

"Please, Landis, this is important." She sounded desperate.

Sighing, "Okay. Where do you want to meet?"

"My place is out. I've got company galore there. My sister and her kids."

"What about a restaurant or something?"

"This is private, and I need to be alone with you when we talk."

"Listen, Jackie, I don't know what's left to say. I didn't want us to part like that. I didn't want you to get an abortion. I tried calling you and seeing you--"

"I know, Landis," she interrupts him. "I need about one hour of your time. I'm begging you to meet me. *Please!*"

Landis did not like the sound of this. What did she want? Maybe she needed to apologize. He rubbed his hand over his head in despair.

"Okay. I'm on my way now to close. Why don't you meet me

back at my hotel at six this evening? I'm at Tyler Inn on the Drive. Room 812."

"Sounds good. I'll see at six. Oh, and thanks, Landis."

"No problem. I'll see you then." He ended the call.

Pier couldn't believe their house was finally ready to move in. Landis was so organized. He'd given his friend, the famous architect, Nicholas Palmer and his wife Trina, an interior decorator, carte blanche to their home. Pier's assignment was to show them what she wanted.

Nicholas was glad to help. He rearranged his schedule to accommodate his friend. According to him, Landis helped him get his first loan and invested his own money in him. "He believed in me even when we were in college." Pier loved learning new things about her husband.

She hugged herself. Tonight they will finally be in their own home. All that was left to do was go home and wait for Landis. She looked at her watch. It was eight. He said he would be back by ten tonight.

She sighed. Together alone with no parents around. Not that she was complaining. Her parents were the best. They gave them lots of space. They didn't blink an eye if they stayed in her room all day or if they went out when her mom was cooking. Her father showed the utmost respect for Landis. Maybe that's because Landis went to church on Sundays.

The ringing of the phone brought Pier back to the present. "Hello?"

"Hi, Baby," Landis voice sounded a little strange.

"Hi, Handsome. What's wrong? Where are you? I'm on my way to the house." Pier knew something was wrong.

"Umm, everything is fine. I'm still in Chicago. I have a few more loose ends to tie up. I'll be driving out first thing in the morning," he said tautly.

"Landis, is everything alright, you sound weird. What's going on, Hunk?"

"I'm okay, sweetheart. Is your mom there? I need to talk to her."

"No, she and Dad are out. They plan to stop by your parents' house. You want me to call her for you?"

"No. I'll catch her later. I gotta go baby. I love you with all my heart, Pier, and I love our baby. You have made me the happiest man in the world. You believe me?"

He sound like he was crying or maybe drunk. "I know you do and I love you, too. Say, you and Keith didn't do too much celebrating today."

"No. Listen, I gotta go, I'll see you tomorrow in our home. Don't go tonight; wait till tomorrow. I don't want you alone. Love you, 'bye, Baby.

"'Bye, Handsome. I love you too." She put the receiver in its cradle.

Landis sounded so strange. Why? Something was wrong. She was sure of it. But what? Who? Jackie! That's who. Did he see her and regret marrying Pier. That's it. Her heart started pounding. She could hear roaring in her ears. Oh God! Oh God!

"*'You have made me the happiest man in the world,'*" she remembered what he'd just said. That wasn't it. No, if Landis saw Jackie it didn't mean anything. Pier was not happy on how they got married. But she knew when he said months ago he was on his way to talk to her, he was telling the truth. But something happened she was sure of it.

She yawned and stretched. She headed upstairs to bed.

A few hours later her mother was gently shaking her awake.

"Pier, wake up, hon. We need to talk to you."

She turned over and rose up. Her mother was crying. "Mama, what's wrong?" Rubbing her eyes as she glanced in the direction of the doorway where her dad was standing. "Daddy what is it?"

"Baby Girl, we have some bad news." He moved into the room. "Speedy just called. He and Micah Rochelle are on their way to Chicago."

Pier screamed Landis' name. "What happen to Landis?"

"He was in a car accident and is unconscious."

"No! No!" Pier sobbed in her mother arms.

"His parents and Speedy's number were the numbers to call in case of emergency. The police were unable to reach Renee or Louise. Thank the good Lord they were able to reach Speedy."

Pier jumped out of bed nearly knocking her mama over. She moved too fast, which made her dizzy. She swayed. Her dad grabbed her and helped her back into bed.

"I have to go to Chicago. I have to be there when he wakes up. He needs me."

"I'm sorry, Baby Girl, but Micah Rochelle made it clear you weren't to leave. She is the nurse."

"I don't care. He's my husband and I'm going to Chicago."

"That's enough, little girl. Now you are in no shape to go any place. Speedy said he would call as soon as they check on him. They should be there in about an hour," her father said sternly.

"Go to sleep, hon. We hate we had to tell you," her mother said as she pulled the covers back over her.

"It will be impossible to sleep. I need to be there. He needs me."

"I'll sit with her for a while, Spence, you go on to bed." Elder left the room.

"I wish I was there with him. If it was me, he would be right by my side," Pier moaned. "Nothing or no one would be able to stop him." She rubbed her hands over her face as the tears flowed down. Lying back against the pillows, the tears cascade in seconds drenching them.

"Pier, Landis knows you are not able to come. He wouldn't have it. Now close your eyes and go to sleep. As soon as we hear something, we'll wake you."

Mrs. Mortimer turned on some gospel music and sat down in the big strawberry chair.

Pier closed her eyes but opened them again. Closed eyes brought about images of Landis. She tried to think. She couldn't. She tried to pray. She was too scared. Her little perfect world she'd worked so hard for continued to crumble. All she wanted was to love Landis and him to love her. She went about it all wrong. Twenty-twenty hindsight gave her the information on that.

Elder Mortimer returned back to the room and sat on the arm of the chair. They joined hands and prayed, as they have done for many years, for Landis. Elder was persuaded that Jesus was the answer.

Pier heard the prayer. She prayed along with her parents. "Oh, Lord, hear my prayer," she whispered. "Let my husband be okay, Lord. Please forgive my sins, oh God. Please help Landis. He is a good man and he loves us," rubbing her stomach. "Please give us the chance to be a family and serve you like we should. My dad always preached you are a God of a second chance. Please give us that second chance. In Jesus' great name, I pray. Amen.

Speedy and Micah Rochelle arrived at the O'Hare airport exhausted and worried. Micah cried all the way. She couldn't believe this was happening to her brother. The last time she had seen him he had been so happy. Going on and on about his wife and baby.

Speedy's last conversation with him had been an hour before the police called. He had sounded strained, as if he wanted to tell him something but change his mind...

"Hello."

"What's up, man?"

"Nothing. Just chillin. What's up with you?"

"Nothing. I'm coming back tomorrow instead of tonight," Landis said tensely. "I've missed my babies."

Speedy laughed. "Somebody got it bad," he stressed the word bad.

Landis gave a hollow laugh.

Speedy immediately knew something was wrong and asked him if everything was okay. Landis hesitated, sighed and said everything was okay.

"I'll see you tomorrow. Please, Speedy, take care of my family until I get there."

"Done deal." They said their good-byes and now Speedy was heading to some hospital downtown Chicago.

Upon arriving at the hospital, Micah Rochelle told them she was a nurse and she demanded to know just what was wrong with her brother. The doctors informed them he was unconscious due to a head wound, had broken his right leg in three places, and cracked a few ribs. All and all he was a lucky man.

"Blessed," Speedy corrected quietly.

Dr. Benson nodded his head in agreement.

"Doctor, may we see my brother?"

They walked into the room, Landis' leg was in a temporary cast, he had a bandage on his head. His face looked like their son, Spency, had attacked him with red and blue markers. Micah Rochelle covered her mouth with her hand to keep from screaming out. Tears rolled unchecked down Speedy cheeks.

"I've got to call the parents," Speedy said hoarsely. "I hope Dad was able to locate your parents."

Micah pulled the chair in the corner up to the bed and sat down caressing her brother's hand. For some reason, Speedy turned back before leaving the room and when he did, his mind went back not too long ago when Landis was sitting in a similar chair next to Pier's bed holding her hand.

He shook his head. Tomorrow indeed was not promised. He had been too laid back about this preaching business. Spencer Trace Mortimer made a vow right where he was to God. He would serve him with all his heart. "As for me and my house," he declared in a stern whisper, "we are going to serve the Lord."

The ringing of the telephone woke Pier who hadn't realized she'd been asleep. She eased out of bed moving toward the hallway. She felt better. She was sure she could get to Chicago and see Landis for herself.

Speedy had called and given them the news that Landis was still unconscious with a head injury, broken leg and cracked ribs. Pier thanked God he was alive and must have fallen asleep.

She knocked on her parents' bedroom.

"Come in," said Elder.

"Who was that on the phone? Was it more news about Landis?"

"No news. That was Renee. He and Louise will be flying out

first thing in the morning. They said to tell you not to worry. Landis will be home before you know it."

Looking at her parents, she wished she was little again so she could crawl into that big bed with them and listen to her mother sing away her problems. As a matter of fact, it was just a few months ago she lay across their bed and went to sleep. It seemed like years ago. Pier held her head down and started walking out the room.

"Pier," Ella called.

She turned around. Her mother had moved to the center of the bed next to her father, with the covers lifted up for her to get into bed with them. Pier needed no second beckoning; she swiftly moved to the bed and got under the covers.

"We spoiled this one Ella," Elder said.

"Spen, we spoiled them all." She closed her eyes smiling. Only yesterday, Speedy and Spency were lying on this bed taking a nap.

Speedy finally got Micah Rochelle to leave the hospital. They decided to stay in Landis' room. The nurse had given them Landis' things he had on him when the accident occurred.

The bed was a welcome sight. Speedy insisted his wife go to bed. She was exhausted and needed to rest. They had to be at the airport in the morning to pick up her parents.

Around four o'clock in the morning, a few hours after they went to bed, Speedy woke to the ringing of the phone. Eyes still closed, he felt his way to the phone only to pick it up to a dial tone. Opening his eyes, he realizes it must be his cell phone. Grimacing, he eased out of bed trying not wake Micah up.

The phone was still ringing when he reached the pocket of

his coat. He checked and it wasn't his cellular phone.

"I am too tired for this," he mumbled. The ringing stopped only to start again.

"Bay, get the phone," grumbled Micah Rochelle throwing the pillow over her head.

"If I can find it." Speedy snapped the light on. "Where is your phone, Mic.?"

"At home. I forgot it," she yawned. "Check yours."

"It's not ringing. Forget it. I'm going back to sleep."

Micah started laughing under the pillow. "It's Landis' phone. Check his belongings. Whoever that is is very persistent."

Speedy grabbed the bag and sure enough the phone was ringing. "Should we answer it?"

"You better after waking me up."

"Hello?"

"Is this Landis Lovington," a woman's weary voice asked.

"Who is this?"

"Landis. This is Carolyn Winters, Jackie's mom. I hate to call you so late or early in the morning, but I'm at the hospital with Jackie. She asked me to call you. She's had the baby now."

"What?" She's what?" Speedy demanded. Micah Rochelle lifted her head from under the pillow.

"Had the baby; She's early and she not doing too good. Can you come?"

"Ms. Winters. I'm sorry, ma'am, but-"

"Please don't say you're not coming. She needs you," Carolyn Winters sniveled.

"No ma'am. Um, this isn't Landis. I'm his brother-in-law, Spencer Mortimer. Well, my news ain't that great. You see, Landis is in the hospital. He had a car accident."

Carolyn gasped like the breath had been sucked from her. "No," she moaned. "This can't be happening. My child needs him."

"Speedy, who is that? What is it?" Micah Rochelle got out of bed as she spoke.

Speedy raised his hand. "Listen, Ms. Winters, my wife and I are here about Landis. If you tell me what hospital, we'll be there."

Carolyn gave him the name and address. They end the call.

Speedy violently threw the cell phone on the bed. He paced the carpeted floor, face chiseled with anger. He stopped in front of the bed where Micah Rochelle sat; wide-eyed bewilderment written on her face.

"Well? Are you going to tell me why you're so angry?

He sat down on the bed. Anger left as quickly as it came. His golden brown eyes filled with sorrow as he looked into her chocolate eyes. Rubbing a weary hand over his face, he held her hand. "Mic that was Carolyn Winters, the mother of Jackie Reynolds. Apparently Jackie is in the hospital, she had a baby, and she needs Landis."

She closed her eyes. "What?" she asked opening her eyes. "Speedy, what is going on?"

"Sweetheart, that's what she said, and she also said Jackie isn't doing well. We've got to get there and see what's going on." He rose quickly and got dressed. He called the front desk asking for directions to the hospital.

Micah Rochelle certain she had cried all the tears in her, started with a fresh downpour. She did not dress as fast as Speedy due to the numbness she was feeling. "What is going on Lord? Please tell us something," she whispered.

"Let's go, Mic." She rose slowly from the bed. Speedy pulled his wife in his arms and held her tightly. "Listen, sweetheart, our downside is we don't know what's going on, but we do know your brother loves my sister and there is an explanation," he sounded so sure. This same man a few months ago wanted to rip her brother apart. She said as much.

"I'd like to think I've grown since then. Besides, today I truly learned how to put God in charge of our life. I'm learning to trust Him."

"Oh, Speedy, I hope you are right. I can't take what we went through in July."

Once at the hospital, they were directed to the floor Jackie was on. A man and three women were sitting in the waiting area. The oldest of the three women stood when she saw Speedy and Micah Rochelle. She was tall with caramel colored skin and light brown short hair. She looked tired, sad and defeated. Her eyes were swollen from crying. Yet she mustered up a warm smile at them.

"Mr. and Mrs. Mortimer?" At their affirmative nod, she held out her hand. "Hi, I'm Carolyn Winters. This is my husband," the man stood, "George, and our daughters, Jennifer and Jeanette." The daughters didn't get up-they didn't even acknowledge the introductions. They only looked like they were in another world.

"Ma'am, call me Speedy, and this is my wife, Micah Rochelle." Carolyn sat down on the couch, moving over to make room for Speedy and Micah.

"Only one person can be in the room at a time, so my son Johnny is in there. The baby is premature. She was so weak. They had to give her a cesarean." She turned her tear-rimmed eyes to Speedy. "It a boy," she said between sobs. "He will probably make it, but they don't think my Jackie is going to. There were complications. She lost a lot of blood. Her blood pressure will not stabilize." Her body racked with sobs.

George leapt to his feet. He wasn't as tall as his wife, but he was solid muscle. He pulled her into his arms, shhing her. Telling her it would be all right. Jennifer and Jeanette decided to scream and cry. Speedy and Micah Rochelle rushed over to comfort them.

Speedy didn't think it could get any worse, but it did. For a young man in a white coat walked into the waiting room area. He walked to Carolyn and George.

"Mr. and Mrs. Winters. We can't get her stable. I'm sorry we've tried all we can. She has come around and is asking for Landis." He raised a brow toward Speedy, asking if he was Landis.

"No. I'm his brother-in-law. Landis had a car accident and is in the hospital." It was sheer stubbornness that kept him from bawling his eyes out. His throat was tight with unreleased tears when he asked if perhaps they could see her.

The doctor ran his hands through his blond hair. He paused in thought. "I don't see why not."

Speedy and Micah Rochelle followed the doctor and Jackie's family into the ICU room. Jackie lay lifeless in the bed with tubes and monitors all over her. Even now Speedy could see she was a very beautiful woman. Her eyes fluttered then open. She moved them around looking at everyone in there. Johnny was sitting by her bed. He stood and moved when they enter the room.

"Landis," Jackie whispered. Speedy stepped to her side, lifting her hand in his. She was looking at him. "Where is Landis? Did he go home?" She became delirious, talking to Landis as if he was there. "I'm so sorry, Landis, for not telling you about the baby until today. I'm sorry I was so jealous that I lied. Tell your little Pier I'm sorry, too. I do love you, Landis." She closed her eyes.

"Where is Landis?" she asked upon opening them again. "You must be Speedy. I saw your picture at the townhouse. Is Landis mad at me and won't come?"

Micah Rochelle moved nearer to Speedy, tears streaming down her face. "Hi Jackie, I'm Landis' sister."

"Micah Rochelle. A pretty name. He's mad, isn't he?" she could barely get the words out. She closed her eyes again.

Speedy had one arm around his wife's shoulders and the other hand holding Jackie's. The tears he tried to keep in check were decanting down his lean cheeks. A nurse came in to check on Jackie.

She opened her eyes again. Speedy was still holding her hand. He didn't know what to say so he went on instinct. Leaning his tall frame down near Jackie, he spoke softly to her. "Jackie, I'm going to tell you what I believe to be the truth. I think Landis was on his way to talk to you again but had a car accident. He is in the hospital. That is the only thing that would prevent him from being here with you." At her whimpering he said, "Don't worry he is okay. Now you get better so you can be with your son."

She shook her head. "Poor Landis. He is a good man. Mama," she mustered the strength to call. Her mother stepped forward. "I want Landis to raise our son. Please, Mama, promise me you will see to it that Landis gets his son." Carolyn was crying uncontrollable.

"I promise," she said between gasps.

She called her stepfather, brother, and sisters. She told them she loved them. Speedy stepped forward again.

"Micah Rochelle," she called. "Ask Landis to forgive me. Ask him, will he tell our son about me when he's older?"

"Jackie," Speedy interrupted with urgency, "Do you believe in the Lord Jesus Christ?"

"Yes, I do. And I accepted him in my life. That's why I couldn't abort the baby. I was warned about the risks but I could not have an abortion."

"Then with your permission, sir, can we pray." He began at the permission of George and Carolyn.

Jackie Reynolds closed her eyes for the final time at seven o'clock that morning.

Her family circled one another and wept. Speedy and Micah held one another and cried. They cried for Jackie, for the baby, and for Landis.

Speedy and Micah sat with her parents in the living room of the hotel's two bedroom suite they had requested after picking them up from the airport, explaining to them what had happened.

"She had a boy! I didn't know she was pregnant." She looked at Renee sitting quietly listening to all that was being said. "Honey, did you know about this?"

Renee was sitting on the blue flowered sofa with his wife; Speedy and Micah were sitting in identical powdered blue wing back chairs. He lifted his wife's hand and kissed it. Speedy gave a corner smile. How many times during these past months has he seen Landis do the exact same thing to Pier?

"Yes, dear, he has shared with me the situation about Jackie, however, my understanding was she had gotten an abortion." He raised a brow to Speedy.

"Same here. He told me she was pregnant and getting an abortion. But Carolyn, her mother," he reminded them, "phoned and said she was having the baby and the rest we've explained."

Renee nodded his head in thought. "And you said Jackie want Landis to raise the baby."

"Yes, Papa, she told us before she died," Micah Rochelle said. Once again the tears ran. Speedy knelt before his wife holding her; Louise sprung up also to comfort her child.

Renee went and stood in front of the window looking at the lake. He sighed. This was such a mess. His mind went to little Pier. What will she do? What will Landis do? What will any of them do? He turned back to his family. He patted his daughter's face. "Everything will work out. I want you and your mother to rest. Spencer and I will go to the hospital to check on your brother."

"They are supposed to call us as soon as he comes to," Micah Rochelle reminded them.

"We will be there when he opens his eyes." He waved his large hand to Speedy. "Go call your parents and tell them what is going on. Get a hold of Shannan and tell her not to let little Pier out of her sight. That little spitfire will be on the next plane moving if no one's watching her."

"Yes, Speedy, I'll let your mother know what's going on," Pier heard her father say as she walked in the kitchen. Was it her imagination or did he change the subject when he saw her?

"Yes, Spency is okay. In spite of everything, we are enjoying him. He's out walking with your mother now." He paused and listened. Yes, son, you do that. Call us as soon as Landis wakes up."

Pier, who was pouring herself some juice, dropped the glass

when her dad said 'as soon as Landis wakes up.' Her Landis was still unconscious. They were watching her like a hawk. They called Shannan, who was on her way even now to play watch guard.

She couldn't see the glass for the tears. "Leave it Baby Girl, I'll get it up. Listen, Landis is still unconscious. As soon as he comes to your brother is going to put that phone to his ear and you can let him know how much you love him."

"Okay. I guess I'll go upstairs and lay down." She walked briskly out the room. Once in the sanctuary of her room, she buried her face in the pillow and cried. She thought about Landis and how much he loved her.

"She remembered a couple of months ago, Landis was in Chicago and he made his regular call to see how she was doing.

"I'm so happy to be your wife. I'm glad to carry your child."

"Why do I hear a but in your voice, Baby?"

"Well, if you had your handsome self here with me, I wouldn't have waked up thinking about Atlanta's peach muffins. I want them so bad. I hate craving. All I was doing was thinking about writing to a couple of friends there, and what do I wake up wanting? A muffin," she giggled. "Now when do I get my husband back?"

"Well, baby, this is my last time for a long time coming here to work. Monroe-Phillips will be opening in St. Paul in one week."

She laughed gleefully. "Oh, Handsome, I am glad. When you get home, we'll celebrate."

"Done deal. I have more news we can celebrate also. See you in a couple days, Baby."

Later that night her father called her downstairs. Standing downstairs were Shannan and Keith with a big box.

"Hi, legs, umm Pier," he corrected himself at Shannan jabbing him in the side. "Your husband sent me to Atlanta this morning to get his wife some peach muffins." He bowed, "the pleasure was all mines. Now are you sharing?"

"What, Keith? You went all the way to Atlanta just for some muffins?" Pier was flabbergasted.

"Well," he grinned, "it was a good reason to get Shannan to skip work and meet me. I hope she doesn't lose her job," he grinned again.

They went into the kitchen and ate muffins and drank milk and coffee.

She called Landis and told him how much she loved him.

"I promised to take care of you and make you happy."

Oh, Landis, I am so glad you married me. You have made a very happy woman."

"Me too. Now go to bed and dream of us. 'Bye."

"Goodnight, Handsome."

Now she lay in bed wishing she could be there for him. She closed her eyes and willed herself to fall asleep. Maybe she'd wake up and Landis would be awake.

When she did wake up, Shannan, was sitting in the strawberry over-stuffed chair. During their stay with her parents, Landis insisted she leave her room just the way it was. It was really funny because her father hated it and he assumed the red would go. Landis laughingly told her if her father knew what he really thought about her bedroom, he would shoot him.

"The parents want you downstairs when you wake up. So let's go." Pier got up rubbing her small round stomach as they went downstairs.

Her mother and father were sitting on the soft beige colored sofa in the family room drinking tea when they entered.

"How you doing, hon?" Mrs. Mortimer asked.

"Mmm mmm, I don't know," she answered despondent. She sat in the beige chair across from them; Shannan sat on the sofa with them.

Elder sat his cup on the coffee table and began to speak, "Baby Girl, I spoke with your brother, and Landis is still unconscious. He and Renee were on their way to the hospital. They promised to call as soon as Landis comes to." He leaned his tall body forward. "We do not want anything happening to you or our baby. So Shannan has agreed to stay here until Landis is better." Elder leaned back against the couch.

Pier said okay. They talked, watched TV and went to bed.

It was around midnight two days after the accident when Landis opened his eyes. Speedy had convinced Papa Renee to go to the hotel and get some rest. He said he would stay until morning and then Micah Rochelle and Mrs. Lovington could come and relieve him. The hospital staff had put a cot in the room and he was laying on it when he heard Landis groan.

Speedy jumped up running to the bed, saw his best friend chocolate eyes looking back at him.

"What's up, Man?" Landis whispered hoarsely. He frowned in pain when he tried to move. His head felt like a sledgehammer was pounding inside. And when he tried to open his eyes black spots prevented him from focusing. He closed his eyes again and tried to move. He couldn't move his right leg and realized it must be injured. He was sure a 'karate wanna be' had used his ribs as target practice. His hands were the only things that seem to be in good working order. From the beeping sounds and the smell, he figured he was in the hospital. He couldn't remember what happened, but as bad as he was hurting, thank God he was alive. Thank God!

"Hey, Bro." Speedy pressed the nurse's button.

"I'm in the hospital? What happened?" he asked between grunts.

"Listen, don't talk until the nurse and doctor get in here."

The nurse came in rushing around, checking machines. "Hello Landis. How are you feeling? Are you in a lot of pain?"

"Yes," he whispered. Then winced as he tried to move again.

"On a scale of zero to ten, what would be your rate? Zero being no pain."

Landis did a half of grin. "One hundred."

"I've notified your doctor and the doctor on call will be here momentarily."

Landis closed his eyes again. His head was banging. He couldn't keep his eyes open. Why was he in the hospital? It must be something pretty serious to get Speedy to come. He knew Micah wasn't too far away.

"Hello," said a man with a heavy accent. Landis opened his eyes. "I am Dr. Lee. Do you know where you are?"

"Hospital," was the curt reply. "Why am I here?"

"You were in an accident. A car accident. Do you remember?"

Closing his eyes again, Landis said no. The doctor examined his eyes.

"What is the last thing you remember?"

"Going out to dinner with my girl. It was Valentine's Day."

Speedy who had been standing quietly let a gasp escape his mouth. February! That was nine months ago.

"What is your girl's name?"

"Why are you asking me all of these questions?" Landis demanded to know.

"You hit your head and we want to make sure you're coherent.

"Okay."

"Do you feel up to a few more questions?" the doctor asked.

"Ask away, Doctor." His voice was sounding a little stronger.

"Give us your full name, age, where you live and the name of your girlfriend."

"My name is Landis Renee Lovington; I turned twenty-nine a couple of months ago. I own a townhouse on the north side of Chicago. My friend's name is Jackie, we have been seeing each other almost a year." He closed his eyes. "Anymore questions, Doc?"

"No. No, Landis. The nurse will give you something for pain and your doctor will see you in the morning." Dr. Lee proceeded out the room. Speedy followed him.

He returned as the nurse finished giving Landis the pain medicine. Landis eyes were open slits. He smirked at Speedy.

"So it took a car accident to get you to come visit. The good thing is you'll get to meet Jackie."

"I look forward to it," Speedy said faking a brightness he didn't feel.

"Did Micah come with you? I hope the parents aren't worried."

"Yes. She and the parents are at the hotel."

"The hotel? Why didn't you stay at my place?"

Speedy hunched his shoulders. "We weren't thinking." The doctor said to be careful and don't volunteer any information. So he couldn't tell him he had sold his townhouse or that Jackie was dead and they had a son. Speedy ran his strong hand over his face. And he definitely couldn't tell him he was married to Pier.

"My head aches and all I want to do is sleep. I'm okay. Go be with your wife."

"No way. Your daddy said stay and that's what I'm doing."

"Still scared of my old man?" Landis teased.

"And you know it." He lay again on the cot. He'd call Papa Renee and let him know what's going on. He needed to call his dad, also. He gave a weary sigh. Lord, help us all.

The next morning when Landis opened his eyes, he was able to see a little and what he saw made his heart swell with love for his friend, who was asleep on an uncomfortable horrible looking cot. Speedy was truly a good friend, Landis thought, as he drifted back to sleep.

This time when Landis opened his eyes, he saw his mother, father, sister and Speedy standing around like a funeral was in process.

"Who died?" They all looked startled.

"Landis!" His mother exclaimed. "You're awake. Good. You took ten years off my life."

Renee, knowing what a rambler his wife was, intervened. "Hey son, glad to see your mother smile again. You gave us quite a scare."

"Sorry."

"Hi, Brother," Micah Rochelle whispered. "Glad to see you."

"Hey, Sis." He glanced around the room, then back to Speedy. "Dude, you're still here?"

"Yeah, Man. But I'm otta here until later."

"Sounds like a plan. Did anyone notify my girl, Jackie?"

Nerve wracking silence followed his question. Everyone looked any place but at Landis.

A horrible thought came to Landis. "Oh, my God! Jackie wasn't in the car with me, was she?"

"No, son. Nothing like that. You were alone," Renee said smoothly. "Spencer spoke with Jackie and she knows. Now listen. Enough questions. We are waiting for your doctor."

As if summoned, the doctor walked into the room. He was talk and wore glasses and had short dread locks.

"Good morning, all. I'm Dr. Steven Wilson. Landis, good to see you awake. You feel up to some more questions." He sat down in the chair Renee relinquished.

"Sure. Go right ahead, Dr. Wilson."

"These are your parents," he gestured toward Renee and Louise.

"Yep. And my sister, Micah Rochelle and her husband, Speedy. He's also my best friend and like a brother."

Dr. Wilson nodded. "Last night you said the last thing you remembered was Valentine's Day and your girlfriend, Jackie. We believe you are suffering some memory loss. Do you remember anything else?"

Landis hesitated, "I do remember something but it's too personal to tell."

"Landis, you must understand, we are concern about your head injury and we want to make very sure your memory is completely restored," Dr. Wilson said with heavy emphasis.

Landis sighed, rubbing his face with his left hand. His head had begun to hurt again. He couldn't tell them in front of Speedy; it took everything in him not to jump on a plane to where little Pier was and declare his love for her. If Speedy knew that he would surely kill him. Not to mention what Elder Mortimer would do.

"Landis," Renee Lovington called, "Son if you remember

anything, please share it."

"Okay. There is this young woman I'm crazy about but it would never work," he paused, closed his eyes as if trying to conjure up that memory, "I remember wanting to get on a plane and visit her and make her aware of my feelings.

"I controlled myself and instead agreed with Jackie to take her out. Don't get me wrong," he said watching his family and the doctor, "I care about Jackie. We have an understanding."

"Landis," the doctor pulled himself up, "you are nine months off. This is November fifteenth. Now calm down," he said at Landis' look of alarm. "We will run some tests and see what the problem is." His pager went off. He looked at the pager hooked on his belt.

"I need to take this. Listen, your family is instructed not to volunteer any info to you until after the tests. Okay?"

"Okay."

The doctor exited the room.

Landis stared at his family. "I don't care what the doctor said. I want to know what I missed."

"Hey, Bro, if it would help, we would do it like that," said Speedy snapping his fingers. "But we want you to remember on your own, not something we said."

"He's right," said Louise. Renee and Micah Rochelle nodded in agreement.

Landis shook his head. "I want to know now what I am missing. Good Lord, this feels weird. This is definitely whacked. Is that why Jackie isn't here? Will someone tell her I remember her?"

"She knows. Don't worry, Landis, everything will work out fine. Meanwhile we are going to go back to the hotel," said Renee.

"Yes dear," his mother kissed him. "Get some rest. We will see you later."

It had been two whole days since Pier heard any news about Landis. Speedy would call and speak with her parents, but when she asked what he said, they merely state everything is fine. Everything was not fine. Her husband was in the hospital and she wasn't there by his side.

She was suffering from cabin fever. No one would leave her alone nor would they let her outside. Shannan stayed with her once she left work at the courthouse. She accompanied Pier everywhere. Her mother stayed with her during the day.

Pier knew they thought she'd bolt and head for Chicago the minute she spent anytime by herself and they were right. As a matter of fact, that's just what she was going to do. She'll demand to go and see her husband. She'd stand up to all of them if necessary. She'd show them, treating her like a child. Huh, she was a married woman. Mrs. Landis Renee Lovington.

She was pacing back and forward in the family room when Shannan, along with their parents, entered the room. They wore a devastatingly shocked expression.

"It's Landis? Isn't it? What's happened?" Pier asked wildly.

"Yes, it Landis. He's fine except, I think you better sit down, Pier," Shannan grabbed her arm and led her to the couch.

Elder Mortimer sat his large frame on one side and her mother sat on the other and Shannan kneeled in front of her.

"Baby Girl, the accident caused Landis to have amnesia. The last thing he remembers is February of this year. He has no memory of being married to you."

Pier laughed. "You are kidding? Right? This is some kind of

joke. You knew you couldn't keep me here, so you fabricate this romance drama with the hope that if Landis doesn't know me, I won't go to Chicago." She scrambled to her feet toppling Shannan over. "Sorry Big Head," she says absently minded.

She paced the floor again. "You know this won't work. I'm taking the next thing smoking and heading to Chicago. And no one can stop me."

"Fine," Ella Mortimer said, standing "We all are taking the next thing smoking, which is the plane. Start packing. We leave in one hour."

"I'm packed already." Her eyes welled up with tears. "This can't be happening, can it, mama?"

"I'm afraid so, hon. The doctor hopes when he sees you, he'll remember."

Shannan had gotten up and was now sitting on the couch. "Everything will be fine, you'll see, Big Head. If I lose my job from taking off so much time from work," she grinned, "I'll get another one. I'm not running home to get any more clothes. I'll buy what I need in Chicago."

Elder Mortimer and his family arrived in Chicago's Midway airport three hours later. They were met by Speedy and Renee. Speedy lifted his son, Spency high in the air. He was so glad to see him. Spency giggled, throwing his chubby arms around his daddy neck.

"Ey, Daddy. I miz you. Where is my mommy?" Spency demanded to know.

"At the hotel, waiting for you." Speedy smiled lovingly at his son.

Spency turned his attention to his paternal grandfather. "Ey, Papa." He threw his arms around Renee neck. "Where my Grammy?"

"At the hotel, waiting for you," Renee echoed Speedy reply.

After everyone greeted one another, they piled in the black Yukon Speedy had rented. They headed for the hotel discussing the tragedy of Landis losing his memory. They agreed Pier should rest awhile after which Speedy will take her to see Landis.

Micah Rochelle and Shannan ended up going with them to the hospital. Pier had been warned to act like little Pier and not his wife. The doctor was clear about let his memory come naturally. Pier was all for that as long as she could see her husband, she would go along with whatever.

She felt butterflies in her stomach pretty much like she did in June when she'd come to Chicago. The ride on the elevator to his floor seemed to take forever. Pier's heart had nearly stopped beating by the time she walked into Landis' room.

Landis had been laying in bed, trying to remember each month from March to November. He came up with nothing. Not quite nothing; he did remember dancing with someone in a red dress. He guessed it was Jackie. God! He wished he could remember. If his ribs weren't hurt, he would've decked Speedy and made him tell him what he's missing.

They've all tread around him like eggshells and he was sick of it. For two days they'd come to visit but tell him nothing. And to top it all off, still no Jackie. It's like he has leprosy.

Landis was so caught up in thoughts that he didn't hear the door open or anyone entering.

Shannan cleared her throat. "Remember me, dear, or am I forgotten." She batted her eyes and leaned over and kissed Landis' neck. "I should bite you on the neck."

"Hi, Gorgeous. How can I forget you?" Landis had a scheming

look in his chocolate eyes. "I hope I did something grand for your birthday."

"Beat it, buster, I know the drill. Don't tell you anything." Shannan said with a roll of her head.

"Look, Landis, we've brought little Pier with us to visit you. When she heard what happen she insisted on coming," Speedy said in a slightly rigid voice.

Landis raised an eyebrow at Speedy's tone. He turned his head to the entry. His chocolate eyes widen, his heart thumped and he caught his breath. This was little Pier. God, she was beautiful. She had on a black wool skirt and big red sweater with red boots. Her light brown eyes sparkled with fire.

She kept her eyes on his as she slowly made her way to his bed. Once she reached him she gave him a slow breathtaking smile and said, "hello, Handsome". Landis closed his eyes, for surely he had died and gone to heaven. How many times had he dreamed of hearing those words tumble out of her mouth to him? That's what she called Speedy and her father. Never him.

Then she did something everyone else in the room was hoping she wouldn't, she leaned over and pressed her lips to his. She heard Landis' gasp of disbelief and Speedy noisily clearing his throat. They must be crazy if they thought she was going to sit around twisting her thumbs and not fight for her husband. She'd fight anyone or anything, even amnesia for the man she loved. She raised her head up and asked him how he was doing.

Landis exhaled. He looked around the room. He grinned. "I see little Pier's all grown up and kissing men now."

"Not men, Landis. Only you."

"I think," Speedy interrupt saying, "ladies maybe you should take Pier to get something to drink."

Pier agreed because she couldn't stay in this room another minute, and Landis looked at her like he did the day they went to the zoo. Interested but you are my friend's little sister.

Shannan and Micah Rochelle comforted Pier as tears ran unchecked down her face. Micah checked her pulse. Shannan wiped her eyes. They fed her crackers they got from the nurses station and hovered. After awhile, Pier said she was fine and was ready to go back into the room.

After they left, Landis shifted his large frame a little and let out a whistle. "Man, you've got your work cut out. When did she start-?" he held his hand up. "I know we can't talk about it."

Speedy with the upper hand said wickedly, "you kinda act like you like my little sister kissing you."

Landis, who had wanted to tell his best friend for years but never could, decided to throw caution to the wind, the worse case scenario was Speedy would get mad and Landis could blame the head injury. "What would you do if I did?"

Speedy rubbed his chin. He knew he had to play it heavy handed. "I think you're too old, but Pier's an adult. It could be worse."

Landis stared at Speedy like he'd grown another head. "Just like that? If I said I wanted to date your baby sister, you would go along with it."

Speedy looked thoughtful and nodded. "It could be worse," he repeated.

Landis rubbed his hand over the injured side of his head. "Lord, I wish I could remember." He kept a watchful eye on Speedy. "I think you're pulling my broke leg."

"Hey, man, in all honesty, I would be upset, but believe me

when I say I'd get over it," Speedy said with some humor.

"She's the one, you know," Landis whispered in reverence. "She's the young woman I wanted to jump on the plane and see." At Speedy shocked look, "I'm sorry, dude, I wish it could be Shannan like you and Mic wanted, but its little Pier." Landis sighed. He didn't believe he just blurted out his five-year secret. And what was amazing, Speedy didn't blink an eye. He wanted to cry after all these years, saying out loud what he felt in his heart.

The reentering of the women prevented Speedy from replying. They stayed about an hour with Landis with Pier sitting next to him periodically caressing his hand or face. She couldn't help it. She had to touch him. Speedy finally decided enough torment for the Lovington couple and insisted they leave.

"I can stay a little longer," Pier, said almost begging.

Speedy shook his head. "We only have one car and you don't need to be traveling by yourself in some strange city." Shannan and Micah Rochelle kissed Landis and headed out the door.

Landis was watching Pier closely. Speedy was actually helping her up. She looked so sad. Why would she act this way about being with him?

"Pier, you promised," Speedy whispered in her ear. Out loud he said, "Say goodnight to Landis."

"Goodnight, Landis."

"Goodnight, little Pier."

She allowed Speedy to escort her to the door. She broke away and ran back to Landis with a strangler, 'Oh Landis' and kissed him hard.

Landis was tripping. He was sure something was up. Then, as if willed by itself, his eyes looked at two things; her ring finger and her stomach. Panic shocked through his body. She was married. And pregnant! No! To whom? His head started hurting something fierce.

Speedy looked back as he escorted Pier to the door again. He paused. "You okay?"

Landis nodded his head. He knew he was married to Pier. He didn't know the how, what, where or when but they were married. And she was pregnant with his child. Maybe three or four months.

"I'll check on you later. I want to get Pier back to the hotel. She's been a little under the weather."

"Okay." He closed his eyes as they left. He drifted into sleep.

He was driving on Lake Shore Drive when his cell phone ranged. Jackie wanted to meet him to talk with him. He said he couldn't. He had to close on his townhouse. He saw pictures of him dancing with the woman in the red dress. It was Pier. He, himself, carrying her upstairs to his guess bedroom. She was in the hospital. Speedy hitting him. The red bedroom. Telling her how happy she had made him. The car sliding on ice and crashing.

Landis woke up, his body drench with sweat. His heading was pounding; his mind racing. It was a miracle he was alive. He remembered everything. Being married to Pier. Jackie. Their baby. Pier. Their baby. Jackie was supposed to have gotten an abortion. She changed her mind. She felt he had the right to know…

He arrived at the hotel, happy that all ties except for business with the bank were severed in Chicago. He had closed on the townhouse and this time tomorrow he would be in his house with his wife and their rosy future.

The thought of Jackie shattered his happiness. What did she want? When he thought of the times he tried calling, her begging her not to abort the baby he got angry; now she needed to talk.

Where was she when he needed to talk?

"Calm yourself down, Landis Renee," he murmured to himself. "Just see what she wants."

He paced the floor until he heard a knock at the door. Two things happened when he opened the door.

One, he looked in Jackie's beautiful face and felt absolutely nothing and two; Jackie stomach was as big as the proverbial house.

"Jackie! Oh, my goodness, you're still pregnant. I thought you'd aborted the baby." He was in shock and just stood at the door gaping.

"Landis, please forgive me," she said weeping. She threw her arms around his neck. "I am so sorry."

Landis' expression went from shock to puzzle. Not knowing anything else to do, he held Jackie to him, and then walked her over to the sofa.

"Jackie, what is going on?" he asked as he helped her take off her coat and she sat down. "I don't understand. The last time we talked you said you were getting an abortion."

Jackie ran her hand nervously through her short hair then laid it on her huge stomach. "I know, Landis." Taking a deep breath, "I thought I could, but once there, it was a no go. I couldn't." She continued to caress her stomach as if it was giving her strength.

"I have not been myself during this whole pregnancy. To begin with, when I first found out I was pregnant, I wasn't happy. Career-wise of course. I'm not getting younger and I can't afford to be out of action for six months or so."

By now, Landis felt as if he'd been founded guilty by a court of law and was given the death sentence. His life was flashing before him and it was telling him his rosy future was now darkened.

Maybe the baby wasn't his. But what other reason could she have for coming clean with him?

"Look Landis," Jackie said, "when you returned the last time from your visit, you were so standoffish and totally different.

"I've always known you were in love with someone else. You told me when we first met remember?" Landis nodded his head. "You've never said who but that was fine, we got along okay."

Landis leaned forward and held her hand. "I also said I was attracted to you. I cared about you. Jackie, I never intended to mislead you. I thought I could never be with Pier, so I tried to lose myself with other women. I am sorry you were one of them and got hurt."

Jackie smacked her lips sadly. "I know you didn't, Landis. I do love you but when I saw how you and Pier were looking at one another that Sunday in June, I realized I wanted me someone to love me like that. The love you felt for her oozed out like a volcano. Although you both tried to hide it, I just knew. I was off the trail with the guess bedroom. But then, you wouldn't dream of making love with her in the bed you shared with other women.

I acted so silly that day because I never suspected little Pier to be the one. You did go on and on about her. Her name was brought up every time I heard you talking to one of your family, but I thought you were just being a big brother. Imagine my surprise."

Landis wished he knew what to say but he didn't so he patiently waited until she finished. He hoped it would be soon.

"I was jealous and an abortion seemed like the best thing. Then my friend, Cynthia, she's a Christian, started talking to me and one thing led to another and I realized I couldn't go through with an abortion."

Landis leaped to his feet. "My God, Jackie, why didn't you tell me sooner?"

"What would you have done? Forget Pier and marry me? After seeing you with her, I couldn't settle for being second best."

Landis was pacing the floor rubbing his hands over his brow. His life was indeed over. Pier will leave him for sure. Yeah, his life was over. Although, something deep inside him kicked into gear at the thought that he still had a baby, that Jackie didn't get the abortion.

"This is incredible. You're pregnant. Pier's pregnant. When I screw up I really screw up."

"Yes, I know. You're married, also. Listen, Landis, I don't want anything from you. I just felt like you should know about the baby. I guess I didn't want you to think badly about me and I don't know." She cried and cried and cried.

Landis held her and cried himself. For Jackie, for Pier and for himself. Deep in his heart he was glad she didn't get the abortion. He comforted her as best as he could under the circumstances.

Jackie stood up after awhile. "I'm leaving now," she said with as much dignity as she could muster. "Do you want me to contact you when the baby is born?"

"Yes," Landis whispered. He leaned back and closed his eyes. He wished when he opened them, everything would be like it was a few hours ago.

"Oh by the way, it's a boy." Jackie opened and closed the door with a soft thud.

"A boy! I'm having a boy." Tears ran down his face. He called Pier just to hear her voice and to see if her mother was home. He called Speedy tempted to tell him but couldn't. He wiped his eyes and grabbed his leather bomber jacket and ran out the door. He didn't know where he was going, but suddenly the room was too small and he had to get out…

Landis remembered jumping in his sports car and driving faster than he should have on Lake Shore Drive; after coming to his senses, he slowed down only to slide on some ice right into the concrete wall.

Chapter Fifteen

"Landis," Speedy was calling him. He had returned to check on his friend.

"Hey, Speed," he was crying, "I remember everything." He held his hands to his face. "I wish to God I didn't."

"Land, don't say that." He sat in the seat by the bed. "I know everything, also."

He took his hands down from his face. "What?"

"I spoke with Jackie's mother. The doctor gave us your stuff. Your cell rang. I answered. It was Carolyn Winters."

"Why was she calling?" Landis queried.

"Listen, man, why don't I buzz the nurse, let her know you remember."

"Why are you changing the subject? Is there something I need to know?"

Speedy was desperately trying to think of what to say. He shouldn't have blurted out anything without consulting the nurse or doctor. Should he tell Landis that Jackie was dead? That she wanted him to raise the baby? The baby was in ICU because he was premature. And when he went home, he was going with his daddy. Her funeral was tomorrow. His parents have been to see his son. They've met Carolyn.

"Look Speed, I know something is going on. What?"

The nurse walked in. "Hi, Landis. Do you need something?"

"He remembers everything."

"That's good news," the nurse replied. "I'll page your doctor and let him know."

Speedy stood up. "I'm heading back to the hotel and let everyone know. I know one person who will be glad. I thought your wife was going crazy. Well, alright, Landis." He exited ignoring Landis calling him.

"You're not home free yet my friend," Landis murmured. "I'll find out what you know."

Speedy, Renee and Elder went to the funeral. Carolyn informed them the baby would be staying at the hospital until his weight increased. He was stable. They would keep him until Landis was able to get him. If he wanted to be let off the hook, her daughter, Jennifer, was willing to raise the baby and Landis could have visitation rights.

Renee assured her Landis was doing better and would get the baby as soon as he got out of the hospital.

Pier stayed at the hotel, unaware of the events. All she knew was the men went out and as soon as they returned, she was going to sit with her husband. As soon as Speedy told her Landis remembered, she was headed for the hospital. It was too late. Speedy promised the next day he would take her to the hospital.

Shannan had called Keith to let him know she was in Chicago and he, of course, came running. Pier sensed marriage was on the way for those two.

Micah Rochelle was in her room with Ella and Louise. She seemed a little depressed. She looked as if she'd been crying. Why? Landis was fine now. Sitting alone Pier wondered why she had to wait for Speedy. She could take a cab. She told a preoccupied Shannan she was taking a cab to the hospital.

"Okay. I'll let Speedy know when he gets here. Keith will be here in a few. You wanna wait for him?"

"No. I want to get there now." She headed out the door. "Let Mama know where I am for me please."

Pier hailed a taxi cab and headed for the hospital. She smiled to herself. Won't be long before she sees her husband and he will recognize who she is.

Landis lay staring at the three men like they had lost their minds. He couldn't believe what they were telling him.

The doctor had been in to see him. He was doing well and could go home in two to three days. He didn't want him traveling to Minnesota for another week at least. Landis was waiting for Pier to come when in walked the three musketeers with this stunning news.

Jackie had the baby prematurely. She died in child birth. They were coming from the funeral. Her last wishes were for him to raise the baby. He felt a headache coming on.

Anger flowed through his body, anger at Jackie, but mostly at himself. If only he had told them how he felt about Pier five years ago, stood up for what he felt. He should have waited to see if Pier felt the same thing. If only he had waited on Pier and not slept with other women, especially Jackie. This wouldn't be happening. Speedy's sermon came to mind. *Lest ye fall.*

Now was not the time for the 'if only'. He messed up. Now how was he going to tell his wife that his former lover had his child after all? She's dead and he's left to raise their son. And according to his father, the baby looks just like him. They will do a blood test if that's what Landis wanted. But he was certain the baby was a Lovington.

"So what am I supposed to do?" Landis asked frustrated. "How can I tell my wife that I have a son? What's his name anyway? We can't keep saying the baby or boy." He wanted to get up and walk out. But he couldn't get up and walk out because his leg was broke, his ribs cracked and he was in the hospital.

"She didn't name him. It's up to you. What do you want to call him? Landis Junior?"

Landis closed his eyes with a sigh. "Will someone please tell me what to do? How do I tell Pier about my son with Jackie?"

Pier stood at the door of the room. The four men were unaware of her presence. *'How do I tell Pier about my son with Jackie?'* is what she heard. She gasped. Four pairs of shocked eyes turned her way.

Landis gave Speedy a helpless look. *Help me, God. Please help me.* "Baby, how did you get here?" was all he could think to ask.

"Cab," she answered as she sauntered into the room. She stood by her husband's bed. She bent to kiss him, exclaimed over him getting his memory back. She talked a mile a minute, all on auto pilot. Jackie had the baby after all and Landis was the father, raced over and over in her mind. Everyone knew but her. They all treated her like she was a child. Even her husband.

Well, she'd show them. They could stand around like it was a funeral if they want to but she would not.

"Can I get you anything, Handsome? Are you comfortable?"

"Baby, I know you heard. Sit down and let's talk about it." A few minutes ago he sounded desolated now he was trying to comfort her.

"Yes, I heard. So what? Jackie had the baby? Isn't that what you wanted? Weren't you devastated when you thought she was going to abort?" She sat down. Her father, brother, and father-in-law were standing as if statues.

Landis sighed. He was in for a long day. What would he do? What should he say? He couldn't ask her to accept a child that wasn't hers. Pier, in this mode, meant show them I'm not a child.

"Can I be alone with my wife please? We have some things to discuss. I'll call later."

They hurried out of the room. Landis held Pier's hand. He was watching her closely.

"They went to a funeral. Jackie died in childbirth," his voice cracked a little. He rubbed his hand across his face.

"No. I'm sorry, Landis, I know how much you cared about Jackie."

"Yeah, well, you know I love you Pier. I did care about her. I hate that she died." He told her everything. About Jackie calling him, meeting with her; finding out about the pregnancy; being angry and storming out of the room. How the accident happened.

"Speedy and Micah Rochelle were at the hospital the night she died. She requested that I raise the baby."

Pier couldn't hide the pained look. Another baby maybe she could handle, but to raise him along with her child. Would she be able to do that? Is she that selfless?

"I see."

"Baby, I know this is a lot to ask. We'll talk about it when I get out of this place. Right now we need to think about it. I don't want to lose you, Pier, but I can't turn my back on this baby." He was holding her hand rubbing it with his thumb. He exhaled. "Please tell me what to do." His eyes filled with tears. He had cried more this year than he had in his entire life.

"What do you want to do?" her voice trembled with unreleased tears. She had to be strong for Landis. He had always been the strength now it was her turn.

"I don't know. Let's sleep on it."

"I'll go now, Landis. I'll see you later." She ran out the room.

"Pier! Pier, wait!"

Landis stared at the doorway after she left. It was over. He knew it. It had been one bump after another. They have weathered every storm to be together. He didn't think they could weather anything else. He grimaced at himself. He wouldn't ask that of Pier. He loved her and needed her, but it was unfair to saddle her with another woman's baby. He'd let her file for a divorce.

Pier ran out of the hospital. She decided to walk around for a little bit. Landis had another baby. What would have happened if he'd known? He would have married Jackie and she probably would've moved back to Atlanta, never revealing the father.

She walked without seeing the scenery. Her mind was racing. Could she cope with being a mother to another woman's baby? Would this marriage survive another hit? She walked for hours and still couldn't find any answers. Finally, totally exhausted, she flagged a cab and headed back to the hotel.

When she walked in, the family was in an uproar. Everyone was talking at the same time. Finally Elder took over and insisted she tell them where she'd been for four hours. Speedy was on the phone telling, she assumed, Landis she was there and okay.

"I needed to think so I walked around for a little while. Sorry you were worried," she said wearily. "I'm a little tired. I'm going to lie down." She ran to the room.

Her mother walked in a few minutes later. "Pier, have you eaten?"

"Not hungry," her voice was muffed from the pillow.

"Hon, you got to eat something." Ella sat on the bed.

Pier rose up and threw herself in her mother's arms, crying her heart out. "Mama, I don't know what to do. I guess I'm still a kid because I can't raise another's woman's baby. I'm sorry, but I can't. I know I'm selfish, but I just can't do it."

"You must do what your heart tells you to do. But remember these things take time. You may not feel you can raise Landis' son now. That's only natural but things will work out, you'll see."

"I hope so, Mama, because right now I don't know if my marriage will survive this."

"You and Landis have been through a lot. This has definitely been a trying year, but God is faithful if you call on Him and not yourself."

When Ella walked into the hospital room to visit Landis, she was devastated to see such despair in his eyes.

"Hi, Landis," Ella said as she took the chair by his bed. "How are you, son? Dumb question?"

"Mrs. Mortimer, I'm so glad to see you." Landis grabbed her hand. "I'm doing well. How's Pier?"

"She'll come around, son, you wait and see. Just give it some time." She gave him one of her gentle smiles, the one that encourages you to overcome any obstacles.

"I love Pier so much, but I can't give up my son. Carolyn offered to take him and raise him and I can visit whenever I want.

So did Jackie's sisters. I can't do it. I want my son with me. I do not expect Pier to do it. I know that's asking too much. I accept that now." He massaged his temples with his hands. "I can't imagine my life without Pier. I've been there; done that. I want things to be like they were.

"I was so angry with Jackie." Once he started talking, he couldn't stop. "For being pregnant, for lying, for telling the truth and for dying. Then I was mad at myself. For being weak and not risking my relationship with Speedy and tell him I was in love with Pier. For sleeping with Jackie, for getting Pier pregnant." He rubbed his hand slowly over his brow. He closed his eyes briefly.

Mrs. Mortimer patted his hand.

"The first thing, Landis, is not to give up, which is what you are doing. You love Pier and she loves you. That's what you fight for. Neither one of you are quitters. Don't give up. Give it some time. Pier will come around. You'll see. Right now she's basically saying the same as you. Only she feels she can't do it."

"I know. She told me," Landis said wearily. "I get to go home tomorrow. Keith insists I stay with him. I'll get to see the baby for the first time. Carolyn and I will discuss naming him."

"I was thinking the best thing would be to take Pier home and when you're better you come home. You'll see everything will be fine, son. Let's just trust God on this matter."

"Yes, ma'am," Landis said despondently.

"Okay, I'm going now. You try and get you some rest. Your mom will be here later to see you. I love you, son."

"I love you, too.

Chapter Sixteen

It had been two weeks since Pier was back from Chicago. She still had no answers. She and Landis talked. Their conversation was strained. The baby was fine, still in the hospital but doing well. If he continued gaining weight he'd be out of the hospital in a week. Micah Rochelle and Speedy were flying to Chicago to accompany Landis and the baby home.

Landis was staying at Keith's place. Keith was here in Minnesota staying abreast of the work at the branch for Landis.

She was sitting on the sofa in the family room when Speedy walked in.

"Hey, little Pier."

"Hi, Handsome. What's up with you?"

"Nothing much. Thought I'd drop in and check on you and the baby."

Pier rubbed her stomach. "I'm getting huge. I look like a blimp."

Speedy shook his head in disagreement. "You look beautiful to me and no doubt to Landis."

At the mention of Landis' name, Pier stood up.

"Is he really doing okay? When we talk, it's like it was before we got married, scared to say how we really feel."

Speedy gently pulled her back down on the sofa, rubbing his hand over hers.

"How do you feel about Landis?" he asked.

"I still love him with all my heart. I'm not sure I can handle Jackie's baby. I feel like every time he looked at him, he'll think of her. I guess I'm jealous of the baby. I guess I'm jealous of his relationship he had with Jackie." Her eyes filled with tears.

Speedy put his arms around his little sister. It devastated him to see her so distraught.

"I'm going to share a secret with you. It's a secret that Mama, Dad, and I have."

He cleared his throat. "When Mama met Dad, he had just gotten a divorce."

Pier looked shocked. "Dad was married before?"

"Yep. He was married to a woman named Lucy James. According to Dad, they had been married for two years when one day Dad went to work and came home and she's gone."

"What? Just left? Didn't say anything to Dad?"

"Yep. She had been gone for about six months when Dad received some divorce papers in the mail. He signed the papers and mailed it. Then he went out to get drunk.

"What?" Pier grinned. "Not the right Elder Mortimer."

"Will you stop interrupting me, little girl."

"Sorry."

"He had gone and I quote, 'to a honky tonk,' and got loaded. Because he was so drunk, he left his car and walked.

"He passed out in front of Mama's house. She was coming in

from church and saw Dad in her yard. She got Uncle Charles to see who he was and get him out from the yard. Uncle recognized Dad and saw he was drunk, decided to bring him in to sleep it off. And the rest is history. Dad woke up to a "vision" and a few months later they got married."

Pier listened in awe at what Speedy was talking about. She wondered why their parents never told her their dad had been married before. Maybe she was too young. But why did Speedy know about it and why was he telling her now?

"Anyway after about a year and a half, a year after Dad's divorce and mama is six months pregnant when Lucy James knocked at the door demanding to see Dad. When Dad went to the door, she stated she needed to talk to him. Mama invited her in and she explained why she left dad.

"It seems Lucy James was having an affair with a married man. She and the man ran off together."

Speedy paused and look down at Pier. "I know you're wondering where I'm going with this story. Just a little more patience, I'm going somewhere," he said in his preachy voice.

Pier nodded her head. If nothing else, her love for Landis taught her patience.

"Now where was I?"

"Lucy James had an affair and ran away with him," Pier said.

"Yes, well, when she ran away it seemed she was pregnant and she didn't know who the father was, so she told her lover he was the father until I was born."

Pier gasped. "*You!* She was pregnant with you? Mama not your real mama?"

Speedy shook his head in dismay. "Of course she's my real Mama, just not my birth mom. You see, when I was born Lucy

James and her boyfriend were happy, according to her but as I got older I started to look too much like Dad for the boyfriend's peace of mind. So she brought me to Dad."

"Oh my goodness! I had no idea. Does Shannan know about this?"

"No. Mama and Dad didn't care. They left it up to me. I didn't want y'all to know."

"But why Speedy? It wouldn't have made a difference."

Speedy hunched his shoulders. "That was when I was a kid, when I got older it just didn't seem important."

"So my situation is similar to Mama's?"

"Exactly. That's why I'm telling you now. They never really explained what happen with them, if Mama was mad or if they separated or anything like that.

"All I know is as far back as I can remember, Ella Mortimer, has never treated me anyway except like her son. I sometimes forget I have a birth mother named Lucy James or whatever her last name is now."

"You don't ever want to find her and talk with her?"

Speedy looked scandalized. "Whatever for? He asked. "If I ever saw her, it would be to say thank you for the best mom in the world."

Ella, who had been on her way to the family room when she heard her son sharing with his sister their secret, strolled into the room.

"I've thanked her enough for all of us." She sat down next to Speedy. "If you want to contact your mother, she's not hard to find. Just a few phone calls and your daddy will have all the information you need."

Speedy shook his head. "Nah, I don't need to talk to her. I

have all the mother I need right here." He threw his arms around his mama and kisses her.

"I guess we have to tell Shannan Big Head now", said Speedy.

"Yeah, she'd die if she knew Pier knew something and she didn't." They laughed.

"Pier! You are an adult now and it's time you make adult decisions," said Ella.

Speedy had stood and walked over to the window. It was snowing outside and he seemed fascinated with the snow. Truth to be told he was holding his breath waiting for his sister's reply.

Pier stood also, pacing the floor. She knew after hearing the *family secret* it made her rethink this whole problem.

"You're right, Mama," she said after awhile. "I am an adult. And I know just what I'm going to do.

Keith was back in Chicago and at his condominium where he so graciously let Landis stay. Speedy and Micah Rochelle were due to arrive any moment to drive Landis and his son back to Minnesota.

Carolyn and her children helped Landis bring the baby home early yesterday from the hospital. They were teary-eyed about the baby leaving Chicago. Landis had assured them they were welcome to visit anytime and see Jackie's son.

Carolyn handled everything well. Landis just knew she was going to take him to court and try to fight for custody, but she didn't. She said she must respect her daughter's wishes. If Jackie wanted him to raise their baby, then she and her family could only respect that.

Sometimes, Landis thought, maybe, just maybe if Carolyn

had fought for custody and won, he would have Pier and still have visitation rights. Shaking his head, he nipped that in the bud. No way would anyone but he raised his son. Somehow, some way he would have both his wife and child. And when his other baby was born it would be the four of them. Living the happily ever-after life.

Keith helped Landis last night with the baby duties due to him still being in a wheelchair and ribs still a little tender.

"Okay, dog, you got everything. The baby stuff is packed; your stuff is packed and I checked the weather and although it snowed, the roads are smooth sailing all the way home."

Landis grinned. "Now all we need is for Speedy and Mic to get here."

"I offered to pick them up at the airport. They said they would take a cab. You think you're going to be okay with the drive?"

"Yes. I should be fine. We had too much stuff to be trying to fly out."

"Man, Landis, I'm going to miss you. I already miss working with you."

"I know, Dude, I know. I'm gonna miss you, too. Hey, man, you know you can visit anytime. Shannan would be glad to see you. Seems to me like you kinda sweet on her."

Keith sat down grinning. "Yeah, you're right. I like Shannan. She's good people."

Nodding in agreement, Landis rolled his wheelchair over to the bassinet. He stared at his son, laying his hand on his head. He smoothed his baby fine hair.

"Good looking kid," said Keith.

"Yeah, he is. Looks a lot like his mother."

"I disagree. He looks a lot like his father with some of his mother's features. He has Jackie's eyes and nose."

"I just hope I can have my wife back. I hope Pier accepts this baby and we move into our house and it's all good."

"It will work out, Landis. You'll see."

"Everyone says that but Pier. This past week, I haven't been able to even talk to her. She's never at her parents' house. I know she didn't move into our house. This is a mess, but a mess I'm going to straighten out. You'll see."

"Man, I believe you," said Keith. "I have all the faith in you."

Landis sighed, "No. Let's make that all the faith in God…

The ringing of the doorbell prevented Landis from continuing.

"That must be Speedy and Micah Rochelle." Keith went to the buzzer.

A few minutes later, Speedy and Micah Rochelle were at the front door.

"Whuz up, Keith?" They shook hands. "Whuz up, Landis? You ready to push out of here?"

"And you know it," Landis said while receiving a kiss on the cheek from his sister.

"Are you sure you're up to it?" Micah Rochelle asked.

"I want to be home tonight. I'm sure."

"Well, my man, Keith," said Speedy. "We hate to leave so quickly but somebody wants to be home tonight. So let's load up this stuff."

Speedy turned to Landis. "I can't wait to see this truck you got." He raised his brows. "And drive it."

They laughed. Landis decided to get a black Cadillac full loaded Escalade truck.

"Brother, this is your first and last time driving my truck."

Everything was loaded in the truck except the baby and Landis. He and Keith hugged and said their good-byes. They were on the road within the next few minutes.

Landis sat in the back so he could put his leg up. He let Mic fuss over him and his son. He was a sleep within the hour.

He woke three hours later because Speedy had stopped. The baby was crying and Micah Rochelle had climbed in the back with the baby to feed him.

"Hey, sleepyhead. Speedy stopped to let me feed the baby." She was rocking the baby back and forth. "Do you need to go to the bathroom?"

Landis yawned. He hated how weak he felt. "Yeah."

"Wait here and Speedy will help you."

Speedy opened the door. "I see Sleeping Beauty is awake. Need to go to the potty?"

"Dude, it's over for you," Landis said as Speedy help him out of the truck.

"Let me get the wheelchair."

"No, Speedy, I'll use the crutches."

"Are you sure that's a good idea?" Micah Rochelle asked.

"Yes. I gotta practice because I refuse to be in a wheelchair when I see my wife after three weeks."

Speedy and Micah Rochelle grinned at one another.

"What's funny?"

"Nothing. Just glad to have the old Landis back," said Speedy.

With the help of Speedy, Landis was able to make it to the bathroom and back in just under fifteen minutes. He was exhausted and asleep before Speedy could pull out of the recreation area.

He woke once again because Speedy stopped. But this time, he stopped in front of Landis house. The lights were on so he assumed his parents were there, waiting to see the edition to the family.

With the help of Speedy, he once again used his crutches. The door was opened by his father.

"Hello, son," said Renee embracing him. "Good to have you home." He helped Landis inside. Speedy went back to get the baby.

Landis hopped toward the living room. He heaved a sigh as he remembered all the work his Pier put in finding the right furniture and patterns for their house. He stood staring around the living room for a few minutes, then headed back to the foyer.

He heard a noise at the top of the stairs the same time the door opened and in walked Speedy with Micah Rochelle, his parents and Shannan. Landis swung his eyes back to the stairs where his Pier was descending. He hopped toward her. She was standing three stairs from the bottom so she could be eye-level with him. He had lost weight but she had never been so glad to see anyone in her life.

She looked into his eyes and said, "Hello, my darling, handsome, husband. Welcome home. Where is our son?" Then she cradled his face in her hands and kissed him.

Epilogue

Two years later

Reverend Wright stood on the podium smiling at the surprise he had for the Mortimers and Lovingtons. It was good to see Pastor Spencer Mortimer and his lovely wife, co-Pastor Micah Rochelle Mortimer and their four year old son, Spency and one year old daughter, Micah Ella Louise, better known for her initials as Mel.

They had been pastors for two years and their church had grown by leaps and bounds. Elder Mortimer and his wife, as well as Deacon Renee Lovington and his wife opted to stay at True Foundation.

How Speedy got Shannan to not only join his church but to be in charge of the youths, Reverend Wright will never know. He had been working on that girl for years. Friend of the family, Keith Monroe sat next to Shannan. Reverend Wright was waiting to hear marriage from them soon.

He grinned at all the heavy weights Landis had invited for this

Thanksgiving service. He grinned even more at what the offering was going to be like. Yes, not only were these families' givers but they only associated with givers. And in the congregation were Keith's parents of Monroe-Phillips Banks, clothes designer, Karseeme LaMarr, architect, Nicholas Palmer and his wife, Trina, and a host of friends.

He smiled at Little Pier, a mother now, trying to get her son and daughter to stop fighting over who gets to sit on her lap.

"Ladies and gentlemen, it gives me great honor to present to you our speaker for today, Landis Renee Lovington."

Landis stood up grinning at the shocked surprise his family and friends gave as he went to the podium.

"Praise the Lord, everybody. It is truly an honor and privilege to be here in your mix to bring the message. I want you to know when Reverend asked me to do it, my first reply was no. As you know Pastor Speedy is the preacher in the family, always have been."

Everyone laughed.

"But at Reverend Wright's insistence, I agreed and here I am. About two years ago, my brother-in-law brought the message Lest You Fall and at that time, I was going through so much. The message pierced my heart and set me on the right path. I am going to attempt to teach on Lest We Fall. You see, we have a tendency of trying to do things ourselves. But if we trust God and one another, we can be more than conquerors."

Pier smiled as she listen to her husband speak. They had come a long way. She looked down at the now quiet Landis Jr. and his sister Shannan Janise. They were blessed. One day when they were older, they would tell them about Jackie. Right now, Grandma Carolyn was both of their grandmothers and so were

Chicago granddad and all the uncles and aunts.

Pier learned to love Jackie's family as they loved her. She and Landis visited often and Carolyn came every Thanksgiving.

She had grown up and was no longer jealous of Landis relationship with Jackie. Yes! They were blessed.

"...so you see," Landis was saying, "It is easy to fall when we put our trust in ourselves. Only when we trust God can we stand with the assurance of not falling or failing. Indeed I am a blessed man. I thank God for my wife and kids and how He directs our life. God is good. Amen." Landis walked to his seat. He picks up his wife hand and kisses it.

Family and friends had gathered at Landis and Pier's home for Thanksgiving dinner. They were also celebrating Landis Jr.'s birthday. This was the only time this year everyone could come.

Elder Mortimer was standing ready to give the speech, ah, prayer.

"As you know, when I was a child, I was too poor to," everyone finished with him, "celebrate my birthday."

Pier smiled at her husband who winked at her as they listen to her dad tell the same birthday story he has told hundreds of times.

"... Today we are celebrating our grandson Landis Jr.'s birthday as well as Thanksgiving. Thank you all for coming. Now let's pray so we can eat."

Landis looked at his wife and the love of his life.

"I love you, Baby."

"I love you too, Handsome."

About the Author

GloriJean Johnson grew up watching old romance movies with her mother. She loved everything about them: from the struggle of two people admitting to their love, to the couple that would sacrifice everything for their love and passion. But this was just the beginning. For it was in these early years that GloriJean realized she was a true romantic and a firm believer in the power of love.

As early as age ten, GloriJean entertained siblings and friends – in fact anyone who would listen – with love stories inspired from her huge imagination. And because of her passion for writing, she shared her gift with her children, and as tradition would have it, her young grandchildren. Her love of teaching the gospel and writing now leads GloriJean to follow one of her own dreams --- to publish the stories she has told for many years.

GloriJean, born in Meridian, Mississippi, now lives in Minnesota with her true love, her husband, John. One of her passions is proclaiming the gospel of Jesus Christ. She is a prophetic preacher, teacher, motivational speaker and author. GloriJean loves traveling, reading, walking and spending time with her family. She also enjoys working and volunteering in the church where she serves as a church leader, board member and co-founder with her husband.

CPSIA information can be obtained
at www.ICGtesting.com
Printed in the USA
BVHW07s1809121018
530012BV00002B/301/P